The
China Caper

BERNARD KATZ

authorHOUSE®

AuthorHouse™
1663 Liberty Drive
Bloomington, IN 47403
www.authorhouse.com
Phone: 1-800-839-8640

Published by AuthorHouse   05/22/2012

ISBN: 978-1-4685-7210-0 (sc)
ISBN: 978-1-4685-7209-4 (e)

Library of Congress Control Number: 2012905363

To my wife whose insights to the Chinese
character were always important

CHAPTER 1

San Francisco

I MAGINE, BACK THEN, me, Jake Diamond, a Korean War prisoner jailed in China. Crazy. Anyhow, just so you understand, I'm an upright citizen. Got an antique store in San Francisco, a seller of things Chinese from the China Trade. You know, Chinese 18th, 19th Century imports of furniture, porcelains, and an occasional wall hanging. Nothing great, but way beyond the dime-store junk you see just down the block on Grant Avenue. Some say it's an odd choice for a guy from Coney Island, but I can tell you the stuff is in my blood. At least I gave up some for the privilege.

I'm lost in my thoughts about retiring, leaving the business for a sunnier place when the bell just above the front door softly jingles. I get a kick from the sound, like those old emporiums in the South you see in the period movies. Anyhow, I'm almost smiling when I see who comes in.

The breed is maybe extinct, something out of those oldies they show at the Roxie Theater out on 16th Street,

1

in the Mission. A taller, thinner, nattier, much older Charley Chan walks in looking like one of those 19th Century edition ambassadors from the Orient. Taking a soft, careful step, while holding a cigarette between his thumb and forefinger, like in the old European movies, he strolls the aisles looking over my goods.

I walk over and in my best San Franciscoeez say, "Sorry Pop, either you or the cigarette has to go." I also want to tell him you don't wear linen in this city but I don't think he would have cared. He's also a guy who carried it off, that kind of old world charm.

"Of course. You are quite right." He searched around for an ashtray and as I don't have any he went back outside and began field stripping the butt by tearing it into small pieces. I hadn't seen that since the army, and it seemed, what? Endearing?

I watch as he walks back and there's a feeling of recognition sweeping over me. "Hey, Pops, we ever meet before?"

Without even looking he tosses back, "Never."

I can't let go cause the feeling is palpable, from somewhere back in time. "You sure?"

He ignores my question and starts looking about my place. Showing he knows quality, he unerringly goes to a late 17th century table cabinet, my most expensive piece. Then he ambles over to a shallow rose-colored bowl, turns it over like he should and checks its Ch'ien Lung mid-18th century seal. But I could tell the way he surveys my stuff he's not a buyer. He kind of glides over to me and stands close.

The man has these Chinese eyebrows, like short pieces of steel wool. His skin is mottled. I can see liver spots on his wrists, about his cheeks, wherever his clothes ended.

But it's his eyes, they had these light reflections, holes you could gaze into and see the stars and heavens of worlds past. If I ever have a Chinese uncle he's what I'd want.

"I believe you are Mr. Jake Diamond?" Without waiting for me to even shake my head he goes on. "I have something you may be interested in."

With little trace of an accent his American education is clear, but he's definitely born in China. There's an awkwardness, or maybe superiority about him, I don't know. Maybe an unruffled way of a man who carries himself born to more than money, to servants. He gives me his card:

Dr. C. Liu, Curator, National Palace Museum, Taipei

"Medical or academic?" I ask.

Normally I'm not this way, you know, cute. In this case I'm kind of flirting with him to show I'm interested, in a good way, if you know what I mean. He stares at me for a second, then with a damn charm seeming to be a Chinese birthright he smiles and says, "Yes."

Now what the hell is that supposed to mean? I like it about him, the inscrutable part but I should tell him puzzles are not my strong suit, I go to Sharli for such things. I depend on her a bunch. She's clever and she keeps me young, if you get my drift.

"Something I may be interested in? Sure, I'm always in the market." From his round case comes a Chinese silk scroll. He rolls out its four-foot length on my 19th Century red lacquered desk from Jiangsu province priced at $2,100. I'd let it go for $1,950 but not a penny less. I take a quick glance at the scroll, I take another, a bit longer. Now I gotta sit down. I'm all of a sudden looking at a world that can only exist somewhere in Chinese heaven. It has mountains way off seemingly never touching earth, clouds suggesting there's a sky somewhere in undefined space and an almost cold silence reserved for the wide-eyed that seek to travel horizons only imagined.

Dr. C. Liu begins talking and I listen. This wise man of three thousand years of Chinese civilization is offering me a deal reserved for caliphs, emperors and thieves. I'm impressed. No, it's an insufficient word. Yet when he finishes I stare at him as though he's demented. If he didn't appear as though he owned the shop and everything in it I'd give him a sawbuck and show him the door. It's a staggering offer. He asks if I want to buy the scroll and gives me a price and adds, "No dickering, please."

Now I know that's not the Chinese way but hell the amount he asked for, well, it's a relative pittance. Big bucks to me, mind you, but a fraction of the scroll's true market value. But then, how much is close to priceless. While he only gave a detail here and there, if what he says is on the up and up it's a golden prize that had to come from Beijing's Forbidden City. And quickly I wonder why he comes to me with it. I mean, my looks don't even resemble an altar boy or a Hollywood Valentino, my bank account is a shy little thing and my record as a player in the world of antiques is, well, even modest is bragging.

There are reams of questions running about in my head. I kept repeating to myself not to screw this up and to find out if what he's offering is legit or not. I needed some time. I gotta think about this and tell Dr. C. Liu, Curator, to come back the day after tomorrow. Then he takes me completely off stride.

"Mr. Diamond, we have never met, but you out-bid me for the Red Official at the Amsterdam auction."

I stare at this walking advertisement for the Chinese secret of aging. He continues, "It's a lovely piece." He smiles. "I hope to own it some day."

Yeah, sure. I'd taken a liking to the little beauty of the ancient arts of China sitting right where I wanted it, in my apartment. It had the best view in town watching the tramp steamers whisk under the Golden Gate.

"I wouldn't count on it old man, but you never know. Even the San Francisco Giants could win the World Series." And he said he didn't know me, the old faker. Son-of-a-gun, so he was the voice from the back corner driving up the price. No, I know him from some place else. It'll come to me.

Before he left I asked, "Why so cheap?" He looked at me uncomprehending. I said, "A Zhou Mengfu must be worth, what, in the low millions?"

Cool, unruffled, he came back with a Mona Lisa smile. Then, in his cultured voice, "But you see, there are conditions, limitations." He leaned close. "The buyer, no one must know he is the owner and it must never be shown to anyone before his demise. And the same condition must pass to the heirs." To win me over he placed his hand on mine. "Our museum will still carry the painting in its catalogs. We would never admit to selling it." He leaned back and with a completely disarming friendliness he again spoke softly, "The buyer, or their heirs, must never place it on exhibition."

I had taken out my cigar, lit my match and almost put it to the leaf.

The flame died and only the burnt sulfur wafted to my nose. Liu went on. "You see if it came before the world purview the Peoples Republic of China would claim it as rightfully theirs, stolen from the Forbidden City by the gangster Chiang Kai-shek. They would confiscate it, haul it to Beijing and put it away for no one to see." He laughed, softly, "I could imagine the row between an American citizen and the Peoples Republic over private property rights. Your anti-Chinese California Congressman would have a field day."

His last words had caused him difficulty. "Would you kindly get me a glass of water." He unscrewed the top of a small nineteenth century Japanese vial and removed a bluish pill. I thought it looked like a Viagra since I well knew its color.

"Foolish doctors," he said waving his hand at some imaginary advisor, "they believe twentieth century medicine can overcome the historical precedent of dying." He paled and I realized I didn't want anything to happen to him, I liked the old man. A minute later his color returned and he went back to his pitch without missing a syllable.

"Which is why the painting is also a bargain to you. Everything must be on the, how do you say it, the q.t., why the price is so reasonable and the profit for you so attractive." He smiled knowingly. "So necessary for your retirement."

"Listen Liu, is all this a cock and bull story. I've never heard of anything so complicated. Is the damned painting hot?" I should have waited for his answer but another question kept pushing to come out. "Besides, why would Taiwan want to sell this national treasure?"

Taking out his handkerchief he touched the corners of his mouth, then, despite the store still having its morning chill, he brought the white linen to the bead of perspiration on his forehead. "We have a President of Taiwan who knows the gangsters in Beijing will eventually claim our country for their own. He prefers to have our treasures in the hands of the cultured West," he actually winced saying it, "rather than those with Chinese blood dripping from between their fingers."

I had no more questions. "Where are you staying? I'll call."

"The Stanford Court on California Street." He offers, "It has a delightful fountain as you enter under the colored glass portico."

Aside from his offer, I liked the old man, trusted him maybe 'cause the guy had class, something I always aspired to but couldn't grab.

Anyhow, I couldn't get any more words out before the front door is open.

"Think it over," he says, "but hurry, San Francisco trolleys go up as well as down."

Now what kind of crack is that?

CHAPTER 2

I HAD TO SAY it over and over, Charley Chan is offering a Zhou Mengfu, a classic from the Chinese Imperial Palace collection. A painting on silk, a slice of Chinese history, a preview into the heavens. With my pulse pounding I know to tell myself to go slow, not to race ahead. A Zhou Mengfu. All of a sudden the things I sell are an embarrassment. No question my stuff is prime, but it's not in the same league. I keep asking myself—Do I buy this classic, this gem, this slice of worlds unseen or am I singled out to be a sucker? Is the old man a scam artist? I wished Harry'd be here. He knew the classics, studied them up there when we were prisoners while I went to the lesser stuff. I never had Harry's eye for the money goods. While only older by 3 days he had the smarts. Dead these, what, 45 years, escaping from someplace along the Yalu from that long gone unknown Brit's house. And my fault. And I still can't shake it. Harry, we shoulda stayed together that night. I shouldn't have let you go alone.

Even if you were the older. Hell. Yeah, the scroll, the scroll, that's what counts now.

You must understand, while history's not my suit I do know Zhou's paintings were taken by Chiang Kai-shek when he ran from the mainland to Taiwan. Once in a while I hear the Chinese Nationalists let the world line up to see a few of Zhou's brethren. But they've never let those kinds of goods leave Taiwan. The De Young Museum in San Francisco would sometimes get an exhibition from the Nationalists but never of this quality. Hell, every curator of every major China collection in America would gladly shorten his sex life for a two-week exhibit of that kind of stuff. The old Chinaman is offering me what? culture, great art, even early retirement. As my Hebraic sainted mother would say if she'd been Irish, "Oh, lordy."

I learned long ago trusting the seller was more important than the deal itself. But C. Liu, for crying out loud, he's twenty-four carat, Honest Abe, Captain Courageous and I coulda sworn I met him someplace, long ago. It'll come back. But I got more pressing problems. Make no mistake, I wouldn't go into this deal like a Bar Mitzvah boy with his first two dollar whore, no sir, I'd make sure of everything, all details. Believe me, I'd do my due diligence.

Right after Liu left I called Taylor Davis knowing his collection and his bankroll. More important, he'd accept the condition about not exhibiting it. Taylor's a true collector. Ownership was the key allowing him to be swept into the beauty of the work at his own time and mood. He picked his Chinese pieces with the eye of a connoisseur and he almost never haggled. He knew I always gave him the right price. It's the way I did business.

One price and always the best price, always, to everyone. Almost. In all truth I could easily envy Taylor with his Connecticut good looks. An ex-tennis professional, he'd been on the tour before Lendl. While he reached only a twenty-six national ranking, he always performed as world class.

We agreed to meet in neutral territory, in Golden Gate Park, near the carousel. The merry-go-round was a joy. It had all those repainted horses and rabbits, and chickens. They had one in Coney Island when I grew up, owned by a Japanese family whose daughter sat in my classes. I wanted to talk to her but didn't know how to start. That hesitancy stayed with me too long. I missed out on knowing a lot of good people.

I waited sitting on one of the park benches in the bright sun. Surrounded by mainly green space alongside the spinning colors and animals, the oom pah pah of the carousel's organ music and it was all so damn comfortable. Close to the Children's Playground, the antics of the kids and their unexpected exuberant laughter always gave me an emotional high. To me there is no other town that comes close to San Francisco for charm, even the damn buses had it—don't ask me why 'cause I'd tell you I liked the warning sound they made when they lowered the first step to allow the disabled to get on.

As Taylor had yet to show I'm thinking over the transaction of the scroll and I smile to myself, that old codger. I asked the old man, "Hey Liu, Chiang Kai-shek took all those paintings with him when he left China for Taiwan. Isn't that stealing? I mean, Zhou's painting came from the Forbidden City, right?" I don't wait for an answer cause I know it's so. "Won't I be stealing from China?" What happens? He gives me one of his inscrutable looks,

"Jake," he says smiling, "that's philosophically possible."
You had to love the guy.

Figuring I still had some minutes, I picked up the
newspaper the wind had wrapped around my leg. I needed
to see the date of this kind of historic meeting, September
19, 1998. I liked all the nine's involved and less than two
years to the Millennium. It sounded like good omens.
Must be I've been around this Chinese stuff for too long.

Watching as Davis came over the last rise, the breeze
was whipping his blonde hair and white cotton trousers.
He had trouble keeping his tie within the folds of his
blue blazer. A picture of a man who would have been
comfortable as one of the group which paled around with
Cole Porter back in the 20's and 30's. No question, I was
jealous.

"Jake, you are such a romantic, meeting here."

"Romantic, huh? Guess you're right. I have three
ex-wives to prove it. The alimony is killing." I tell
everybody that 'cause it gives them a simultaneous sense
that I got money and I take care of my mistakes. None of
which is true, even the wives part.

I didn't want to waste too much time with small talk
as I needed to get back to the painting. I told Davis about
the *Late Autumn* and everything Liu laid out. We talked
about it for a while and he asked if he could come see it.
I told him no, not now, 'cause I want to get Wyatt, the
historian and chairman of the Asian Art Department of
Berkeley to give it his blessing, to authenticate it. There
was no higher authority than Zhou Mengfu himself. I
told Taylor if anyone even had the slightest doubt about
the scroll we would both walk away.

He kept after me to name a price. I wasn't sure what
to ask but he wouldn't relent and neither could I. The

temptation of saying those high numbers was too great. Took a deep breath, held it and then let it out carrying the amount of three point three million. Davis didn't even blink, but he did counter. We played for a few minutes and came to a number we both knew would be the clincher and, son-of-a-gun, the deal came off. Pat, another dealer, had told me Taylor became a born again Christian some years back and turned heavy into this conversion stuff. I couldn't care as long as we now agreed to the two million eight-five for the painting. Not too shabby for a guy who got cast off clothing from his uncle and guessed weights in a summer job back in Coney Island. After the deal with Taylor I called Liu at the Stanford Court and we arranged to show the painting to the eminent Professor of Oriental Art, Wylan Wyatt the next morning at the private rooms of the Bank of America on Montgomery.

When we met the next day this guy Wyatt was a sight to behold. I had never seen the gentleman up close as I never crossed the Bay Bridge into Berkeley except for that fine restaurant, Chez something or other. The climate there was a bit heady for me with all those learned gentlemen, unwashed students, down in the heels homeless and the almost Republican no-man's land. Wyatt came into the bank looking like an antebellum Southern gentleman, a yellowed straw hat, rumpled white suit and a belly pushing out the waistcoat four inches beyond the belt. Perfect. We shook hands, said our hellos and he steps up close, "You have some fine pieces in that shop of yours on Gold Street," and all with a bit of Boston in the background.

"You been to my shop?"

"Don't be modest, Mr. Diamond. The word is out. If you want some fine and authenticate 19th Century

Chinese furniture made for the European market you go see Harry Diamond in San Francisco."

I liked the guy immediately.

Wyatt examined the scroll in a private cubicle of the bank. He had brought his equipment of lenses, chemicals and later even left to get some X-rays of the painting. Eight hours later he shook both our hands, replaced all his stuff in his doctor looking bag. He walks up close to Liu and says, "I've never seen that Zhou before. Congratulations, it's a classic" and smiles thinking how cute he was. He asks if he could get the scroll for an exhibition some time. Lui smiles. Damn, they know each other. Wyatt hands Liu and me a photocopy of his Certificate of Authenticity. Absolutely no question now, Wyatt put his imprimatur on the *Late Autumn* by Zhou. The damn scroll is kosher. Then I'm thinking there's something about that guy I don't trust. Too soft? Too effete? Too close to Liu?

Raising the necessary money for Liu now became my next job. I took all my cash, and turned in my IRA's while hating to pay the tax on them. I told a faceless voice at Ameritrade to sell, at market, all the stuff I had hanging around. It broke my heart to sell those lovelies, but what the hell, in for a penny, in for a pound. My total liquid assets came to one hundred and fifty thousand. Donald Trump I'm not.

If the gross is unimpressive you gotta remember I have two ex-wives, and while they aren't rapacious, there are obligations to meet. Next, I listed the entire inventory from my shop, The China Trade, the entire stock. I put the value of all my cloisonné plates, chairs, tea caddies, brass lions, ceramic dragons and Chinese-made Queen Ann chairs in neat columns.

My worldly possessions sat there in black and white, line by line, all my assets except my mortgaged condo and my Red Official. My net worth sat staring at me. To tell the truth, even I couldn't get excited. Taking the tally of my shop's inventory to the Bank of America I asked for a loan against all my little beauties. I also offered my past loan history, and a short plea to the Gods. Somebody listened as the bank gave me a demand loan for two hundred and fifty thousand. I suspect the prayer didn't do half as much as the interest rate charged. I know it pressed just beyond all usury laws. Now came the insanity.

I took the same inventory and sashayed into the Wells Fargo on Samson. Again I offered the list as collateral and sure enough the same prayer enabled another two hundred and fifty thousand loan under the same terms. When I walked out of the bank a bead of sweat wet my upper lip. Big shot, I couldn't even handle a grand larceny of borrowing twice on the same assets without peeing in my pants.

"Jake," I asked myself, "what are you doing, looking to reopen Alcatraz?" I had become a felony in the making, and wondered if California gave seniors a discount on hard time. Hell, I've got my buyer and the cash for the scroll. I'm feeling big time. I'm going to pull this off. Still, my heebie jeebies got my knees knocking. I gotta get some distraction, some loving. I call the wonder of my life, Sharli.

We've been seeing each other for five years now, about as long as the longest of my marriages. I know, I know, after all this time why didn't I make an honest woman of her. Well, I'll be perfectly straight, she not an honest woman, she's a real estate agent. She also owns this sweet 1920's Edwardian on Russian Hill, near Polk. It has three two-bedroom apartments and she hasn't raised the rent in two of them for the time I've known her. "Jake, I can't. One is an old Chinese couple raising two grandchildren and the other family is Irish with two lovely boys. The man is a house painter and has a delightful brogue but no green card."

She recently told me what the third goes for. "Yikes," I said, "how can you charge such numbers?"

"For those two computer nerds, it's as easy as embroidery."

Did I tell you she's half-Chinese? The other part? It doesn't matter.

"Jake," she once said, "I'm like the progressive income tax, taking more from those who can afford it."

Of course I'm lying about why I've never asked her to marry me. The tone about her being a real estate agent, an answer I give to the wise guys who live down in Miami when I visit my brother. The real skinny hurts. I'm gun shy. Married two times and a failure at both.

Sharli's place is out on Sacramento Street, just past Fillmore, near a small park. It's a neat U-shaped building with a Spanish fountain in the courtyard. On her walls hang those gold painted Chinese screens of long legged cranes standing in leafed ponds. You see them all over Grant Avenue, in the tourist stores.

My sweet lady actually prefers her Chinese name, Chai Ling. While it's on the door to her apartment it's not my preference. I have a reason for it but not now. One thing I've kept secret about the lady I love, she has a slight limp, and she thinks me terrific, clever, sweet and I walk like John Wayne. You know, the way he placed one foot in front of the other in a pigeon-toed fashion. Maybe I do, I don't know. What I can tell you is her exotic aura reminds me of an oriental Hedy Lamarr. She tells me I'm crazy. I don't think so.

Sharli answered my knock.

"You look great, kid," I offered on entering. After awhile you're bound to learn something right. But she really did catch my breath in her embroidered red blouse and soft brown wool skirt. Younger than me by fourteen, no, fifteen years, it always depended whether we were talking American or Chinese time. This business of the Chinese becoming one-year-old as soon as they're born always threw me.

When I lived back in Coney Island I got a job with Izzy Klein guessing the ages of those who would sacrifice two bits for the privilege. Anyhow, the Chinese always screwed me up with their one year old at birth business, but who can tell how old they are anyhow?

I suggest to her we go to Sam's for fish. She says, "Oh, goody." Now why does that please me? At the restaurant the first thing out of her lovely mouth, "Jake, you look worried." That's why I never play poker, 'specially with her.

"Naw, nothing. Just a shopper from Taiwan, a Mr. Liu. He said he'd be back."

She gives me the fish eye but it dies there, thank heavens.

The salmon in dill mustard sauce couldn't be beat and she's off telling me about her day's business. There's an energy there, an up-beat cadence and I always get the feeling tomorrow there's going to be world peace. I don't think she's ever down except when her mother creeps into the conversation. Seems the old lady still misses her family in Shanghai. Anyhow, I catch the feeling knowing

I gotta hold up my end so I start to tell her about the Baptist preacher and the cowboy.

"Jake, not another one of those terrible stories you hear from those other dealers."

I ignore her irreverence.

"This cowboy's on a flight to Texas," I begin, "and the hostess asks him what he'd like. He orders a whiskey and soda. The stewardess gets it and returns. She then asks the preacher next to him if he'd like one. The preacher rises half out of his seat, "I'd rather be tied up and taken advantage of by women of ill-repute than let liquor touch my lips."

The cowboy hands his drink back and says, "Me, too. I didn't know we had a choice."

Sharli looks at me and I get a kick under the table but she breaks out giggling, demurely, of course, so no one would turn their head. That's my gal. I could take advantage of the situation cause once you got a lady laughing the evening is yours.

I call a cab and we leave for her place. Just so you know, sex between us is always a delight and tonight my thoughts were right up there with Utamaro's Japanese prints of sizable phalluses, errant pubic hairs and reticent tits. For those of you who haven't had the sensual pleasure of your lips trailing down female Oriental skin, allow a bit of advice—do it. I'd like to say it's like spring rolls, once you start in, well, you know. Sometimes I think that's why we're made, for the sheer extravagance of pushing sensuality till there is nothing but that. And after, I can assure you, counting sheep has become an unnecessary art.

CHAPTER 3

T HE FOGHORNS ON the bay wake me. I'm smiling
as I'm imagining the heavy cotton candy rolling
in under the Golden Gate. Sharli stirs and I say I'll call
later as I'm closing the door. In a few minutes I'm in my
office and back fighting my nerves about the deal with
Liu.

There's a devil on my shoulder repeating a Chinese
adage, "You can always cheat a foreigner, you can always
cheat a foreigner." It's something that's always with me
and I never buy anything in Chinatown until I see what
the Chinese are paying. Even then I count my change, at
least twice. But Liu, oh, he is good. He's has me on the
fishing line with a hook in my mouth. All I have to do is
jiggle.

I can't find an argument against myself so I go and
clamp down on the wriggling worm and give Liu the call.
He asks if I need another day or so. I say, "Naw," like it's
just another everyday transaction.

Liu comes by early, just after 9:30 AM and with just a few polite but unimportant words we go ahead and exchange my kraft paper bag full of bills for his scroll wrapped in older manila paper. That quick. I loved the way it came off, like something out of Dashiel Hammett. Without even a glass of champagne or even a bit of kosher wine sealing the deal Liu tells me he's catching the afternoon flight to Taiwan. I wish him well and I'm back in my office basking in Zhou's genius.

Yeah, I admit it's a hell of a risk buying this little baby but it's going to provide Sharli and me days in Cancun, nights in Vegas. That little painting, that *bubbala*, it's everything.

I have a safe in my office, it's a big Mosler left over from the previous tenant, a jewelry maker. When I rented the building he told me the Mosler reeked of security from prying eyes, thieves, and fifteen hundred degrees Fahrenheit. In my quaint old way I still didn't trust any of it. I kept my real goods beneath two floorboards under my swivel chair by the roll-top desk. Silly, but it's the way I am.

Yes indeed, I'm feeling good. Yes, indeed. I've got a classic painting under the floorboards and a buyer just down the street. All those worries about, money, the future, all solved. I notice my telephone messages have been piling up and I suspect they're all from Taylor. I'm right. I punch his number into my keypad and he starts right in.

"Jake, my Zhou, when can I get it?"

"You have the cash?"

"C'mon, Jake, you know, almost 3 million, it'll be a few days."

"Well, that's when you get delivery of the Zhou."

In all truth, I wanted the scroll just for myself over the next few days. I didn't plan on handing over the gem until I'd had my fill. The longer it'd take him to pull the money together the better I'd like it.

"Taylor, you can take a couple of days. I know you're good for it and you know I have it" And that's the way it went for just over two weeks until Taylor's anxiety and phone calls got the better of both of us. I promised him delivery the next day.

Still early, the sun is starting to melt the clouds and I'm back in my office a bit sad knowing this'll be the last time I get to spend time with my classical beauty. Sitting by my roll top desk I reached to the floorboards and gently pulled out the Zhou. I needed these last hours with the eleventh-generation descendant of the founder of the Sung dynasty. A hand scroll, ink on silk, about ten inches by forty-eight long—personal art made specifically for the Emperor. I rolled it open and sat it on a broad easel.

The scroll is simple ink on simple silk. A coming winter scene with clear mountains and broad valleys, islands in a watery lowland punctuated by clusters of raggedy trees, and pavilions seemingly lost among the branches. Not a soul, not a boat, nor bird, nor cloud, nor wind, nor snow. Just quiet, coming cold, great space, and great loneliness. The master's touch. I smiled. The artist stands off as simple recorder in cool detachment. Pure style. I knew enough Chinese to read the equivalent date, 1302 AD. The Yuan Dynasty, a heritage established under Genghis Khan's grandson, Khubilai.

I bathe in all the painting's provenances, its documentation, and its pedigrees. There is Zhou's signature in vermilion ink chops; Chinese characters first carved into soapstone, inked, and pressed to the silk. His calligraphy, its rhythm, proportion. The master's touch. There's even a chop of the emperor who subsidized the painter. There are the official papers from both the caretaker eunuchs of the Forbidden City and the directors of the National Museum in Taiwan, all guaranteeing authenticity. And now I even have the imprimaturs, the affidavits of the expert, Wylan Wyatt, Winslow Professor of Chinese Art, UC Berkeley. The only other authority would be old Zhou himself. No question, everyone signed on, it's the real McCoy.

Deciding to shut off the overhead fluorescent, I went to my desk and focused the clean light of a halogen lamp to the painting. I reached for my cigar, placed it in my mouth, and it stayed there, unlit. The power of the work is pulling me into its space. I felt myself cold, alone, lost among the mountains, an eerie feeling. Another minute. Okay, enough. I turned to close the lamp. and hesitate. Something wasn't kosher, somewhere.

I walked up to the painting and my eye cataloged each hill, every tree, and all branches. My senses followed each stroke from start to finish. My attention went to the top right corner where Zhou's stylistic chop, his seal, in red ink, dominated. There! Right there! Oh, God.

How the hell did I miss it? Easy to overlook, just a few off-colored strands of silk. A subtle shade difference melding in among the others. But it's not just the silk, it's also the chop's vermilion ink. It appears, what, somehow wrong, too thick for something done all those centuries before, almost wet.

Taking a step to the desk I opened the top drawer and brought out my penknife. Moving back to the easel the small blade steady in my hand I scraped carefully, gently, along a single off-color silk thread. It came off easily.

Now between my fingers it is pliable and yellowing at the ends. I didn't like it one bit. The older the silk the less its moisture content making it whiter, more brittle. Damn, damn, I'm in trouble, deep trouble. I figured the thread I'm holding is maybe, what, fifty, a hundred years old, tops.

I go back to the scroll with my knife and tried to keep my growing anxiety at bay. Placing the tip of the blade to the vermilion ink of Zhou's signature, I gave the slightest flick and the smallest piece of red flakes off. Placing it on my forefinger I rubbed my thumb over it, once, twice. What I'm afraid happens, the color shows on both fingers.

While I'm not an expert in these things, the making of the ink is well known. A red dye is mixed with linseed oil giving the mixture a certain lump quality and color intensity. With time the linseed oil coagulates, hardens, almost to stone. I take a deep breath, attempting to gain control, but I can't.

Dammit, it's supposed to be almost a thousand years old, it shouldn't give off color. I look to the painting then to my thumb, there's no question, the red is there, even bright. I had to sit down.

"That bastard." I kept looking at my fingers, "the smooth talking bastard." My eyes rise to the ceiling, "I should have known. I should have known." That friggen Charley Chan.

CHAPTER 4

I'T'S FUNNY ABOUT trust, once given it's almost too difficult to take back. To me the old man oozed confidence and honesty, like Ronald Reagan, and now he seemed more like Richard Nixon. Damn. I sat there staring into a cold scene of loneliness of classic ink on silk. The painting is still taking my breath away like one of those calendar Vargas women who I'd dream about as I reached puberty. And now I had to admit this three million dollar painted piece of silk is maybe nothing but a three-dollar bill.

Rising from my chair I shut my door and close the light. The room became raven black, the way I wanted it, the way I felt. I sat there stewing, mad at Liu, myself. I let my anger run through for a little longer, brooding, thinking.

Wait a minute, wait a minute, it hit me.

I put the lights back on in my office and reached to pull out the affidavits Wyatt had given me, photocopies of his Certificates of Authenticity. While my earlier impulse had me ripping them in half, a second's thought told me I have his professional opinion of the painting's legitimacy. Hell, if I'm not mistaken, he'd be financially responsible. I acted on his expertise. I could sue him for damages, my losses. Yeah, I felt better.

Copies? I need the originals for them to hold up in court. I rummaged my desk for the phone number and quickly dialed.

"Is Professor Wylan Wyatt there?"

A woman asked my name.

"This is Jake Diamond."

Some voices off to the side, muffled. She came back. "I'm sorry, he's not in"

"He's where?"

"China."

"China, what the hell is he doing there? Where in China?"

"Please, sir. In Hangzhou.

I calmed. "And he's returning when, my dear?"

She hesitated, not knowing whether my tone had insulted her or not. "In four weeks," a pause, "sir."

Panic. "Damn it, do you have a number for him?"

It became her turn. "No, and keep a civil tongue in your mouth." She hung up.

What the hell's going on?

Friggen experts, all of 'em, bastards. Years ago, I hit a guy with my Honda. He sued and they brought along an expert, an economist to set personal damages. This whore then goes ahead and begins to estimate this, that, whatever. He's sitting up there, straight faced, talking about the dollar value of the guy's denial of connubial rights. They were charging me because the guy couldn't get laid, and all for a sprained ankle for crying out loud.

I went back to the painting and hold it at arms length. A whore in Queen's clothing. I brought out the knife and became sorely tempted but only took off two small strands of the discolored silk and carefully picked off another fleck of red ink. Placing each in a different glassine envelope I put both into a larger one, walked out to the street and set the outside accordion gates. As they say, before they gut you for cancer, "You'd better get a second opinion."

In ten minutes I stood waiting for the Number 48 bus on Van Ness heading to Hayes Valley where Teddy owned the Bamboo Lantern, an Oriental curio shop.

Teddy impressed. He is a big man harboring a small ego with kindly acts. A Stanford dropout he had gone to teach English in China, Kunming.

"Jake," he said, "you should go there. I always wanted to see the last stop of the Burma Road, the place where the Flying Tigers landed."

Teddy lectured there during the eighties and knew more things Chinese than their ambassador. More important, he had a small lab in the back of his current shop where he would test paints, porcelains, metals, just about anything Asian and for any purpose. I always believed he enjoyed that part of his business more than anything else. "Teddy, Teddy," I called entering his shop.

"Jake? Back here."

You really couldn't tell what Teddy had in his place as everything was hidden by heaps of things of apparent Chinese or Japanese origin. There were complete stone gates from Chinese towns long destroyed, copied brass horses from the Sung Dynasty, yellow and red silk Chinese and Japanese robes hung on black lacquered screens. There were *mah jong* sets everywhere. To make matters worse, every thing he had existed in some sort of disrepair, damaged or crushed, some beyond redemption. It appeared he only cared for birds with broken wings, club footed dogs, and canaries that wouldn't sing. I adored him.

His six-foot-six frame came out of his flotsam fortress with a dust cloud trailing. He had a habit of eating beetle nuts and those purple drippings had stained his gray-blond goatee. His black eyebrows could have hidden one of those sideshow black Malay birds who find your fortune if you put a quarter in its beak.

"My good friend, Jake," he said as he placed his arm about my shoulder, "you need something fixed?"

I pulled out the envelope containing the red ink and silk strands of my *Late Autumn* painting. "Could you tell me something about these?" I hesitated. "Today. It's important."

He didn't even glance at what I gave him. "Of course. Give me two hours. I'll come by your place. We'll talk."

From Teddy's I caught the Market Street trolley to Montgomery and started to walk. I like my shop's location centered in the middle of Gold Street. Jackson, only a block over, has a whole slew of antique shops, but none strictly Chinese, or even Asian but almost everyone carried something Oriental.

Patrick has a classy place selling Louis the Fourteenth stuff. My interest had always been his seventeenth century map of China, a wood block engraving on rice paper by Junyi Cao. No question, a real doozy. But the price, absolutely beyond my reach, even with my professional discount.

"Jake, when are you going to take it off my hands? I know it'll be more comfortable with you. You must have memories of the country."

Patrick, a stand-up kinda guy would never stoop to just selling me.

"Yeah. Maybe pretty soon Pat, pretty soon."

Looking at the map it hit me. All I really knew about Chinese geography has always been the one big house in the damn cold part of Manchuria. The Chinese kept me prisoner there during the Korean War. I too vividly remember when their damn bugles and heavy cotton coats crossed the Yalu and minced the 5th Army and our chicken-shit lieutenant surrendered the entire squad. They never did give us to the North Koreans. Instead, they brought us to this sprawling house in the black hours of night and returned us to the 39th parallel when the Armistice was reached in the same fashion. I never knew where they brought us.

The sprawling house had windows doubled to keep out the cold. When winter came they sealed the panes to the frames with tape to keep the Gobi desert from blowing into the rooms. An inhospitable large place, it had varnished black rippled wood paneling and an awkward central stairway, neither circular nor logically angled.

We were five American POWs, including Harry, and it's all that mattered. It was only proper Harry and I were together. After all those years of childhood in Coney Island we were, well, brothers. I say it now but you know, and I even dislike the thought, there was something, some place way back in my head which always buzzed when I gave Harry something of my inner thoughts. Harry was too often too smart, if you know what I mean.

There were also about a dozen Chinese officers in that isolated house whose names and faces kept changing. They lived in the comfortable bedrooms upstairs. They were arrogant as hell with us being Westerners and them Chinese. You know how it is. While never nasty they did bang us on the occasion, more for show than cruelty. But Qin, now there's was guy who liked to hurt. No, hurt is too mild a word.

We slept in the cellar where the large coal furnace provided heat keeping us warm and perpetually filthy. From a large front porch there loomed a city some miles away. I could make out smokestacks and even church spires. Imagine, church spires. One of the guys who understood some Chinese thought it Mukden. What do they call it today, Shenyang? Anyhow, I didn't believe it; we were too close to Korea. I still think so. Harry, who quickly picked up the lingo of the Chinese never said a word but I think he knew. Hell, I've pored over maps for years and I could never really figure out where we were even after Harry and I tried to escape.

My finger traced along the Korean border of Junyi's map when Pat tapped me.

"Should I roll it up for you Jake?"

"Thanks, Pat, not today."

I had to leave as I knew Teddy would be on time. On my way out I called back, "Let me know if someone makes you an offer," as though I could buy anything more than a pair of chopsticks.

I walked onto the street and almost ran into Mickey on his way with my coffee and Danish. "Oops, sorry kid. Come on, walk with me, help me open the store." But I could see things were not right. A furrowed brow replaced the high-keyed alertness he usually carried.

Mickey is American down to his slang. His parents are Chinese, from Taiwan. He's a good kid, quick eyes, and slow hands. While I had to gaze down to meet his glance he still had good size for a Chinese. I figured his family originally came from northern China where they grew 'em taller.

"Jake," Mickey says to me on the sidewalk, "I'm glad I found you. My apology. I don't have any time. Please take the coffee, I must run, my mother, she is old, she is waiting."

"Sure, sure," I said reaching for the containers. "What's wrong?"

"Her brother, he's dying. My uncle." As he said it his quick eyes welled. "He is a good man. Very respected, very honorable," then, as an afterthought, "he took care of me one summer when I visited my family in Taipei."

"I'm sorry kid, tell her so."

He didn't hear a word. "I must run, Jake. My mother is waiting."

Damn, my mother would have liked him. No, I'm exaggerating. Always her baby and as good as Mickey, I thought of her dying while I stay imprisoned by the Chinese. It's not fair, not to be able to say goodbye. The world never seems to turn the way you think it should.

CHAPTER 5

I WATCHED THE KID leave. Seems nothing ever comes easy but I know I had the advantages. All my limbs functioned, I could do numbers in my head, and on the occasion women thought me good-looking. That's enough to win most games.

Now I'm back standing across from my shop on Gold Street and taking in the red brick building. It's a narrow structure with some length. The front has a single gentle arc window surrounded by lime leached San Francisco brick. In the left-hand corner on the large expanse of glass is my name in small, but tasteful gilt lettering.

The name of the place, China Trade, is printed in large yellow letters following the curved contour of the window. Underneath is, "Asian Antiquities" also in gold. I always get a kick out of it. Me, a lifeguard with hairy arms from Coney Island, a dealer in Asian antiquities. Imagine.

I took out my cigar and stuck it in my mouth. It immediately worked its way to a comfortable place by the right incisors. I'd still be smoking cigarettes if we hadn't started playing pinochle on Friday nights back in Brooklyn. For pinochle you need a cigar.

Walking across to my place I unlocked the accordion metal shutters, pulling them to the side. While they serve a purpose I really dislike them, installed only after a break-in some twelve years ago. I told a big Irish cop I thought they might have been Chinese. He didn't seem to care.

Inside the store my world dominated. A hush always overtook me each morning—the kingdom of old China. Here were the gentle bent lines of Chinese chairs, cabinets, storage chests, cut, joined, and finished without regard to time, things made specifically for western consumption. I liked everything, the textures, the woods, the intricate carvings, even the simple Chinese latticework, and yes, the smells. But it's in the porcelains the Chinese had the secrets.

The old Chinese craftsman originated those magnificent blues Delft ran to copy. And it became the Germans and French who salivated for the secret processes of cloisonné that delighted the courts of the Chinese Emperors. Sitting on their own pedestals like the Grecian caryatids were the startling blues and whites of Canton and Nanjing pottery. The Chinese, yeah, they had the goods. Always did.

When I walked back to my office I sat heavily in my chair facing the roll-top. I had to get to Taiwan, to get to the old Chinaman. Absentmindedly I opened the top drawer. An Army .45 pistol lay there, glistening. I've cleaned it every week for the past twelve years, since the time of the break-in. When I fired my previous .45 back in Korea the damn weapon always made a big noise and a bigger hole. To remove temptation I kept the bullet clip in the bottom drawer. I looked at the piece and wondered if I could get it through Chinese customs. It might come in useful when I caught up with Liu. Who am I kidding? Guns were never really my style. I put it gently back on its cloth and closed the drawer.

I sat back and waited for Teddy.

The soft bell over the front door tinkled. I smiled calling out. "Back here, Teddy."

Lowering his head as he walked into my office, he came straight to the point. "I have a feeling you know the threads and ink you gave me are of fairly recent vintage."

"Uh huh," became my intelligent reply.

"I figure jus tabout the time the Second World War," he continued.

"Anything else?"

"Yes, unfortunately. I've seen the same materials on forgeries of ancient Chinese silk paintings, copies of Forbidden City stuff. Is this where these came from?"

I stayed quiet.

"Jake, there's a lot of stories about these forgeries, about journeys across China. Cloak and dagger, Nationalist and Communist confrontations, Chiang Kai-shek and Mao's generals. His brow scrunched. "Are you involved?"

"Me? Just tell me what you know."

"Don't rush me Jake, okay. I'll tell you the way I need to.

"Sure, Teddy, take your own pace.

He sat on a stool with no back, interlaced his fingers behind his head and closed his eyes. "In 1937, some 20,000 crates of China's great art from the Forbidden City were shipped to Szechwan to escape the Japanese onslaught.

Jake, imagine, 20,000 crates packed and catalogued. A few years later the Japanese were defeated. When Chiang had to run to Taiwan before the victorious Chairman Mao he had the world of Chinese art at his disposal, but his generals said he could only take 4,000 of the 20,000 boxes. Those 4,000, Jake, the best." His eyes went to the heavens, and settled back to mine.

"Chiang figured he had a better chance of them getting to Taiwan if the crates took different routes. So he split the shipments into three, one going down the Yangtze, another by train to Shanghai. Three barges of the crates were sent through the longest route, through the Grand Canal." Now he spoke quickly, unsure. "Anyhow, there are some stories about that canal shipment, supposedly the Communists discovered the barges and took off after them. All kinds of cloak and dagger. Even sinking of the treasure."

The Grand Canal, huh? I didn't have the foggiest, but I figured I'd better shut up. "Teddy, anything more?"

"Nothing hard, Jake, just some wild rumors about a dealer gone looking for the crates but coming up empty." He gives me an odd look. "Jake, what's going on?"

"I'm not sure, Teddy, I'm not sure."

I almost had to push him out the front door as he kept telling me he needed to see what I had. He started up the street giving me a half-wave. I became too caught up in myself to return the salute. No question, I had to get to the old shyster, Liu.

I walked back to my office and pulled out *Late Autumn* and gave her another look. No question, a charmer, lovely. All I had imagined. But you know there's always a danger when you're married to a gorgeous woman, particularly when you are a kind of palooka guy like me. Need I say more?

I sat there and let time pass holding the scroll, kinda stroking its silk. I started talking to it, quietly cursing its lie. It became the second time I took something inert and Chinese and made it alive. Back then, in that cold dark house in the middle of no place Manchuria were rooms full of antiques; chairs, vases, plates, and even Chinese lanterns. Surrounded by handicrafts from the Chinese factories of Canton, Peiping and Shanghai I had to ask what the hell did the owner find so bewitching? What brought him to surround himself with these curios? Like a seed in fertile soil, I tried to reach the light beyond and like most discoveries it took months of searching and, of course, I found it in a moment.

Back then I had sat on an Elmwood horseshoe-back armchair idly gazing at a row of cloisonné vases, nothing spectacular. I moved my palm along the chair's curved seamless rounded crest rail and adjusted my position looking to the pierced key designed brackets joined with a footrest and wooded stretchers. That's all there was to it, a quick simple feeling of comfort and the esthetic touch of craftsmanship, pleasing to the eye, to the intellect. Now I know that sounds highfalutin, but that's the way it came to be. The lacquer, the dovetail seams, the patience in carving the ruyi-head medallion. The whole room emanated talent and the patience of the Orient. I can tell you I became smitten with the chair, the cloisonné, and all the things that engulfed me. The attraction of the lesser art and handicraft of the China Trade simply took me to a place not on the map. It happens.

I had too much time back then. I took every inanimate Chinese artifact in the dark rooms and made them a woman. I grew to understand the craftsman's eye, watched his fingers cut the wood for nailess joints, studied as he lacquered the wood for the highest sheen. Holding it, stroking it, I would ask it questions, and sooner or later it would tell all. By the time I left that cold house I had my love affair. It's still with me and while my little darlings spoke and revealed their secrets, my Chinese jailers had no such compunction.

"Ah, Mr. Jake. You are a foolish man, studying these trinkets like you do. We did not bring you here to improve your education, only to hear your English."

I liked my jailer, the guy in charge. Not the prettiest fellow, but he knew his men, his charges, the other POW's. "And all the time I thought we were brought here for the grotesque entertainment of Lieutenant Qin."

Qin's name brought him up short "I would keep away from him Mr. Jake. He likes to hurt. Just remember you are here for the odd way you speak English."

I figured this became my chance to find out things about my jail. "Lieutenant, whose house is this?

He glanced at me strangely, but gave what I wanted. "The man who owned this manse of little taste was English, of the Foreign Service. In his retirement he sought the cold, the loneliness of this place. So unlike the British, don't you think?"

Unlike the Brits? Hell, they always went for the extremes, the intolerable heat of the desert, and the numbing cold of the frozen North and South Poles. So the owner was a bureaucrat, son-of-a-gun. "Where is he now?"

"Dead." He witnessed my reaction and laughed. "Of old age. He had no family and loved China giving his estate to the State."

Later I would spy the Lieutenant as he picked up one of the pieces and inspect it with his eyes, his hands, and then place it back gently. I liked him for hiding his interest and figured all these Communist guys couldn't be bad. In one of our late night conversations he confessed he had an older brother who also liked art, but the more sophisticated kind.

In those years as captive I became expert, a champ, in the very best of things in the China export trade. I learned the names of the ships that brought them to Europe, to the United States, the dealers that sold them to the Oriental starved hungry Europeans, and the foreigners who collected them. After I got back to Coney Island I never again set foot in the land of Marco Polo. I couldn't, you see, Harry was still there. I left him in the black night, alone, to die.

I finally tired of looking at the scroll and thinking of those past years. I placed Zhou under the floorboards, shut the light, drew down the outside accordion shutters and walked away. When I got to the middle of the street I turned back to my building, and then to the sky. My words were soft "Please let some nice looking arsonist come along and burn the friggen place down." My God, I'm wishing my fire coverage would bail me out of my predicament. Talk about losing it. I had to find soft words and assurance.

My concern with Liu must have been hanging on my face for as soon as Sharli kissed me she asked if anything happened. "Actually, no. I just need you to make a call for me to Taiwan, to a Mr. Liu I told you about." I peered at my watch. "It's still too early there."

"Liu? Some thing's wrong isn't it?"

"Naw, nothing's wrong." I'm not about to tell her anything, at least not until I knew for sure. If I gave her the slightest hint she'd be all over me like an octopus, sucking out every little piece of information. I'd save that delight for later tonight, if you get my drift.

I went right to business. I had Liu's home and museum number and had Sharli try his place first. The phone kept ringing until the answering machine picked up. My darling spoke in her perfect Mandarin, leaving an urgent message to have Dr. Liu call Mr. Jake Diamond.

Let me tell you, if you haven't heard well-spoken Mandarin you've missed out on diphthongs and harmonics pleasing to even Henry Higgins. Well, maybe it's still a taste you had to learn to appreciate. Not like Yiddish, which is all sugar. Sharli dialed the museum where Liu acted as curator. His secretary hesitated, then said he was out. My sweet lady then repeated the message for him to call Mr. Diamond.

I knew I appeared too worried for her to keep her questions in check.

"Are you going to tell me what this is about?" She had her hands-on-her-hip stance. Confrontation or confession. I had no choice but to tell her the whole story, the suspected forgery, my stupidity, my debt.

With never a recrimination she came to action. "Jake, we must go to Taiwan. A telephone call won't do. Liu could put you off forever."

That's her—no nonsense. Let's close this deal, now. "Yeah, I know, but believe me, Liu is a stand-up guy, I'll bet anything on it."

"Jake, you already did." Damn that lady. Then she threw out a remark which I was even afraid to think about. "You know," she says, "it's possible he stole the painting from the museum and he's trying to pass a copy to you for the blame." I listened with my face all screwed up.

We sat on her blue couch watching some old reruns on TV, waiting for a call from Taiwan until it became early evening in Taipei. As time moved beyond my aging ability to stay awake I called it a night. For all I knew, C. Liu, Curator, never existed. Just before the sky lightened we went to Sharli's bedroom.

I can tell you I tried. Sharli would tell you I tried and that she tried in helping me try. The sadness of it all became the heavy burden of being a damned fool. Maybe the day just couldn't carry more excitement.

Chapter 6

I woke to familiar clean sheets and a loving voice.

"You up, Jake?" Sharli's voice came from the kitchen.

I peered down under the covers. Sure enough. "Yup," smiling as much from the thought as the odor of the coffee, and the feeling of the light starch in the sheet. What really gets me when I stay over Sharli's place are the fading remains of the scented fabric softener. Waking up to fresh sheets and dry towels—it's a whole new world.

"Did we get a call from Taiwan?" I asked.

I reached over and started to put on my pants. I wear jeans every day, including weekends, to restaurants, shows, and even the opera but only if it's Madame Butterfly and we come in at the second act for *Un Bel Di*. I tucked in my Pima shirt and like Superman in the phone booth I'm ready to take on anything coming my way.

"Jake, sweetie, we should fly over to Taiwan tomorrow and get this straightened out with Liu. You can't let it run too long."

I've always believed a, "sweetie" in the morning is worth two "darlings" at night. It's almost as good as a Starbucks's to get your day going right. I leaned over and kissed her.

"Sharli, you're right, but there's a couple a things I gotta do first."

There's always a chance with a new day yesterday's conclusion could be proven wrong. Anyhow, there were chores still to be done. As soon as she left for her office I called Taylor Davis. I had to prepare for the worst, a trip to Taiwan. To finance the journey I'd needed to sell the Red Official I had squirreled away, the one Davis and Liu liked.

No question, the sixteen-inch cloisonné figure of a stooped venerable bearded Chinese with a wide hat and flowing diaphanous red robes is a stunner. The open scroll he held spoke to his official status. What caught you were the details, the lines about the eyes and mouth, Chinese characters on the parchment paper. The cloth of the flowing cloak caught your eyes, its changing hues creating a rippling effect along its folds shouting craftsmanship.

The auction description when I bought it? Yeah, "The Red Official." I knew Taylor would be the buyer. He came over to my place once, picked it up and wanted to know all about it. I showed him the catalog of the 1987 Christie's auction of the salvage proceeds of the, "Geldermalsen," a Dutch ship sunk in the South China Sea some two hundred years earlier.

Taylor gave me a price back then but I wasn't ready. I knew he'd buy it today. I'd hate to get rid of it, but if you're a dealer you shouldn't be a collector.

I dialed his number. We smoozed a bit then made my offer. His quick okay told me I should have asked for another few thousand, but what the hell.

"I'll be there, Jake, later this afternoon. Your office."

Selling the red beauty almost broke my heart, like when Sylvia. my first love, told me she decided to go to the prom with Harvey. She said, "His prospects are better." Women know those kinds of things. The night of the dance I played nine-ball at Weepy's pool hall. Won forty-two dollars. I shouldn't remember such things.

I took the Red Official from my apartment to my Gold Street store and waited for Taylor to come with the money for my lovely figurine. The cloisonné sat on my desk in plain paper, probably ashamed I would sell him. Still, I had a stronger sentiment for the forty-two thousand, five hundred.

At 4:30 the ex-tennis pro tinkled the front door bell. He walked to my office and handed me an envelope, one of those large manila kind.

"It's all there, forty-two thousand five hundred."

The heft of the package felt good.

"It's all in hundreds, they still made a big bundle," he explained.

Taylor leaned over my shoulder and watched as I placed the money in the big Mosler safe. I reached over and handed him the paper wrapped package.

"Is this it?" he asked as he began to unwrap the figure. "Oh. Oh," he said now holding it paper free and turning it in one hand. With the other he caressed it as if a woman. "It is perfect." His eyes never released the Official. You knew he had the connoisseur's appreciation.

Then he asked, "Jake, the *Late Autumn*?"

Hesitating I offered, "It'll be delivered on schedule." What is the lie I ask myself? He hasn't even made a down payment, and I bear the burden of the fake.

Taylor spun slowly to leave then took a step back to me. "You know Jake, you're a fraud."

Oh, boy.

"You like to make people think you're hard and uncaring, but I know differently. You're soft, Jake, full of tender mercies."

Son-of-a-gun.

I turned away before Taylor left my office. I didn't want to see the Official leave my place. I know, I'm a dealer, but for this one I wanted to be a collector.

Taking out the money I had just placed in the safe I closed the shop and walked swiftly to the bank. I changed ten thousand to five hundred dollar travelers' checks and put the rest into my Bank of America debit card account. Now it became instant cash anywhere with an ATM. This modern world, miraculous. After my deposit I just kept walking up the hill to the Huntington; it had the classiest bar in town.

Chapter 7

Sharli picked me up in the morning and we drove to the airport, to long-term parking, caught the shuttle to international departures and walked to the first-class ticket counter.

My darling stared up at me with wide eyes. "You bought first class tickets? What's come over you?"

"I know," I said searching around to see if anyone listened. I moved close to her. "You know how I am on long trips, with the bathroom and everything."

We found our seats and became comfortable. Sharli's hand reached to a gold chain around her neck and started to rub her jade amulet. Now you know what jade is to the Chinese, well, to Sharli it's, as she once told me, her mojo. If it's working everything will go well. In order to get that voodoo going her green iridescent stone needed a little warming, a little kneading, like my baseball glove back in the sixth grade.

I love Sharli. She's organized, educated, and cool headed, most things I'm not. So maybe opposites do attract. She has one drawback though, she likes to hold hands while we're walking. But what the hell, every relationship requires some concessions.

Sometimes a feeling sweeps across and I need to ask her to marry me, but there's always a fear she'd run, so I never do. I mean, what am I? A wise guy from Coney Island, slugging it out to make a living. And every once in a while when I'm in the funk and realize the mess I've made, I'm thinking of Harry back in China. He kept urging me to escape with him. I kept insisting the word hero didn't fit my body type. I also reminded him there were the rumors of a cease-fire.

"You going to sit here till you're old and gray. Not me, Jake, no sir, not me. I'm going. Can I count on you?"

When a buddy asks, "Can I count on you?" you ain't got much choice.

"Sure, Harry, sure."

I shoulda kept my mouth shut. He'd be alive and I'd still have my pinky.

The flight over was a piece of cake. While I needed to catch some sleep, my thoughts were caught up in my stupidity of being cheated, and the disappointment of owning a fake. It's like having dirty hands. I needed to wash away the grime to make the world clean again. Damn, I didn't think I'd ever get snookered again. When I was fourteen it stunned with the same intensity.

Harry and I would walk the Coney Island boardwalk and sometimes end the evening at an auction drawing small crowds, selling what they said were factory closeouts. I believed. The auctioneer, "Just call me Al," held up this watch, "It's a genuine Gruen, fourteen carat gold case, sapphires for the hour marks."

I started to reach into my pocket when Harry nudged me, "Don't do it Jake. He's a hustler." Harry gave me my first big rule of business: You had to trust the seller as well as the deal. Harry, he always seemed to know, well, everything.

At the airport terminal Taiwan hit me head on. Noisy, crowded, pushing, hot, luggage all over the place and sounding like a tower of Babel. I'd been here a number of times in the past, usually for China Trade stuff auctions when a dealer went bust. Sometimes I'd get a call from a Chinese who heard I was a fair guy and would I like to buy his inventory. For some reason these deals worked out to where I did well, extremely well. I figured I must have a hell of a reputation but felt something else was at work. Anyhow, this time I'd only be here for two, three days. I'd get my money and head home. I had the scroll under my arm and it only went places if I came along.

My reservations were for the Golden China Hotel. Since my shop stood on Gold Street, I figured it had to be a good omen. You think me a little foolish? Not in this land of superstition and belief in gods. Talk to the love of my life who pays half her commissions to her Chinese astrologer. Remember, she grew up in Mainland China where Chinese Gods run amuck.

The Golden China Hotel stood on Sung Chaing Road and when the driver went up a wrong street my sweet lady was all over him with her longshoreman talk. The cabby cowered in fear. Arriving at the hotel the hours in the plane and the taxi had taken its toll. We were asleep before we could decide to go out to eat or just play around a little.

The next thing it's "Jake, get up, you know I have to leave tomorrow night. We must find Liu and get this thing straightened out."

"Yes, dear."

She scowled at me and unsheathed her fangs. "This is my town, Jake. You fool with me and you're on your own, for good."

Liu lived at Number 8, Lane 14, just off Changchun Road. The taxi stopped at the corner where some kind of celebration had cornered the market on noise. We pushed our way forward into the crowded narrow alley. A brightly decorated limousine with an electric organ strapped to its top blasted screechy tunes. The entire vehicle appeared festooned with flowers of every color and arrangement. The music twinged and twanged in Chinese fashion. Even more terrific were the girls in brief white bikinis singing and dancing in the middle of the street. I took a double take, three girls danced with absolutely no clothes at all. I liked this new China.

With the music becoming hard rock and those nude girls I expected the cops momentarily. Until then I just let my eyes take in the chaotic scene and reconsidered my views on Chinese civilization.

"Somebody died," Sharli whispered to me.

"Yeah, it must be me and I went to heaven," I said glaring at the naked women with bouncing tits.

"Jake, for God's sake I'm serious. All this is just a celebration for a good man who led a good life." She walked over to an elderly woman collecting white envelopes. From where I stood, it seemed as though they were brimming with Taiwanese dollars. I edged closer. Yup, hard cash. Sharli and the woman spoke a few minutes, then my darling reached into her purse and placed a few bank notes into the open envelope. The woman shook her two clasped hands for a thank you in traditional Chinese fashion. Sharli walked back without a happy face. "Jake, Liu is dead."

"Stop kidding. It's no joke."

"You're right, it's not a joke. He had a stroke about two days ago and this is the family's goodbye. It's his funeral."

If it's his, it's mine as well. She had to be mistaken. "What do you mean Liu is dead? How could he be dead? He owes me six hundred and fifty grand!"

"Jake, stop screaming. He's dead, Jake, he's dead."

"I'll kill the son of a bitch."

"Jake!"

Charley Chan, a handsome old man who had to sit down in my shop and pull out a blue pill, dead. I knew it, I knew it. He turned pale then, as though he wouldn't have made the next full moon. Well, he didn't.

Damn you Liu, I hope you're in Chinese hell. No, not there, I mean with Confucius, or whomever you're supposed to be with. Jeez, I liked you. You bastard.

"What the hell am I going to do now? I'm in debt up to my ass. No, beyond. I'm in a country where I can't understand more then a spoken word or two and I've got a painting that's, that's . . . ." I didn't have the slightest idea of what I wanted to say.

"Jake, stop *kvetching* for God's sake."

I should never have taught that lady a single Yiddish word. "Don't get cute with me Sharli. I'm not in the mood. My world is collapsing."

Sweeping the scene I see most of the Chinese were down the street celebrating with food trays being passed around. Almost alone now, Sharli and I looked at each other not knowing what to do. My face must have reflected the way I felt. My future became a life in debt, and time in the hoosegow. What a way to end up, me Jake Diamond, doing five to ten.

"Jake, maybe your brother Sam could help with some money?"

My older brother, Sam, the salt of the earth, he'd give me anything. He moved to Florida ten years ago and keeps telling me to come down and get away from the fog and the *shiksa* women. I went down three years ago and got talked into a game of pinochle, partners. I told those guys with the Brooklyn accents, and white shoes I'd be rusty. "No problem, it's a friendly game." Hah!

Just so you understand, pinochle had always been mine and I hadn't forgotten a thing. I sat down, put the last bit of the cigar in my mouth, near the incisors, and lit the match. By the time the sulfur burned off I had a perfect read of the table. My playing? Seamless. My bidding? Even the kibitzers had nothing to say. The other players, they tore into each other, complaining about everything, every card thrown, and those not thrown. The harangue became incessant.

"Yeah, I guess so, there's always my brother." I stood there staring at Sharli, not knowing what to say, not knowing which direction to go. Not knowing which vein to cut.

The celebration of Liu's death drifted out of sight and we stood like two orphans without a home. I expected some Good Samaritan to come along and drop some coins at our feet. Any little kindness would have been appreciated. I'm staring stupidly up the street and I see hands waving, like trying to get my attention.

"Jake, Jake, is that you?"

Jake? There's another Jake in Taipei? Looking up the street there's a big smiling face come running toward me. The grin became Mickey, the kid, the Chinese Gentile who brings me my morning Starbucks. It hit me as he's waving his hand he's a Chinese version of Archie Comics, something out of the '40's and '50's. Picture him: crew cut, innocent, a girl friend named Jia who he took for some noodles at the local dim sum hangout. Could I ever have been so young in Coney Island?

"Mickey," I ask incredulously, "What the hell are you doing here?"

He blinks at me, a little befuddled. "What am I doing here? I'm Chinese. It's where my parents come from. What are you doing here?" Then he reacted to the stunning looker who stood by my side. "You are Miss Sharli. You are from Shanghai."

You can't surprise my gal; no one can shock a Chinese San Francisco real estate agent. "And you're the young man Jake gets to bring him his coffee." How the hell do the Chinese know so much about each other?

It soon became my chance. "Kid, what's going on?"

His eyebrows rise slightly. "I told you the other day in the city, Jake. My uncle took ill. I had to go to my mother. Well, he died. There," and he pointed to the end of the street, "we're having his, what do you call it, his wake?"

"Not in my world." When you're Jewish and somebody dies its certainly not a joyous moment. Later you go to some relative's house where all the mirrors are covered, and you tell lies about the good deeds of the deceased, how young, and, my, such a good-looking corpse. Then after a little schnapps, a little Mogen David, a *yenta* remarks maybe he appeared better with the embalming fluid. Oops.

"Kid, you're part of the Liu family? You're here for the funeral? I don't understand." Then I think maybe it's not coincidence the kid is here. "What do you know about the *Late Autumn*, the painting Liu sold me?"

"The what? The *Late Autumn*?" then, almost proudly, "but I'm the one who told uncle Liu about you."

"You told him about me? You're the son of a bitch sent him to me?"

The kid reacted, stunned. "Jake, he said he needed an honest and honorable art dealer to sell a valuable painting. You were the one I thought of." He thought for a moment. "But I think he knew all about you even before I mentioned your name."

Funny thing about the kid, he came into my Gold Street shop about a year ago, peered around, picked up a few pieces and checked out my prices and asks do I have any thing in the Ching Dynasty. We start to talk and I can see he's picking at my brain, like a little parakeet feeding from the little porcelain basket attached to the cage. But still he knows things, more than he could pick up from the street, from going to other dealers. About two months ago I gave the kid a broken Indian red and blue Japanese Imari bowl to give to Teddy for past favors. Couple of days later he calls me up to thank me. I told him never mind as it came with a bunch of stuff I had picked up in a steamer trunk at a Butterfield auction.

"Anyhow," he says to me, "I fixed the two halves the way the Japanese do it, with a rivulet of gold and Urushi lacquer as the adhesive. It gives a lovely muted glow to the repair seam." Even over the phone I could tell his self-satisfaction. He adds, off handedly, "The kid, Mickey, he knew how to do it, even corrected me when I was into it. Smart young man."

"Mickey, the painting your uncle sold me, it's a forgery and the guy you're celebrating, he stole my money."

The kid gazed at me with one eyebrow higher than the other, a trick I never did learn. "Jake," he said with his palms extended like a Buddha asking for alms, "my dead uncle hasn't left Taiwan in years."

Whoa. "What are you talking about? You said Liu was your uncle, and a moment ago we both agreed he's dead."

"Yes, Jake, my uncle, Lu Liu is dead."

"Lu Liu?"

"He's my mother's youngest brother. An ex-officer in the Red Army. She said he stayed in China with Mao and fought against the Americans in Korea. After he developed lung cancer they let him go to his brother in Taiwan."

"Kid, slow down, relatives is not my best language."

"My other uncle, Chun Liu, the one you know from San Francisco, he's alive," paused, "in Xiamen."

Did I tell you I love the kid? "C. Liu is alive?" I pivot around to face Sharli "See, Liu is alive, in Xiamen. In China?" I cocked my eye back to the kid. "Xiamen?"

Sharli steps on my toe. "Jake, Xiamen is the old Amoy, a port city just across the straits on the mainland. The scholar's desk you have, the Hua-li wood, you told me about the craftsmen in Amoy."

"Oh yeah, the nice one done by Huang." Yeah, Huang. I always liked his stuff, made without nails, with corners dovetailed. He did good work. I felt my smile widen. I regarded my lady. "If you know so much, let's go get the old rooster."

She glared back at me. "Jake. You know I can't go to Red China, how I feel, about what happened."

I did forget and felt like a fool. Me too, I can't go back. Bad memories. "No, you're right Sharli." Then I became sensible, realistic. My financial life hung in the balance. "Sharli, I need you with me. What happened is the past. China, it's a different place." I hesitated, not sure of my next words. "China and America, we're friends now." Oh sure, tell that to the California congressman.

"You're right, Jake. Everything changes." But I can see her thinking and I can tell I don't come out a winner." I can't go and face my brother after all these years."

When Sharli has that tone I know to find another way. "Whatever you say Sharli, is jake with me." Ho, ho. I shift back to Mickey. "What's your uncle doing in Xiamen? Making some more classic pieces of art?"

He ignores me, properly so. "Jake, my mom tells me he's doing some diving for some lost art objects. Well, not him, but he's running it."

It figures. "Look, kid, you speak Chinese, right? Give me a number where I can reach you."

Sharli's never really told me why she won't touch the soil of the Peoples Republic. I have my suspicions and it has to do with an Irish doctor from Boston, Kevin Hamilton. He joined the Chinese Overseas Hospital in Shanghai to help the country come out of World War II. China's allure smothered him and he married a Chinese woman. They had a child, Sharli.

Along come the Commies, right, and you'd think the good doctor would take the family and leave for freedom. Hell, no. "A sick Chinese is the same under either government," so said Kevin. Then Chairman Mao became a little nutsy, purging all foreigners sending them to the countryside, to work in the fields. For two years Sharli ate only sweet potatoes. Anyhow, the Shanghai hospital desperately missed the doctor's expertise and called him back.

All's well that end's well, right? Not in China. What's that German word? *Freudenschade*? The neighbors bristled that Sharli's family benefited by the foreign doctor's position. Somewhere, somehow the good doctor was either pushed or fell off the roof of the Shanghai hospital.

I could feel Sharli's fear of going to the mainland by telling me to go on without her and find Liu. As she said, she's just not ready yet to face her brother. Her brother? She has no brother. I stood there dumbfounded, again.

We went to the hotel after I told the kid I would contact him. In the room things were kind of strained. I didn't know why exactly and I didn't know what to ask. At dinner Sharli loosened up a little, but nothing about her brother and I didn't have the courage to ask.

"Jake," she said, "I'm glad you will be going back to China. I know this time it'll be an education. The Chinese, well, they're different."

You don't live in San Francisco and not realize the idiosyncrasies of the reigning population. I always figured dealing with their odd ways was a cheap price to pay for their magical cooks.

She kissed my cheek. "Be careful there, Jake. I don't want to lose you."

Lose me? What am I? A kid's mittens? I just leaned over the shrimp in lobster sauce and kissed her cheek.

CHAPTER 8

EARLY NEXT MORNING Sharli and I took a taxi to the airport. While the cabbie fought the traffic I tried a high note saying I'd go to Xiamen with the kid, get the thing straightened out and be back as soon as possible. "A day or two; three, tops. A piece of cake." And she comes back with a bit of reality.

"Jake, damn you. You know very well this thing won't be over quickly."

"Sharli, give me my fantasy. If I think of all the possible outcomes, I get too depressed." I don't know, is optimism congenital or simply learned? You know I believe all things will turn out right. Well, maybe not everything. I once believed the Brooklyn Dodgers would play in Ebbets field forever. Branch Rickey, hah. He's an anathema to the Brooklyn race.

We went through airport scrutiny and it's sensing devices. At least we kept our shoes on. I had brought the scroll with me not wanting to tempt the chambermaids back in the hotel.

"Sharli, hold on to this. Put it back in the office. You know where. I don't want to carry it around the Peoples Republic."

We kissed again. Except for my brother, she's the closest thing to family I have in this world. She walked through the gate taking with her a bit of my confidence. I'm getting convinced living alone in my latter years isn't much of an idea.

When I came back to the hotel I called the kid who came right over.

"Kid, I need you to come to Xiamen with me to find your uncle. Its worth a hundred and fifty a day plus expenses."

Without a moment's delay he came back with, "Make it two hundred and I'm yours."

"Pack your bags, kid." I just love bargaining.

"Jake, slow down. The Communists require a visa to get into the Peoples Republic. I'll meet you back at your hotel in a few hours."

I took another taxi to the northern edge of the city, to the National Museum where Liu said he was curator. I needed to see the previous home of my Zhou. When I entered, and I don't mean to be rude to my Chinese readers, but some of the rooms in the museum, well, let's just say the Guggenheim didn't have to worry. They should have hired the guy who did the Getty in L.A.

I'm having a look-see at all these treasures and walked to a back office asking some guy with a ratty suit if I could see the works of Zhou Mengfu. Whatever blood may have been in his face took a two-week vacation. You would think I asked for my admission fee back. The guy immediately ran to another office and a better-suited mendicant appeared.

"We are sorry, but currently all of the Zhou's are on loan. To foreign countries. On long-term exhibition. Perhaps you can come back, maybe next year."

What the hell's going on? I'm getting the run-a-round. Did they ever have any Zhou's? Or if they did, were they fakes like the one Liu sold me? I stared at the guy square in the eye and he came right back at me. I couldn't be a winner here. When I got back to the hotel Mickey said he had the visas and we're leaving early.

"What kind of hotel do you want in Xiamen, the 4 star Xiamen Inn or a smaller Chinese hotel called the Lujiang?"

I asked the prices. "The Lujiang it is," I said knowingly.

The kid left for his relatives and I went up to my room. Anxious to get a hold of Liu, I knew I wouldn't be able to sleep. To kill some time I went to the bar. I'm drinking a Tsingtao, nice beer, and this Chinese lady took a seat next to me.

Just between us, I never really get lonely as married has been my natural state. I mean, at first blush you'd think I'm tough, independent and would have the broads at my beck and call. Ah, I wish. You see little Jewish boys like myself, outside of Tony Curtis, are always out there scratching for it. Do I really have to tell you about little boys, those horny little bastards. At about the time I had my first orgasm I worked on the back of the Brighton Laundry truck after school. I took the wet wash to women and brought down the week's dirty clothes. My fervent wish, the hell with the tips, was to be seduced.

One lady, years younger than my mother, lived alone. She seemed a little scary because she had big boobs and always stared me straight in the eye. My world changed when she bent over to tie her laundry bag and those marvelous, warm, abundant breasts, popped into view, and all the way down to the nipples. I found heaven.

Smiling at her I said, "Yes ma'am, no ma'am." I even gave her the right change, and warmly refused her nickel tip. All the goodness just to get her attention, to fulfill my dream, to take her will of me. Anyhow, my real problem has always been lying to the ladies; I'm just about incapable of doing it. If I told them I loved 'em, hell, I had to marry 'em.

Anyhow, this Chinese lady leans over allowing me to peer at her décolletage. "Buy me a drink?"

"Sure." I called over to the bartender, "A beer for the lady."

She gives me one of those looks and a not too kindly, "Thanks, sport."

For a hooker she had a longer road behind than ahead, and you could tell her heart simply wasn't in it. I figured her at thirty-five, maybe forty, though still neatly turned-out. A well-paid secretary for sure. The hell with it. How could I even think of insulting Sharli? I never even made it to a second Tsingtao.

The flight over to China took the same time as driving over the Bay Bridge at rush hour. I asked the kid about the pronunciation of X-i-a-m-e-n, I mean X is a pretty tough letter to start a city name.

"Jake, before the Communists took over it probably would have been Shiamen, based on an English spelling system."

"No kidding?" I figured the Reds changed the spelling as they wanted nothing to do with the West. Of course they could have given it to some Brooklyn guys where pronunciation also has little to do with anything.

I took out a pencil and wrote out my old prison guard's name, C–h–i–n. He smiled.

"I'm sorry, Jake," and he wrote Q–i–n.

To me the old spellings were better, but hell, it's also true for the songs.

We landed and walked to customs where a red line separated those who had things to declare from those who didn't. There were two guys in uniforms off to the side with small side arms wearing sneakers and pale sissy green uniforms two sizes too large. Who the hell could take these guys seriously? I should talk, they taught us a lesson up by the Yalu.

A guard with a red band across his cap put his arm across my way. He spoke to me in Chinese, and I just stood there facing him. I knew he wanted to know if I had thirty pounds of heroin in my bag. The guy tried again. I shrugged my shoulders, a universal sign of dumbness. He got pissed.

"Do you declare anything?" he finally asked in exasperated English.

"No" and walked straight on, waiting for maybe a bullet to my head. The kid followed.

"Jake," he says, "you're a piece of work."

I ask him where he picked up that expression.

"From listening to you."

The ride to town approached the word dull except as we came closer to the port then every thing changed. The Lujiang Hotel lay at the end of the center white line and the beginning of the water, right by the bend where a ferry docked.

"Like it?" the kid asked

"Yeah, I like it."

The building with its brown brick looked like a forty dollar a night 1930's Chinese hookers style hostelry. Its steps swung around the front of the building in a semicircular fashion, facing both the port and the main street. They housed a school for hustlers.

"Change money, change money, buy jade, gold, cheap, buy me." Free enterprise in a Communist State. You had to love it. The players had the moxie of ticket scalpers at an old Ebetts Field Giant-Dodger game before the traitor Branch Rickey sold out.

A white-powdered faced lady with deep vermilion lips sauntered by. The kid elbowed me in the ribs and whispered, "Stay away from her." I looked closely. The kid had to be dead wrong as she appeared the sanest considering all the mayhem going on.

We made it to the lobby where things were a little more peaceful. It had a small bar and pool table off to the left. The reception guy turned out in a resplendent soiled white shirt and a frayed black bow tie. He gave me a welcome usually reserved for white guys in an all black bar.

I sent Sharli a fax with all pertinent information. We each went to our room with the kid saying he'd call his mother. I put away my stuff and we almost ran into each other exiting our doors. At the roof lounge we took seats by the window overlooking the neon lit harbor. Pretty scene.

I asked, "How old are you kid?"

He laughed. "C'mon, Jake, you know everything."

Eyeing him carefully I added four years to my estimate and said, "Twenty five."

"Not too bad Jake. You're closer than most. I'm twenty-eight."

"Okay then, what'll you have?" The little stinker ordered a scotch with a water chaser. Sure, why not, his wallet stayed closed. I took the local draft.

Leaning back I gave the kid a good going-over. Nothing unusual. Just black hair, brown eyes of the Chinese, and an innocence you could reach out and touch. No, a purity, kind of like two-year old blond girls you find in malls pulling at their mother's skirts to buy them a doll, which they are. I didn't know too many Chinese kids, but Mickey had an angelic quality.

"Why are you here, Mickey?"

"What do you mean, Jake?"

"Don't con me kid. The two hundred bucks a day hardly covers your bother. Did Liu tell you to tag along, to report my actions?"

The kid gave me one of those honest faces, like an altar boy giving the chalice to the priest, fearful of making a mistake. "No, I wouldn't do that Jake." He paused, appeared sheepish, then said, "My mother told me to go with you."

"Your mother? Kid, you're twenty-eight."

"She also said I should see the home of our ancestors."

"And?"

"I should visit with my Uncle Chun, we're the last he has." Then he lowered his head, raised his eyes to me, and confessed, "He may leave me his money."

I had to laugh. I also had an uncle, an old vaudeville second banana. He had a room and bath in an old ratty hotel just off Broadway at 47th Street. He lived there for thirty-seven years. I think maybe he had two suits and a tie, all bought in the '40's. Oh yeah, he sewed his pockets tighter than timpani drums. My mother told me, "Visit your uncle. He has no one else. Go, go, you'll get his money." Ha! Israel is 300 trees richer. I hope the kid makes out better than I did.

"There's something else, right?"

"No, Jake, that's it." He hesitated a half-second too long.

"Kid, you'll never make it with the women if you can't lie to a friend. What is it?" I took him off the hook. "Forget it. What's the plan for the next coupla days?"

I may have told him to forget it but we both knew his motivation was more than, what's that Latin phrase, filial piety. Anyhow, I figured it no big deal. Hell, he was just responding to hormones, or some such. Besides, the kid still didn't have a road map as to exactly why I wanted to see his uncle. I couldn't tell him I'd like to break the old geezer's neck.

He says to me, "My uncle telegraphed money to my mother for his brothers funeral from the Xiamen Inn. He's may be there."

We sat around a little longer and talked about nothing. I pegged him from the beginning, a good kid, smart, and fast eyes. He had a 50's sense about him, like Ron Howard in his TV show, *Happy Days*. After the beers we left to find Liu. And I foolishly thought it would be a piece of cake.

CHAPTER 9

COMING OUT OF the hotel the street appeared as a Chinese fire drill—all helter-skelter. There were cops all over the port area as traffic and people sprawled to all compass points. Although, I gotta tell you, the cops, they just weren't fearsome, at least not like the Guardia Civil in Spain. You know those guys, they carry .45 caliber burp guns slung over their shoulders and wear shiny triangular black hats. Some old geezer at the Plaza Real in Barcelona once told me they were made with the flat side at the back so when they lined them up to shoot those bastards they'd fit neatly against the wall. I bought the old guy *un cortado* for that one.

We braced ourselves for the streets and made it to the Xiamen Inn's entrance in a straight shot. As we walked up a bunch of glass doors were opened by short guys with tight colorful uniforms who seemed to have escaped from the old Philip Morris cigarette ads of years ago. They had these little red pillbox hats with matching tight jackets and gold buttons. Inside the registration desk sat off to the left in black and gold. To the right, a restaurant with a too wide smiling maitre'd at the entrance.

"Hey, Mickey. Go check to see if your uncle is here. I'll be in the bar."

Someone put some money into the place. As you walked into the lounge you faced a glass wall some fifty feet across. Behind, a waterfall maybe twenty feet high. I liked it, hell, I loved it. It had an almost mystical feel as you watched the water making its way down among rocks, foliage, ledges, but heard nothing. I scanned around the room to see if maybe the Chinese bandit Liu also enjoyed the view.

At the first table were three Chinese army officers. They had the look of command and were busy with their cell phones. Along side sat two small tables with some of the best looking hookers I'd ever seen, ever. They glowed with an iridescence of the hippest clothes, makeup, and costume jewelry. Someone had taught them well.

Did you ever see the movie of Shanghai in the '30's, you know, *Shanghai Triad*? Those little singsong girls who chirped and showed gleaming thighs had nothing over these birds. Sweet little attractive things. None of them broke twenty, Chinese or American time. I couldn't take my eyes off them.

I ambled over to the black plastic upholstered bar and ordered a beer, whatever they had on tap. Down about five stools three guys were speaking American. Two of them I found out were Vietnam vets, guys who tried it back home after their discharge but found it too tame. The third captured my eyes by his size, but I could see only his back. He must have felt me staring as he turned my way. Of course, Blacky.

The Red Official, the one I bought in Amsterdam, it's where I met this scary guy with big arms and tattoos. A diver, he had worked the salvage operation on the Dutch ship in the South China Sea for Swans and Son. He stayed around for the auction, and we became almost friendly. Well, that's overstating it. I never met anyone who became close to Blacky or even wanted to. We had a few beers the first night back then until a tasty little tart walked past and gave him a smile. He took off after her without even a by-your-leave.

He's looking at me with curiosity. It kinda comes back to him. "Jake, amigo, Jake Diamond, right? Chicago?"

Three things about Blacky, he had an irritating habit of always calling you "friend" in some language other than English. The other is you don't screw around with him. You give him straight, honest answers, always. You don't want him on the other side. Lastly, he's a kinda case of arrested development with a foul mouth. And, oh yeah, he was albino. But you'd better not remind him of it.

"San Francisco, Blacky, San Francisco," I corrected.

"Right. What are you doing here, Jake? How they hanging?"

"I'm searching for a guy."

"Me," he eyes fell to mine, "I'm looking for cooze."

My glance went to the girls at the tables. "You came to the right place."

"Damn, fucking right I did."

Blacky is easy to spot in a crowd. Imagine a gaggle of black hair all over his white body, Popeye forearms, and a perpetual scowl as though nothing could please him. To make matters even more dramatic, he's prone to Italian black silk suits with white on white shirts and matching ties. I figured he had a very boring closet—like mine.

An imposing figure all right, a frightening giant. In a moment of alcohol narcosis he once told me he hailed from St. James Parish in Louisiana. As he said it I could hear zydeco back country music. In his professional life he claimed expertise at two things, diving and whoring. One other thing, Blacky had something I'd love to have, a great gravelly voice, like an ocean wave drawing back over rounded shore stones. It makes him sound like he's seen everything and been everywhere.

We stumbled along for a few minutes talking about his dive those ten years ago. He started in on his women, went on for a few minutes and then hits me with, "I meant to tell you, Jake. I'm doing some diving off the coast."

I'm listening now, maybe there's something in it for me. "Big outfit?" I ask.

"Naw. Some old guy, works for a museum in Taiwan. He's freelancing. Fancy-dressing little bastard."

My jaw had fallen in some kind of disbelief. What the hell is this, a Russian novel where everything is coincidence?

"His name Liu by some chance?" I asked with trepidation. I didn't want to hear the answer.

His eyes brightened like a lighthouse as the beam came around your way. "Nothing gets by ya, Jake, does it? Is that why you're here?" Then his attention went over to a taller Chinese woman who just joined her fellow workers at one of the tables. She had on one of those classic dresses, you know, where the slit goes up so high you're embarrassed just looking. Blacky cuts the conversation in mid-stride with, "See ya around, amigo," and joined the *mah jong* table with the newest Dragon Lady.

One of the Americans seeing me alone ambled over. I felt good about his Yank friendliness. He bought me a beer and we started to schmooze. The guy dressed in a soiled light blue shirt with a white collar, an older plaid suit and a patterned tie. Brrr, low income stuff, but he has twinkling eyes and a terrific smile bringing you right into his world. He's built like a running guard for the Washington Redskins, the kind of guy you want on your side because he'll always be there for you.

We started off trading war stories, him telling me about the heat of Nam and I'm relating the cold of Korea. Very dull material. I asked what he's here for. Told me, "Couldn't take the States, they wanted me to work from nine to five. Now who the hell can do a thing like that? So I came back out to Bangkok and drifted here. I'm married, a local woman. I started a bike factory, on contract, mountain bikes, you know, K-2, Dyno."

"Oh yeah, sure, sure. Yeah, ride em all the time."

He gives me a once over and smiles. We finished the beer and it's my turn to buy. I called over the bartender and the Nam vet leaned back against the bar and his attention moved to the table with the women.

"You friends with Blacky?"

"Not exactly friends." I know he's going to tell me something.

"They say he killed his partner in Florida, in the Keys." And he sipped a little of his beer. "Blacky said they were diving together when his buddy swims away. He washes up on Marathon the next day with nothing but his fins."

"You know different?" I asked.

"The word is he and Blacky were in the treasure business. That Blacky cut away his air cylinder when they came across a pot full of gold coins from some buried galleon." He sees my astonishment. "Yeah, it's the word."

The other American down the bar called his friend and they put their heads together with the hotel manager. I sat there sipping my beer feeling kinda at odds with myself. The story about Blacky, totally believable. Then it appeared the conversation and evening had run down at the other end of the bar and the Nam vet gets up to go. He picked up a chair half-wrapped in brown paper and starts out. The long trip must have caught up with me as I watched until he only had two more steps before leaving the lounge.

"Hey, wait up." The chair. Damn it! I knew it as part of the China Trade, a piece I had sold in my store years ago. I took him to a seat in the lobby, and asked if I could take the paper off.

"Sure. Go'head."

My heavens, a friggen Chinese Chippendale side chair with its pierced stretchers, cutouts in the braces stabilizing the two sides. It had the Cabriole legs popular in the early 18th Century along with the excessive carving of the Chinese craftsman. I spun the chair over. Sure enough, pegged construction, not a nail to be found. It couldn't be, no one made them like this today and yet the chair I held had to be spanking new.

"Where the hell did you get this?"

The fire-plug came back with, "What's the big deal, I'll get you as many as you want."

"As many as I want?"

"From Huang. He has a small factory out near the University. If you're interested in this stuff he also has some old looking scroll paintings."

Of course. Son-of-a-gun. Huang of Amoy. Alive and well? Couldn't be. "Take me to him."

Almost exasperated he barks, "Hey, give me a break. It's Saturday night. I have a wife and little girl at home." Then he backed off a little, spoke softer. "You can find it, he's near the little hurricane port for the fishing boats, out by the Buddhist temple. Ask any cab driver."

Ask a cabby? Where am I, Hoboken? Then I saw the kid walk in, waving to me. He came over and the Nam vet walked away.

"Jake, my uncle is registered here, but he's not in. I left a message."

"Damn his hide." I don't know what to do. "Let's just get outta here."

Back at our hotel neither the kid nor I were tired. Mickey asked if I wanted to shoot a little straight pool. Now nine-ball is usually my game but it's been years. I always knew if I put a little more time into it I could have won serious cash but as a kid living in Coney Island, hell, for the big bucks you had to get to the city, mid-town, the hustler's world. No matter, if you're an adult shooting money pool, well, it's a mug's game. Even at sixteen I knew a nine-ball player operated just this side of society, kind of like bookies, and cops, close to the criminal. I think Woody Allen once said clowns sit with the children. I guess pool hustlers stay with the hipsters.

When I played it only amounted to walking around money. In Coney Island summer was the time when I made the money with Izzy Klein and his Mid-way hustles. He's dead now, but he taught me.

I racked the pool balls and let Mickey break. He ran three but I could see he wasn't competition. I sunk the balance. Putting some power into my break I put away the three in the corner and the seven just about made the side pocket. Getting back into the game I felt my stroke working well, smooth and straight. I put away the one, four and five when a freak carom scratched me into the far corner pocket. It became the kid's shot with a wide-open table.

"Jake," he says stroking, "there's another reason why I'm here," and his eyes lifted to meet mine.

I figured the kid's conscience finally got him. He rose up from the table and chalks his cue, hesitated, like he's thinking things over. He found something interesting on the floor and began pushing a cigarette butt with the toe of his shoe. "My mother said my uncle wanted me to stay with you," he said it fast, like he's ashamed, "to tell him what you're doing and where you go."

I'm disappointed.

"Jake, I would've come anyhow. I wanted to see China. And, and," I get a Cocker Spaniel look, "you know I respect you."

"I like you too, kid, but you're spying on me and I don't care for it. Worse, I can't tell you to screw-off, but I'll tell you Mickey, those two hundred bucks a day, gone, no more, vamoosed." I paused. I didn't want to get too nasty, "just expenses."

He's talking low, kind of like repentance. "I figured that, Jake."

With nothing more to say, we both put our cues back in the rack on the wall, we headed upstairs. It didn't take long to fall asleep.

CHAPTER 10

THE PHONE RANG. I rolled over, "Get that Sharli, will you?"

It rang again. I opened my eyes. The room's colors were the special bright blue and white wash of the Greek Islands. Naw, couldn't be. Then the bells, the hoots, and even a foghorn told me. Hell, it's China. I picked up the phone. "Yeah?"

"Ah, I do believe it to be Mr. Diamond."

I knew that cultured voice. Sitting up real quick in a hushed scream I say, "Liu, where the hell are you. We gotta talk."

"That's an unusual greeting, Mr. Diamond." There's a moment and I can tell he's smiling. "I feel I am getting to know you quite well," he tells me. "I'm anxious for us to get together. I am with the gentlemen you call Blacky, at my hotel."

"You're with Blacky?"

"Jake, my boy, I've asked my nephew whom you have kindly brought along to meet me in about an hour. I shall expect both of you, of course."

"Liu, you bastard, stay there. I have things to say to you. It's your friggin painting, it's . . . ." I'm talking into a dead phone.

If he keeps doing what he's doing he's going to join his brother among the naked dancing ladies. Who am I kidding? I gave up violence with the Korean War. Actually, I never had it. I sometimes envy these guys who get physical, but I think its been bred out of us Jewish guys. Maybe I should tell that to Murder Incorporated and Lefty Buchholtz or any of those Israeli terror groups, like the Irgun. Or even Ariel Sharon. I know it's just me, I don't have a large enough violence gene.

Downstairs I join Mickey and order a cup of coffee. I'm always the optimist.

"Kid, you got any college?"

He kept eating the rice stuff, what did he call it, congee. He finally put the spoon down. "Sure Jake, I went to college."

I'm staring at him and realize he's almost indistinguishable from the other Chinese in the room. I mean he doesn't look American except for the way Americans have, a kind of a natural easiness.

"Stop playing cute kid. I heard you know a Japanese plate repair process not too many others discovered."

His eyes came up. "I never meant to hold back, Jake. You just never asked." Now we're eye to eye. "I have an MA in Fine Arts from Berkeley, and I spent a year in Japan studying ceramics under Yamada."

For some reason I'm not surprised. It's always the quiet ones isn't it? If I asked him about women he'd probably

71

pull out some Playboy centerfolds and say I had this one, that one. Naw, he's still a virgin. And Yamada, I heard of him, ceramics, but I never understood this modern stuff.

I think about the kind of protected life my little side-kick Chinese Pancho has led. I had the poolroom and ethnic fights of Coney Island, the war, the prison camp and the hustle to get enough money to open my place on Gold Street. I know I shouldn't be making comparisons, lives are lived in their own time and place, but it would have been good to go to college, to lose my Brooklyneez.

For a guess I throw out, "Mickey, you know Professor Wyatt?"

Without coming up from his plate he says, "Sure, I know Professor Wyatt. I took his class, Classical Chinese Art."

Oh, my God. "And you gave your uncle my name, right?"

"Sure, I told you he wanted a respectable dealer who had good customers." He hesitated just long enough to make me wonder.

"And," I tried to help him along.

"I don't know, Jake, he already seemed to know about you."

I wanted to reach over and grab him by his shirt. Maybe things were only just starting to fall into place but I still wasn't sure, about anything.

"Do you know Blacky?"

"You mean the guy I saw you with last night whose arms seemed to stretch forever?"

"You'd better not say that within his earshot." He had to be innocent, of everything.

Once outside the scene hadn't changed since yesterday. We side slipped our way down the steps between those who wanted to change our money and those who wanted to sell us something for it. We took pedi-cabs as they'd be faster than a taxi, given the crowd.

I watched the melee of the streets and wondered how the hell I ever got snookered into this deal with Liu. Every day in San Francisco hustlers came into my store selling me Chippendale chairs saying they were made in China some two hundred years ago. I'd turn 'em over and they'd be stamped, *Hecho en Mexico*. They'd try to pawn off vases from Portugal, rejects from Delft, and Qin Dynasty horse castings from California. Guys would come in with fake prints by Hiroshige and Yokusai. They didn't even know they were Japanese. I had one hero offer me the Mona Lisa. And now I'm chasing Liu as he became the master con man of them all. Damn!

Blacky waited for us in the lobby. I walked right past him, glancing around, "Where the hell is Liu, he's has my money?" I tried to keep my temper. I think I failed.

"Hey, tomodachi, what are you so upset about? Liu's here. He's waiting for you."

It took awhile but my question finally hit him. He squinted his eyes. "You have some deal going, mon ami? You buying or selling something?"

I felt a little better. Blacky's always transparent and if anything existed between them besides the diving employer-employee relation it didn't show.

I raised my voice. "Where is he? I gotta see the faker, that *momzer*."

"Easy boyyo, you don't talk to me like that."

I gotta watch my words. He'd break me in two. Just as I calmed Liu came out of the elevator. His eyes lit up and it's a warm, genuine light.

"Mr. Diamond, your timing is impeccable. I have some marvelous news."

He walked toward me with his hand out, cool as can be as though the only thing between us is a long-standing friendship. The old rascal is sporting a cream-colored linen suit, walking stick, and a Panama hat set off with a thin yellow band and a flick of a red feather. Definitely a rogue. I'd say he appeared in good health except he's leaning heavily on his cane. I don't care. In a second I'm on to him like a Monarch butterfly holding fast to a honey laden Morning Glory on the Monterey Peninsula in October.

"Liu, I gotta talk to you. It's important. And I bet you damned well know what it's all about."

As though he didn't hear a word he comes up close. "You know, Mr. Diamond, your face, it is like the sacred mountains of China, replete with crags and ravines. It shows all your good deeds and sweet thoughts. Yes, it reaffirms my judgment, we are kindred spirits."

I mean you gotta love the guy.

He faced the kid. They talk in Chinese and Mickey kissed him on the cheek as the old man came back to me and placed his hand on my elbow, steering me away from the others. "Jake, I can't stop and chat now. It's urgent for me to go north, to the canal, by Suzhou. But I, you, we will talk. My interests are the same as yours." He gave me a squeeze on my shoulder as if to assure me he's on my side. "It's very important, Jake. Rest assured I will always care for your best interests." A calmness comes over him. "May I call you Jake?"

This is crazy. He takes me for 650 G's and he asks if he can call me Jake, and he'll always take care of me. What kind of swindler is he? I had a cousin who spoke in kind of the same way to his customers, in the same reassuring tone. His occupation? A stockbroker. "Damn it Liu, you sold me a fake." Now I held his elbow.

He actually smiled. "Yes, Jake, it's possible. I'm thrilled by the possibility the one you have and all the other Chou's in the Taiwan museum are fakes. Wouldn't it be wonderful, Jake? Isn't it marvelous?"

"Wonderful? Marvelous? You crazy?" I figured he's lost it as all the liver spots from his hands are coagulated in the arteries to his brain.

"Jake, don't you understand? It's why I'm leaving to find out if the Grand Canal holds the Imperial treasures," and he pulled away from me, smiling broadly. "With any luck Jake, you may end up with a two-for-one special. Imagine, Jake, another Zhou for your retirement."

He waved goodbye to the kid as he walked briskly out of the hotel to a waiting car. I'm standing frozen trying to figure out what the hell is happening. Just as he gets into the taxi he turns and kind of yells to me.

"Jake, the Red Official, I'm delighted you took good care of it for me."

I chased him through the open glass doors. "What the hell are you talking about, you crook?" I yell reaching out to him and the best I can do is, "you, you, *shyster.*"

But he's gone.

As the car leaves I'm standing there, shaking my fist at the exhaust. Blacky came running over and grabbed me with both hands. The gorilla whispers, "Be nice, Jake, be nice. Liu told me he'd be back, and maybe you might not want him to go." He loosened his grip and I pulled away.

Blacky had the last word. "He said he'd let you know where he is."

I took a step to the kid. "Did you know this?"

"Honest, Jake. He just said he'd meet us here."

This is a helluva way to get my money back. I had no control and Liu could have me hang around China until my cash ran out, or the authorities decided to make me an honorary citizen. Screw em. I'll dog his every step. I wheeled back.

"Blacky, just what the hell are you doing for Liu besides strong arming me?"

"Hey, he's paying me."

"Why has he hired you?"

"Your buddy, Liu, he called me in Florida, told me to come out here to a little island just off Xiamen, says it's about a fifty-foot dive, for some antiques. I go down, see some wreckage, but it's only a shelf. Beyond there's a fall off to a hundred and fifty."

Mickey and I both stared at him as though he's speaking Hindi. Blacky did the same, looking at us as though there's not an ounce of intelligence between Mickey and I.

"Compadres, I'm not diving now because I don't have the equipment for a hundred and fifty feet. Liu said the goodies would be at fifty." We still showed no signs of intelligence. "You pricks! Don'tcha know anything? I have three Chinese guys, top divers, but they're sensitive to the cold. At one fifty those wet suits don't keep you warm. Another thing, at a hundred and fifty feet ya need different mixtures."

"What's that?" Mickey asks. The kid is braver than I am.

"Jeez, you are dumb. If you go down far with a straight air mixture you get too much nitrogen in yer blood." He laughed. "It's a cheap high." Then he became serious again. "Put too much nitrogen in the air mixture and you may never see daylight."

"Blacky, stop me if I'm wrong but if you dive for treasure the Government is always in for a piece."

He peered right at me. "There's a Chinese guy at the pier every day checking on my dive. I need to show him everything I bring up. He writes it down in his book." He makes a face of disgust like I do when I mail my income tax. "Hey, I never met a country who didn't want a piece of the action. But it's Liu's concern, he gets the permissions," and he waved his hand as though its not his business. "Me, I just dive." There's a seconds delay, and he almost laughs, "Governments, ha. Think they're smart." He gives me a shove in the ribs and winks, "Know what I mean? Everybody's got a fiddle." He gives me a wink and another easy elbow in the ribs. Yeah, like we're both in the know.

Mickey and I walked back into the hotel's dining room needing some coffee. Blacky is crazy and my big meeting with Liu just comes and goes. Charley Chan brushes me off with an enigmatic smile and then those last words of his about the Red Official. Maybe I misunderstood him. Anyhow, I'm the worst for wear and back to square one. Hell, maybe there's a way I can salvage the day.

I turned to Mickey who's now sipping a cup of tea, "Do you know where the university is?" He shakes his head, yes. Terrific. "Let's go, we gotta find Huang of Amoy. Maybe I can make a buck out of this day yet."

The pedi-cab guys knew exactly where to go. There were a bunch of boys, maybe fifteen, sixteen years old with black school bags on their back. They were horsing around, punching each other. I watched them make their way and wondered if they ever cut class. Hell, Mal, Harry and I did it all the time. We'd head to Manhattan to see a movie and a stage show, Stan Kenton, or Dean Martin and Jerry Lewis. The New York Paramount could have held as many morning classes as the city high schools; it had the same number of teen-agers.

I figured it out much later. We told the system we could do what we wanted, when we wanted. I mean, we had almost maybe a buck apiece, just enough to get to the city, catch the show and wolf down a hot dog. Hardly high living, but independence. The trip was also worthwhile because of this guy in the window on the poor side of 42nd Street. Only a kind of high-class soda jerk making malteds, but he had the moves, really. He'd dip a metal ladle into a fifty-gallon can and pull up the right amount of milk. Hit the chrome lever for a jab of chocolate, move to a scoop of ice cream add a clip of malt and then he'd let the Hamilton Beach do its job. The man had become the Merlin of Malteds.

My bicycle rickshaw driver stopped and started talking to me and pointing to a moon gate, the only break in a long wall. Mickey took my arm and we walked through, kind of Alice in Wonderland like. "Well, dis must be da place," I said, trying to imitate some long forgotten comedian.

Before us stood an open yard of bits of carved wood, furniture legs, chair arms, and parts of drawers, all the makings of a house of furniture. Most were intricately carved with sticky layers of lacquer drying in the morning sun.

"Can I help you?"

Remember Key Luke, the number one son of Charley Chan? Well, here he is, simple smiling face perfect English with a touch of extra politeness.

"Yes." I shifted my footing to peer into the small building. "I guess this is Huang of Amoy, the furniture factory?"

"Huang of Amoy. Son-of-a-gun." Key Luke laughed. He put out his hand. "I'm Si Huang." He gave us the Western way, his first name before his last.

We introduced ourselves, and I gave him my card. I put off the natural question of how he learned his English with his little lilt of the Brit.

"The American with the bicycle factory, he had a chair of yours. I hadn't seen one of those in years, at least not as fresh."

"The Chippendale? You liked it, good. Come inside, I have a few more if you are interested."

Who? Me? Interested? A China Trade dealer who finds the mother lode, interested?

No doubt, inside was a veritable treasure trove. A Queen Anne occasional chair standing on its claw and ball, a Chippendale urn table with a square tray top, pad feet, and a rosewood Teapoy with swept legs and scroll feet. The next one put me back, a Chinese export lacquer worktable, and a copy of an 1840 piece. I knew it well, I had an original back on Gold Street. This one also had the distinctive carved ivory inlay and damask workbag, and a gilt painting of a garden in a fictional crowded palace. Delightfully excessive, so typical of the export trade.

Picking up a Queen Anne I stood a moment before I could speak. "Just terrific, nicely done, Si. No nails or glue, the old way." I hesitated, not sure how to say what I wanted to ask. "You have plans, detailed drawings?"

The sophisticated Chinese gave me a knowing smile. "Yes, I have all of those. They were kept among the family papers." He gently touched the arm of the Chippendale. "In China good things survive."

Where the hell has he been these past thirty years with the savagery of the Red Guard? Their hatred for anything before Mao had them destroy the really good stuff, the classic pieces, buildings, arches, temples.

I walked around and stopped when I caught sight of the auction catalogs, the illustrated price lists. They were from the same firms as those I had studied in the cold nameless place up in northern China. "You copy from those?" I asked, pointing to the stacks of journals and papers.

"Of course."

My face must have reflected all the questions I needed to ask. He stared inside my eyes and answered almost all.

"Our family moved to Hong Kong just before the Japanese occupation. As a young boy I went to St. Mary's School. You see I still drink tea with milk." He laughed and took another glance into my pupils. "My father took his library with him when he left Amoy for Hong Kong. I spent my childhood studying it." Turning his eyes to Mickey he continued, "The furniture came back to life when I returned to Xiamen, my ancestral home, when China reopened." He caressed the back of the chair. "My hands itched until I could resurrect the family business."

I started to take in his entire inventory. I stopped when I spied Chinese scroll paintings on silk, all beautifully done, not the amateurish things I had seen downtown. I asked Si about them.

"No, we do not do them here. I have many contacts in this business, artists, and manufacturers. Some very good."

An understatement. My eyes swept along the wall appreciating the skill of the painters. Then, like King Kong chasing after Jessica Lange, I pushed over Chippendales, Edwardians, Queen Anne's, throwing them aside like a kid searching for an interesting plastic toy in a child's game box. I had to get to the far corner.

There, right there. My *Late Autumn*, on the wall, behind the furniture. I couldn't believe it. It also had all the right signatures of Zhou Mengfu, of the Emperor, the right ink color, and the aged silk. But it was different. While it had an out-of-this-world sense of the one back in the States, it lacked its true loneliness, the sense of impending cold, the floating mountains, the genius only a master could include. I reached over and scratched at the red ink, sure enough, a fleck came off. Another clever copy attractively painted. At least this forger didn't come close to be as good as mine. I must have gotten the pick of the litter. How dumb could I have been? Liu really pegged me. Yeah, I must have a sucker face telling the hustler he has a mark.

It's like that time Harry and I were out in Texas with a weekend pass. Under a bare light a three-card Monte dealer was plying his trade. Did you ever see a talented mechanic whose fingers had no motion, just dazzle.

"It'll cost you twenty bucks, soldier. Pick the queen and yours gets mine. Harry laughed as I paid up. Now I'm in China searching for the real Zhou and Liu keeps moving that lady of spades.

Huang says, "You like the painting, the artist? He is an old master." He went rummaging in a basket of rolled scrolls. "I have some other copies of Zhou Mengfu. Wait."

I grabbed his shoulder and pulled him to me. "How did . . . ? Where did . . . ? The original, where's the original?"

Startled, Si spoke quickly. "Why a Mr. Liu, he came by maybe six months ago and asked if I knew of some artists who were good copiers. He gave me a photograph of the scroll you examined and I passed duplicates to three friends. Yes, the *Late Autumn*. It once hung in the Forbidden City, in Beijing."

It all came too fast. Maybe the inhabitants of the New World didn't have a chance against the Old. Maybe we needed a few more centuries of conditioning. Si knows Liu, and then Huang of Amoy gives me the topper. "Mr. Liu showed me photos of other paintings by Zhou and asked if I knew of other artists who could make good copies."

For crying out loud, Liu made a business of this, of copying the masters. At 650 G's a clip he's as profitable as Google.com. Maybe I could convince him to start an IPO and I'd get in at the offer price?

"Si, while I don't know what the hell is going on here, you're a helluva furniture maker." I pivoted, "C'mon kid, let's get outta here."

CHAPTER 11

I TOLD MICKEY TO get a taxi knowing if I hailed it the price would just about double. You see, while there were meters in the cabs everything in China is negotiation. When it comes to price it's always a form of collective bargaining, every place, even back in the lonely house in the middle of the cold of Manchuria. The other lieutenant, besides Qin, who shared command of me and Harry and the others caught me studying a blue porcelain vase one afternoon.

"You think them attractive, do you, all of these, curios?" He said this as his arms swept across the room. "I have watched you hold them." He took three steps over to a low black lacquered cabinet whose two doors were decorated in low-relief mother of pearl. He picked up a lamp sitting on top, a Chinese *cloisonné*, a phoenix perched on a branch. I could see he regarded it with disdain.

"Ah, Mr. Diamond, you should inspect the other room, the closed one where Mr. Harry cleans. There is where the work of masters reside, from the Han, Ming and Sung Dynasties."

Sometimes catching glimpses of the glass cabinets in the locked room I could see paintings on silk screens, on scrolls, bronze horses, vessels, bright porcelain vases. The real good stuff lay there but the room stayed strictly off-limits for every one except, son-of-a-gun, Harry. Of course I didn't know then he had negotiated a pact with the devil.

The lieutenant came back to the Phoenix perched on a lamp. "This bird, Mr. Diamond, I would call it, well, something for the foreigner to buy as no Chinese with an eye for sculpture would purchase it. You see, it is pure decoration, not art. It is made for the low Western taste."

I knew all about the lamp. The bird stood fourteen inches high and its claws clutched a bough of a flowering hydrangea. The artist took the phoenix's colors of blue and green and placed them under a startling translucent glaze. The lampshade shone as woven lacquered hemp. Its muted soft yellow complemented the stronger brown hues of the bird. Sold by G. Shen, 76 Wishing Well Road, Shanghai for seven pounds, five shillings, it had the year 1893 burnt into its base. You see, I knew everything of all the pieces in the house which teemed with little gems. Shen's register neatly summarized all the facts of the lamp. While extensive in its contents, the catalog stood beside a long row of publications from China, England, and even France. There were endless price lists from an exhaustive roster of dealers, of auction houses. All of them sold Chinese things made especially for the overseas markets, for the Westerner's taste.

The library had reeked of its emphasis on practicality, its sets of encyclopedias for commerce. And best of all, the Brit accumulator kept records, punctilious financial registers on all his transactions. With his kind of record keeping I figured him to be a merchant, a small industrialist, an accountant with a penchant for numbers and detail. The lieutenant later proved me wrong.

"Kid, tell the driver to take us to the Inn." I didn't want to face the chaos by our hotel.

Walking into the hotel Mickey started immediately toward the lounge. I took him by the elbow and we sat in a corner of the lobby where they had two wing back chairs decorated with red and yellow silk brocade. I asked what he thought about Huang's work. His reply, "A little ostentatious, a tad too much carving, but not bad, not bad at all." I liked how he put it, he had the eye.

Mickey started describing the style of chair legs utilized in the different periods during the 18th and 19th centuries. He did it easily. Then I asked him about the painting, "You know, the *Late Autumn*?"

All of a sudden he's quiet.

I said, "How come you got nothing to tell?"

"Jake, I don't know what you're thinking, or what's going on between my uncle and you." He peered right at me in a kind of *mano e mano* eye contact. "For some reason the *Late Autumn* scroll is causing trouble between us." He reached over and took my elbow, "Don't let it Jake. We like each other."

Now how the hell can you fault a kid when he says things like that? It's like all of a sudden I have a son, and you gotta trust a son, don't you? But then again, the kid had an uncle who I also trusted.

We got up. The kid said he'd head back to the Lujiang. I needed a little more time before facing my four walls so I headed for my waterfall in the lounge. Two Americans sat at the bar playing liar's dice with the hotel manager. Over by a table Blacky leaned over chatting up a stunning hooker I hadn't seen before. She had a string of matched pearls, and blond streaks running through her very black hair. I'd say stunning except for the flaw of rolled up stockings ending just above her knee.

My conversation buddy from last night leaned over to me and said, "Blacky and the hooker were arguing over the price."

I asked, "Does Blacky speak Chinese?"

He smiled at me. "Naw, he only knows numbers." He went back to the game.

Two older Chinese were smoking at one of the nearby small tables. Finishing, one ground out his cigarette on the carpet floor. Lieutenant Qin had the same ugly habit. The carcasses of dead butts spotted the Persian rugs in the long deceased Englishman's house up north.

Lieutenant Qin shared charge of the POWs. While we were to keep the house and the grounds clean, our main function was to teach English. Actually, that's not right. We were there to simply speak American, as the Chinese called it. None of us could have taught the language. Well, that's not entirely true as Harry shone at book learning but always kept it hidden. He could have taught them English, he knew everything, even spoke their *ni hoa,* how are you, stuff. Every once in a while I'd catch him off in a corner with Qin who's English rivaled ours. Harry once told me Qin had grown up with a missionary family. I don't know why our Chinese guard hated us, but he did.

Anyway, I passed the afternoon sipping away at my beer watching the waterfall in the classy hotel when this woman, American, no question, sat down a stool away. She ordered coffee. It happens. Our eyes flirted and we both smiled. Not at all bad. Hell, she looked fabulous, just the way I like them, a banana cream pie.

I'm pretty sure she heard of Fred Allen, had almost white hair with some old blond left, and wolfed down a few too many dumplings in her time. She had the skin, kind of opalescent, with some fat layers just below the surface. If I pressed my thumb into her arm it would go down a quarter inch or so and then ease up slowly. Oh my, I just loved to do such things.

"You visiting?" I ask.

Her eyes blinked coquettishly a few times and she smiled at me. Most do. "No. Actually I live here. I mean, I work at the university."

I gave her a quick review up and down and believe me her clothing styles were purely Sears and Roebuck.

"Here, in Xiamen? What a terrific idea."

She smiled again and nodded her head yes.

"Good job?" I continued.

She stared at me with those blue's whose clarity are like the marbles I played with back in the Coney Island streets. She says something quizzical, "It's what I must do," with an honesty which draws me in. But I didn't want to push too hard.

"Where you from?"

"Kansas," she tells me in bell tones.

"I've been through Kansas. It stretches from Paterson, New Jersey to just this side of Reno, Nevada. Big place."

She laughed a little. I'm in love, but just don't tell Sharli. I moved over a seat to get closer to her.

"I'm Jake Diamond. From San Francisco."

"Oh, I love San Francisco. The World Christian College who found my position is in San Francisco. Oh," like an afterthought, "my name is Allison, they call me Allie." She extended her hand, and I touched it gently.

Oh my, a baby's cheek.

She asked if I believed in God. The way she asked I knew I had to say yes. Well, I do kinda. Well, maybe. She glanced up at the clock above the bar then at her watch. "Oh, I'm meeting someone."

I walked her to the lobby where she became a little nervous as she peered about. Apparently finding what she was looking for her faced relaxed then broke into a smile. She then reached into her purse and handed me a card with her name and address in both Chinese and English.

"If you're here in the morning," she pointed to the card, "there'll be a number of other Americans at my place. We always meet on Sunday." Leaving she said, "God bless you," like those Hari Krishna guys at the airports.

I watched her go and checked out the performance of those hips. Now don't get me wrong but you know I like women. Those sweet things are small adventures. Actually, women are great novels, they take you to places you never been, introduce you to people you wouldn't ordinarily meet, and you share late hours together. She joined this tall guy and strolled out of the hotel. I'm busy following those hips when my eyes go to the guy. Son-of-a-gun.

"Hey," I yelled, "Taylor, Taylor Davis. Wait up." I run outside to catch them and all I get is the exhaust of a taxi. I'll be damned. He had to have seen me, had to.

I stood there watching Miss Sweet Cups and the buyer of my Zhou drive out of sight. I wondered what the hell's going on when behind me I hear, "Hey, Jake." Not now, Blacky. Not now!

"Hey *amigo*, did I interrupt anything?" He didn't wait for an answer. "Appears we're going to Suzhou together. Liu says all the Zhous in the Taipei museum are fakes," he ends with a puzzled expression. "Anyhow, I'm packing up all my equipment. Have you done any diving before?"

"What are you talking about?"

"Ya didn't get the phone call? Liu said you were next on his call list and he'd tell you everything. See, I told ya not to worry, he's an upright guy."

"What did he say?"

"Just that he'll tell Mickey to bring you to Suzhou. He told me to bring along my divers, wet suits, tanks, I'd be doing some diving. Hey, maybe you'd like to do some?"

"What's this stuff in Suzhou?"

"Beats me. Liu, hey, he speaks good, don't he?"

I gotta take an aspirin. I just didn't know tourists had such busy times in China.

CHAPTER 12

I HAD NO DIFFICULTY getting back to the Lujiang—I simply allowed the crowd to push me to the port. As soon as I entered the room the phone rang. I'm almost too tired to answer. It couldn't be important, I didn't have any creditors in this town.

"Jake, it's me, Sharli."

I hate phone calls. They're almost always trouble of one kind or another. I learned that at my father's knee.

My old man was a hell of a dresser and he always bought the newest cars. The only trouble, he rarely had the money to pay. To answer the phone at night only meant some guy asking for my father and my dad gesturing he's not home. No question, the phone is almost always trouble, even when it's Sharli who I love.

"Jake, are you alone?" she asked.

I actually turned my head to check. I laughed at myself. "Yes, I'm alone."

"Jake, I've have some news so don't interrupt me."

"Do I ever cut into your . . ."

"Jake!"

I felt silly. "Go ahead."

"Well, I did what you told me. When I came back I went to your office and put the scroll under the floorboards and went home. I sat on my deck and had on a yellow halter and red shorts thinking my colors were so Chinese. I knew you would have liked me in one of those new thong suits, but I know my thighs wouldn't allow it."

"Sharli, what's this about?"

"Jake. Let me tell it. Okay"?

"I'm sorry."

"I watched as a dull blue four door Ford Taurus pulled up across the street, Lucky to get a parking space so easily. Two Chinese men exited from the back doors. The third, the driver, appeared medium size with blond hair, very mid-Western. He carried a straw hat which meant he didn't come from the city."

She paused.

"Sharli?"

"All three men crossed to my side of the street and I knew they would be coming to see me. I felt sure they weren't here for a real estate deal. It had to be China, something happened to you."

"No. I'm okay. I'm okay."

"Jake, stop it. I ran inside and put on a pink terry cloth robe and waited for the knock. I opened the door up to the safety catch. A very American face appeared asking for Ms. Hamilton. He introduced himself as Charles Dupont, from the State Department, and his wallet and an identification card replaced his face. He said the two men with him were from a similar agency from the People's Republic of China. I didn't know what to do so I let them in.

"Sharli, you shouldn't have done it, you couldn't . . . ."

"Hush, Jake. They came in and I almost apologized for the mess then thought better of it. The Chinese immediately went to my bedroom. I yelled at them, 'Hey, where the hell do you think your going?'"

The American State Department guy said they didn't speak English, so I yelled in Mandarin. Only glancing at me for a moment it didn't even slow them down. They even went out to the deck."

I asked softly, "Sharli, are you okay?" She ignored what I said and continued talking.

"I guessed they came from the Western part of China where life is harder and the gene pool more mixed. I don't mean to sound racist, but they had the size and cheekbones of the Muslim minority, the manners of the country people. I asked the State Department man just what the hell he wanted? He told me they were looking for a painting stolen from China about fifty years ago. They said you gave it to me at the airport in Taiwan."

"Damn it, Sharli, I'm sorry I got you into this."

"Jake, let me finish." She paused. "Then I asked why didn't they take it then? He said they were afraid of the Taiwanese police. I told him they were nuts, that I took some of your extra clothes because you wanted to travel light."

She paused, and I could hear her drinking something, tea, I hoped. She continued, "I told him to go to hell. Then I asked him why he escorted the Commies? He said, "Reciprocity. They help our embassy in China." I asked him what our people did in China needing Commie help? Anyhow, I'd had enough. I went up to him nose to nose and said if they weren't out of there in two minutes I'd call the San Francisco police. Amazing the power of those words, it really moved them, and I waved good-bye."

"You did good, Sharli. You did good."

"I'm not through, Jake. Then your insurance company called me the next morning because you had left my name in case of an emergency. They said someone broke into your shop by disabling the alarm and cutting through the iron gate. They asked me to come down to see whether any items were gone, helping the police in their investigation. I told them I'd be right there. I knew it had to be the Chinese who had come to see me. It couldn't have been anyone else."

She paused and I knew her eyes were filling and she would have cried because the whole thing had to be emotional. She came back on the phone. She's one hell of a lady.

"Jake, they placed yellow plastic crime scene striping across the front of your store. I had to explain to the officer I came at the request of the police. Walking through the show room I could see nothing seemed missing. In the office your desk lay on its side, papers all over the place. Lamps were smashed and even the wood paneling and ceiling molding were torn down. And the safe, the big Mosler, well it didn't seem to be a problem to those Chinese. The police explained to me about the four drill holes around the safe's combination dial."

"It's okay Sharli. Nothing in the safe had any importance. Well, not exactly. After our first date you sent me a card telling me how much you enjoyed it. I treasured the note and kept it in there." It's a good thing I took the money Taylor gave me and put it in the bank.

"Jake, I looked down to the floor boards where I'd put the painting, it lay undisturbed. They never thought of getting on their knees. You're so clever so I smiled to myself but spoke out loud, 'Big shots, ha.' The police turned around and scowled at me."

"Could you see if they stole anything?"

"Jake, I have to tell you. I rummaged around your desk, but I couldn't find your Army revolver. I couldn't find any shells either. Jake, I think the Chinese took them."

I thought about her last words. "Sharli, you'd better report it to the police. I've got a permit so it's okay," then, "you did good."

I felt proud of her, the way she held together. I knew I had a helluva lady. "You're a smart, brave woman Sharli, and I love you." Oops, I said it.

She waited a moment, absorbing what I had said. Another went by and she offered, "One more thing, Jake. I've been talking to my mother. She says I should go to China and find my brother."

It takes a second. "Brother? Who? Sam, my brother? Whatta you talking about? He's in Florida." I'm asking questions to a dead phone. I figured I heard it all wrong and hung up. I found my aspirins and lay down.

I didn't know what to make of Sharli's call. Why would the State Department be with the Chinese? And why steal my gun? Hell, I'm not about to worry about something happening seven thousand miles away. I had to get back to Liu. And what the hell did that old Chinaman mean when he said isn't it good all the Zhou's in the museum may be fakes. Crazy old coot. I'll catch up to him. He can't keep running all the time.

CHAPTER 13

THE NEXT MORNING I'm again watching the kid eat that rice stuff. It's like the movie with Bill Murray in Groundhog Day where the character is stuck in a constantly repeating day.

"What do you hear from your uncle?" I ask.

"He called me early."

"Yeah, he wants us to meet him in Suzhou."

He jerks his head up and stares at me like somehow I became the Wizard of Oz and stepped out from behind my screen. Of course he probably never saw the movie.

"Just prescient," answering his unspoken question.

The kid gives me a big smile.

"Forget it. It's a Sharli word. When do we leave?"

"Early evening. My uncle insisted we take a train to Hangzhou, then a barge on the Grand Canal to Suzhou. He said it would be interesting and, oddly, his other word was, arduous."

"That's Charley Chan. Okay, we go the arduous way." After saying the word I thought about it. "Hey kid, how can a train ride be arduous?"

"I don't know, Jake, I have a feeling it's not Amtrak. Uncle said there are only two classes of seats, either soft or impossible." And then as if to make things okay, "Uncle Liu said he'd pay." Definitely an aces kind of guy.

"Soft seats?" I asked. The kid just shrugged his shoulders. I came back at him. "You said the Grand Canal?" I wasn't about to let on Teddy's story. I figured I'd hear his spiel.

"Jake, China's Grand Canal, it's one of the great wonders of the world. It stretched some eleven hundred miles, connecting Hangzhou to Beijing, bringing rice from the south to the northern capital. It changed the course of Chinese history."

"Still in operation, huh?" I asked.

"From what I've read most of it's silted over. Now it only goes up river from Hangzhou for about a hundred or so miles. But it's a major artery Jake, still important." Mickey's expression is as though he's at his father's knee.

In case you're interested, the kid, even when I first met him seemed a little lonely. Not like he didn't have any friends, just detached. We shared a morning coffee one time and I brought up the subject of his parents. He brushed me off, politely of course. It never did become a subject of discussion and I stayed away from it. Patrick, the French antique dealer, the one with the map of China on rice paper, he let me in on the kid's father. We had been smoozing as he closed up his place about two months ago. "Jake, the kid Mickey, he's over your place often?"

"Yeah, what about him?" I got a little aggressive without meaning to but by then I had grown to like the kid.

"Is he the one who's father got hit by the Powell Street cable car just at the bend near Clay, 'bout the time of the last earthquake?"

Son-of-a-gun. I remembered reading about it and the city settling with the family. A gruesome death, dragged along about ten feet under the carriage. Kind of explains things like why the kid didn't seem to need a regular job. Maybe also why he sorta adopted me.

I let the kid flow out of my thoughts and went back to thinking of Liu and him taking us north to the canal. I remembered Teddy broaching the puzzle of the Forbidden City treasures being sent to Taiwan back in San Francisco. I speculated if the pieces would all come together. Screw it, I'll wait and see.

I walked out on to the hotel's busy steps and looked around in a kind of awe of the 1930's feel of the street. Lots of older stores, chipped concrete, green shutters on the above level windows and tons of action. I expected a guess-your-weight hustle around every corner. Yeah, Izzy Klein, he taught me a deal is solid when both walk away with a bargain. It's what I thought I had with Liu. I guess he just wanted more. More? Hell, the old Taipan wanted it all.

I'm standing by the port in a Chinese city in a Sunday morning. I had a friend, Sharpless, with a wife from Bogota, Columbia. He said there's nothing duller than a Sunday morning in a third-world country. I figured it's what's in store for me today.

I put my hands in my jacket pocket and there it was, my morning entertainment, the Banana Cream Pie's card and invitation. I took the address to the concierge. He pulled out a map and like the California Auto Club clear crayoned a route to a street near the University. They called a taxi for me, argued with the cabby, and paid the fare. They told me they would add it to my bill. It's not pleasant to be a helpless, aging white male in never-never land.

The driver let me off before a high walled compound by a gatehouse with a carved inlaid wooden plaque declaring in English, "Xiamen University Foreign Teacher Residence." Inside were the Chinese versions of small garden apartments garden apartments. Further back sat another set of flats requiring entrance through a Chinese moon doorway. The place had a Communist austerity about its plain stucco exteriors.

Singing came from one of the back upstairs apartments. I knocked softly, turned the knob and walked in. At the head of the room, before a large cross, were maybe nine, ten Westerners in some kind of, well, trance. What they were chanting wasn't English and sure didn't sound like Yiddish.

I took my eyes away and swept the apartment. I could see a kitchen pretty well dated with a cooling unit atop a refrigerator, like some giant coil. The living room had a set of windows overlooking a courtyard. There were bits of furniture here and there, old and overstuffed. I would have chosen a wall color more cheerful than the Mao jacket gray but at least the place had a new coat of paint.

Allie leaned against the back wall, and next to her slouched, surprise, surprise, my very well bred tennis pro, Taylor Davis. I had heard he became a born-again. So this was his church business mentioned back in San Francisco. It hit me. The chanting was in tongues. Son-of-a-gun, Taylor Davis, a Pentecostal.

I can tell you my education about such things amounted pretty close to nothing. I had to get into the army before I discovered the complicated spin-offs of those who believed in Christ. While I admired their dedication to their god of choice, I never could fathom their beliefs. As a result I trusted none of it, nobody's.

Allie and Davis were both peering at me as I stood there. They quickly huddled and Allie made her way over, took my arm and we went outside. "You're early," she said.

"Yeah, maybe five hundred years. Who were they, Druids?"

She laughed politely. "Come with me and I'll tell you."

We walked along the main path of the campus to a newer building having a small, white-walled cafeteria with stainless steel chairs and tables. Kind of like a hospital place. We both went in line and took coffee. I had to clear my throat and tell her I had no Chinese money. I could see she thought me kidding but as I continued acting as a mute she reached into a small change purse and gave the cashier some crumpled notes.

"Allie, when we met the other day, you should have given me some warning."

She smiled at me. I liked it. This woman is attractive, but this Jesus business puts her into a different kinda place. "I thought the name of the organization sending me here would have told you."

I remembered. World Christian University. Damn. I'm just dumb about these things. Disappointed? Damn right.

"You mean I can't kiss you?"

She laughed softly. "Sure you can, Jake but my heart belongs to Jesus."

"Can I get your body to belong to me?"

"Jake," she said softly, with her eyelashes flipping up and down faster than a humming bird's wings, "stop that kind of talk. It's not right."

I just loved the way she called me Jake, in a kind of breathless manner. Not at all like Estelle, my last wife, pure *shiksa* with golden hair, and very red, full lips. When she used my name it came from lack of patience, at least toward the end. Bathing in the way Allie said my name I almost forgot my next question. "Where does Taylor Davis come in?"

Then she had a whole new face, brighter, even more tender. "How do you know Taylor?" she asked.

"Never you mind darlin'," answering as I did in the Southern fashion.

She filled me in. "He is the World Christian University, finding schools in China needing English teachers. Those of us searching for a way to get to China, well, we find him."

"Who are the others, Allie?"

"Christians, needing a way to carry out God's word, those who want to bring Jesus to China, like me." She answered my look of surprise. "Jake, every American in the room is here for the same reason. It's our calling."

What did I tell you about women taking you to places you hadn't even thought about, I mean talking in tongues.

"I hate to say this Allie, but isn't there a law in this country against proselytizing?"

"Oh, Jake. We're not missionaries like before. We just talk to the Chinese and tell them about baby Jesus.

If they want to find out more, we invite them to Sunday service."

It became my turn to say, "Oh." Maybe she never heard of the government's attitude to the Falun Gong and they don't even have an infant in swathing clothes.

She stood there in the white simplicity of her dress, an attractive, intelligent modern woman convinced her efforts could only bring good to all concerned. Sipping the coffee and still gazing at the lovely white haired lady I see a policeman's uniform come through the door.

Actually I knew it's a cop even before seeing the dark green uniform and the Sam Brown belt with its black patent leather holster. Cops, in or out of uniform, have a way of carrying themselves. It tweaks the male ego, a declaration of war, an immediate in-your-face confrontation. Women, on the other hand, see the attitude and the uniform and immediately put on lipstick. Then it's a double, no, triple take. It's the Chinese army guy who ground his cigarette into the rug of the Englishman's house. That dirty mother-humping bastard from years ago, Lieutenant Qin, my captor, the bastard that liked to kill us in the big house near the lake.

CHAPTER 14

I CHECKED ONCE MORE. Damn it. No mistake. Qin. Without even a hesitation he comes directly to our table.

"Ha. Private Diamond. We meet again. Apparently you could not stay away from China. Shall I shoot off your other small finger?"

Never a smile with Qin. And he calls me by my POW rank. Now that's a memory. He finishes with, "I believe you should have made a stronger effort to stay away. Like your friend, Harry, you should have made a stronger effort."

Qin is ordinarily an easy man to forget. Of average height, no distinguishing features to speak of and heavy black hair, even after all these years. You know the man by his calmness. An equanimity belying the sub-surface churning. Back then he would make me kneel on sharp edged steel for hours while talking in a calm voice about the necessity of keeping rooms dust free. He didn't know it but I had my revenge.

Seared in my brain, a cold night, dark. I had come up from the cellar to put the mops away. I don't know what happened between them, but he and the other Lieutenant, the one who told me about the house, the one whose brother went to Taiwan, well, they were going at it, pushing and tugging and yelling in restrained whispers. I could tell how it would end so ferocious were their faces. And it did. Lieutenant Qin hit him and the other went down. Bending over his prey Qin now had his pistol out, its butt poised for another, more powerful blow. While I didn't really like the Lieutenant on the floor, I hated Qin and didn't want him to be victor, over anything. I picked up the closest thing at hand and smashed it over Qin's head, hard. While it did its job I should of chosen my weapon more carefully. In my hand I had the remains of a delightful Canton blue tureen, auction value fifteen shillings, ten pence. My tormentor went down and the Lieutenant on the floor got up and told me to get out of there, he'd take care of it. This other Chinese officer, well, he also had no appetite to confront Qin and he skedaddled. The next day, at his own request he transferred to some other outfit. I was told it was a thousand miles away.

"Qin. What the hell are you doing here?"

Without smiling he tells me, "You may regret coming back to China. If you do anything to break the laws, anything, you will be in my jail."

"Me, in your jail? No chance. I didn't care for your act years ago. I can't imagine you've improved."

"You are friends with Mr. Taylor Davis?"

Taylor Davis, the sweetheart, the guy with his handsome features, family and money. "Taylor? Why the hell do you care?"

"I can tell you he leads an illegal organization in China. We tire of his promulgating a religion whose loyalty is not toward China. That, Mr. Diamond, is illegal. And you," giving me a sweep of his eyes, "your privilege to remain in China can be rescinded very easily." I always admired Qin's command of the language. I now admired Allie's fearlessness. She spoke directly to his eyes.

"Colonel, we all know your parents were killed because they told the missionaries they believed in Christ."

So the Lieutenant Qin is now a Colonel of the police. That's new, and so is the startling information his parents were also Christians. I remembered the end of Sand Pebbles, with Steve McQueen, when the missionaries ran and the Americans and some Chinese were killed in the church courtyard. I thought how the introduction of Christ confused the tightly wound Confucian and Buddhist religious tapestry of China. And now I knew I still bore Qin's hatred.

Things were happening pretty fast and I could see they were going to speed up. Taylor Davis just walked in. Qin hadn't seen him as he had things to tell me.

"Yes, Private Jake, you will regret being in my jail. Your friend, the thief who stole the treasures of China from the Englishman's house, he regretted it."

"Who?" The treasures of China?

"I'm afraid your Harry couldn't quite handle our jails." With a devil's smile he said. "He simply could not conquer the loneliness of the dark."

What the hell is this guy talking about? Harry died out there, someplace, in the black night of Manchuria when Qin shot off my pinky. While I needed time to think, events simply swamped any reflections or questions.

Taylor Davis strode up with his long professional tennis player gait, confident and smooth. In a weak moment years ago I told the tennis pro all good sounding names were really two last ones like his. He just smiled, but I knew it to be true. The Taylor Davis's of this world were usually Gentiles from the East, with long family histories and big time money. Usually blond, they dressed in casual blazers and tasseled loafers. It's guys like him who knew God and Government were on their side. No one from Coney Island had two last names, but a few had tasseled loafers. They were Irving, or Izzy, or Shlomo. The Chinese, on the other hand, always gave their kids great first names, Eternal Love, Auspicious Life. They gave 'em poetry.

Taylor's eyes were on Allie and I wondered if something real serious existed between them. I wouldn't be surprised. As he walked to Allie's chair a slow smile began but died as he caught sight of Qin. I could see him fight for control.

The Colonel now viewed Taylor and while his eyes followed the tennis pro's every movement his face remained icy calm. Taylor stormed to our table, pushing away a chair before standing above Qin. An unstated battle raged between the two and I had no idea why they hated so. Taylor inched toward me and began an incredible tale, both in its subject, and its telling.

"I see you have met Qin, and I imagine he has promised you my head. Am I right?"

The Colonel's eyes never strayed from Taylor.

"You see, Jake this heathen country refuses to recognize Christ. Qin and his government have made my ambitions of bringing God to China illegal. He hates me beyond reason, but within understanding. He is a proselytizer for the antichrist."

"You push, Mr. Davis, you do push." Qin said quietly.

Taylor continued speaking to faces unseen. "His parents were rice Christians, Chinese who gave lip service to Jesus for their daily bread and indeed they sung their hymns fervently. After all, they could not discard the possibility of the promised salvation." Taylor stopped to see the effect of his words on Qin, but the Colonel's face remained placid. The once 29th world ranked tennis player continued in the same accusatory tone.

"Those handouts of food they sought for themselves, for their children. All so understandable. As their first son, Qin's life was sustained by small things, those pittances of sustenance that found their way to China from New York, Connecticut and the back roads of Mississippi. The American offerings of pennies, nickels, dimes, allowed the rice Christians to exist." Taylor stopped to take a breath. Me, I had become breathless. He resumed. "Imagine Jake, how the Colonel must have seethed knowing five thousand years of Chinese history brought only hunger while the ignorant hymn singing poor white trash of the American South were filling his stomach."

"How do you know all these things?" I asked breathlessly.

He gave me a terrible smile, and then looked back to Qin. "Tell him Qin, tell him." The silence became palpable. "I'll tell you what Qin won't," and a tear shone as a single diamond. "My great aunt and uncle were the missionaries in the cold mountain village."

Stupidly I said, "Oh."

Taylor's quiet rage had become an irrepressible fury. He had begun his tale and he would not stop until finished, until the tsunami had crashed on the shore and left nothing standing. "The Communists later shot my aunt and uncle and stuffed them down the well that drew water for the compound, the well my uncle dug." I could see the torment behind Taylor's eyes as he must have pictured the scene over the years. He gave me a false smile.

"Jake, don't you just love irony."

Man, this Taylor. You never know, do you?

The tennis pro sat back and I thought the horror had ebbed. How naive of me. He only took a few seconds to regroup, coming back strong, leaning into the table.

"Qin grew into his role of a child of the revolution. They made him an officer in the army, a person of importance." Taylor drew his face up close to Qin. The spray of his words dampened the tight-lipped face of the cop. Great drama, marvelous theater, but somewhere in the back of my mind I worried. The buyer of the Zhou, my deep pocket angel, threatening the local constabulary. That, I knew, had bad tidings.

"They gave you power where you never had any, didn't they Qin? They gave you the right to be Chinese."

Qin, still hiding any emotion, rose from his chair, kicked it away and everything changed. He unfastened the flap on his holster and slowly and easily removed his revolver. He held it in the palm of his hand, gripping it so tight as to make his knuckles whiten. His arm pulled back, and like a tidal wave it swept across the ocean and crashed on the shore of Taylor's left cheek. Davis splayed across the floor, face down, sliding, as if he had taken a Joe Lewis right. Blood ran from his face. I had seen it all before in northern China. Allie sat next to me, crying softly.

Oh, hell and damnation. Qin, are you nuts? My two-point-zero eight-five million, my retirement, had his blood all over the cafeteria floor. I didn't know whom to worry about first, Taylor, me, Allie or even Qin.

The violence immediately drew a crowd but not to help, to stare. I tried to bring Taylor back to his seat but his body fought my strength. I left him on the floor and went to find something to stem the flow of blood.

We took him to the infirmary at the college where they sewed his open wound. Allie spoke softly and told me to go back to my hotel; she would take care of him.

"Allie, I've known Taylor longer than you have, from back in San Francisco, from his tennis playing days. I'm staying to make sure he's okay and he gets the right attention." I didn't tell her he would also be the source of my retirement. I had to take good care of him. That sounds too harsh, and it's only half-true. Taylor's an honest man, and by itself qualifies for a foundation of friendship and respect.

"Jake, what can you do? How good is your Chinese? Do you know any doctors? Anybody?" Then, in finality, "Go back to your hotel. I'll keep in touch with you."

"But, but . . . ." And as I spoke other Americans and Chinese crowded about Taylor shutting me out. I had no place to go but back to my hotel.

Returning to my room I tried to call Allie, but couldn't reach her. I had the hotel telephone the college infirmary. They were told they took the foreign devil to the police station. Didn't they know? Qin had become the devil. Taylor? Only foreign.

I went downstairs and found Mickey in the poolroom. He asked, "How was your day?"

I stared at him. "Uneventful."

I picked up a cue stick and we shot a little nine-ball for no money. There were no telephone calls. I marveled how we people survived life.

CHAPTER 15

MORNING GOT HERE pretty quick. I planned to join Mickey for breakfast and discuss joining up with Liu in Suzhou. But first things first, as they say. I reached Allie by phone.

"Jake, Taylor's in jail, and they won't let us visit him." I could hear her wipe away her sniffles. "We've all been praying for him. We know Jesus will not let anything happen." I wondered if the police were in contact with the All Mighty.

"Allie, we're leaving to Hangzhou this afternoon. I'll call when I get there."

"God bless you, Jake."

I believe I've only been blessed by two people in this life, Allie, and my Third Grade teacher. While I appreciated the thought, I don't think either did any good.

I didn't want to leave Xiamen with Taylor still in jail, with my retirement hanging in the balance. Now don't think badly of me when I say such things. You know part of it is for effect. The other part, always the truth.

Taylor and the money were really the same. If one works out so does the other. I should first put my priorities in order. While Taylor has to be *numero uno*, finding Liu ran a close second, or should it be visa-versa? Yeah, I guess so. I could only survive if I found the old man.

Funny thing, despite my protestations to the contrary —I believe I picked that expression up from some movie—I trusted the old Chinaman. Why? Well, he's always talking to me like I'm an old buddy, or a second cousin or he's my Dutch uncle. He speaks to me like he trusted me, even respected me. Some one gives you such honor it should be returned, in spades. Yeah, or at least until he screws you.

The kid, Blacky and I caught a taxi. The train station appeared normal for China, chaotic, what I imagined Ellis Island would have been at the turn of the century. Crowds of Chinese were milling about, kind of lost, waiting, sitting with bags of clothes, others lining up for tickets.

The kid pointed out some types who were scalping. He said tickets for the big cities, Shanghai, Beijing, Xian, all required a few days wait because of the demand. Scalpers would get you on the train today, tomorrow, for a premium. Knowing the Chinese I figured there had to be a printing shop down the street creating reservation knock-offs.

Our train came chugging up, puffed, gave off some white steam with the appropriate noises, and settled in. I knew some guys in Florida who behaved the same way. We found our soft-seat car with no trouble. I glanced over to third class. They were climbing through the windows to grab any space representing even a few inches. Living in China could never be for the faint of heart, and getting there never half the fun. I saw life here as basic, gritty, and downright uncomfortable.

We found our car and compartment, and without doubt, pleasantly surprised at our digs—ample room for four, about the size of the European trains sitting eight. Each side of the roomette had one long settee. At night you simply placed a pillow on one end, took your shoes off and swayed with the train's natural rhythm. Strapped to the wall above was a similar bench becoming a berth at night. All four cushioned sofas were protected with white cotton covers and antimacassars. The oddest part, considering the Peoples Republic, everything proved to be reasonably comfortable. As there was no physical separation between occupants, it became a pretty cozy setup if you liked your neighbors. The compartment had piped in martial music and nary a tune you could whistle. They never heard of John Philip Sousa and we never did figure a way to shut the speaker off. We couldn't even find the blasted instrument.

From the start there were vendors either on the stations or coming trough the cars selling most things I couldn't eat, you know, dried pickled chicken feet and such. As a kid in Coney Island during the winter there were these old men pushing metal pushcarts selling knishes, or sweet potatoes. Now those I could eat. To keep their inventory warm they had a separate compartment with a coal fire. You walked by and you got a whiff of sweet smelling stuff and a warm breeze. Between the two, a real joy.

We all kicked back and wriggled to get comfortable. Blacky had his beer, and almost immediately began to snore, sleeping off a night of, what did he call it, "Seven fucking hours of debauchery." Pleasant guy.

In getting comfortable I asked the kid, "Does our going to Suzhou have something to do with the crates of antiques Chang Kai-shek sent from Nanjing to Shanghai?"

He gawked at me as living proof of the alien landing in Rosewell, New Mexico. "What? Crates? Going where?"

"Forget it kid." No one could fake his level of ignorance. I tried something else. "The Grand Canal Mickey, what else do you know about it?"

He started in without further ado. "In its best day it ran about eleven hundred miles, connected the South to the North."

"I know kid, you told me."

He gave me one of his odd expressions, like if I knew so much, why ask.

"Jake, it took four Emperors and two million dead to complete the canal. It crossed the Yangtze and the Yellow Rivers despite their floodings, their changing course, their silting. Jake, today they would have called it China's Interstate Eighty."

"Not bad kid, a nice turn of a phrase."

"Jake, don't make fun of me, I don't care for it."

He's right, and more important, he has moxie.

"The canal, Jake, it brought the rice of the south to the emperors in the north. It allowed Beijing to exist, to grow, prosper. It supported a ship building industry, thousands of coolies, stop over points, hotels, becoming its own military-industrial complex. At some points the canal joined the lakes, and so lucrative the barge trade that pirates roamed the waters." He ended in a down voice, "Today, only good for carrying tourists, coal and rice, but not really very far." His voice rose, accompanied with bright eyes. "If you want to know more I'll find a good library reference for you."

The kid's beautiful. "Its okay Mickey, its okay. You don't have to get nasty."

"I'll tell you what else I know, Jake. When we get to Hangzhou we only have one night in town. The next morning we catch an overnight ferry going up the canal to Suzhou. Afterward my uncle has the plans."

Well, they say your life goes full circle. I began this China trade rigmarole as a prisoner at the hands of the Chinese. Now it seems for sure I'll be in the hands of another Chinese as this gets wrapped up. Damn. When the hell do I get to be the captain of my own ship.

I had hoped to see China from the train window but I should have known better. Rustic and pastoral scenes, quaint villages, town markets and women washing in the rivers were what I had hoped. What I witnessed were dusty, gray unappealing stations and almost gray countryside. Green appeared to be a color left off the Chinese palette.

A big guy came on the train and into the compartment at Gonzhou in late afternoon. Definitely kinda spooky, like a country bumpkin, unkempt hair, and a few stray strands sprouting from his chin. He had on a gray Mao jacket and duller everything else. But the garlic, he just kept chewing cloves of garlic. There's this Stinking Rose restaurant on Columbus in San Francisco where garlic is the spice du jour, but this cop had it beat to hell. I figured he would stop after his first clove, hah, he had a bucket of them, and already peeled. With the window open it stayed tolerable, but whenever we went through those long tunnels with our coal burning locomotive we had to shut the portals. The real test became whether we could live with either the pungent fumes of the garlic or the soot of the locomotive. When you brought Blacky into the equation with his snoring and beer breath also permeating the closed space I knew I had to get out of there.

Making it to the narrow aisle outside the compartment I pulled down a little spring-back seat and watched the black night pass. Listening to the lonesome sound of the occasional train whistle became my entertainment. Occasionally we passed a weak yellow light nailed to a lonely lamppost. Once in a while a car or a truck's headlight would break through the black, but even then the world stayed lonely. Surrounded by the comforting silence of the car's corridor and the rhythm of the wheels as they crossed from one set of rails to another I started to doze. To stay awake I thought about Qin's remark about Harry, the one about dark and loneliness. I had no idea what he meant.

With the light finally rising in the East I watched China come to life. First a woman drawing water, then a man hitching his pants, pulling a mangy horse. The day lightened and men, women trudged up the road carrying full buckets hung on both ends of wooden yolks across their shoulders. Men and oxen in the wet fields both straining at the harness, binding them in unending labor. A woman with a child at her breast watched as prancing children giggled their way to school with black plastic bags on their backs. Even for the kids China stayed hard, tough, unbending. Pleasure became observing the humdrum of ordinary people's behavior. I'd almost forgotten most of life's pleasures were simple human actions be it in China or San Francisco. Sitting back I watched the entertainment of civilization in motion. Swaying with the train made it even more comforting.

The ride had become a kick until Mickey came out and sat on the aisle seat facing me. "Jake, the guy in the compartment with us, I think he's a cop."

I know I'm world famous, but this far West? Naw. "C'mon, he's probably some Communist official."

"No, really Jake, I saw his badge. It's under his jacket."

About time something really exciting happened. I liked being tailed, a touch of romance. At least I thought they were following me. It could have been Blacky, even the kid, I mean his family escaped from the Communists back in the forties.

You know I don't like cops. No question, they're always trouble, needing to validate their uniform by hassling you. Remember what happened in the cafeteria? First Qin threatens me, then the brouhaha with Taylor. Cops, they're always trouble or is it just the Coney Island in me.

CHAPTER 16

WE PULLED INTO Hangzhou late afternoon and met by one of the assistant managers of the Shangri-La Hotel. Apparently Liu has clout. Even as we approached the hostelry you could tell it had the stature of the kind of place Ronald Coleman would have stayed. Expensive and sophisticated. Even Blacky seemed impressed. This Liu really knew how to spend my money.

The Chinese cop stayed close until he watched us go into the hotel. I went up to my room to catch some sleep. I had about three hours shut eye before the kid woke me.

"Jake, come down, its a nice town."

Now the kid was never into hyperbole so I knew it had to be something. "Mickey, if it's not as oriental as the Mandalay Bay in Vegas you're in trouble."

Just so you know, I'm not a big fan of Vegas, but Sharli, she goes for all those Chinese gambling games, you know, the ones you can't pronounce. So we go to Vegas maybe once a month. With no pool-hall I had to shift over to my other best game, craps.

Sharli said it wasn't a Chinese game. She asked, "Are there many Chinese playing it?"

"Why must Chinese be playing?"

"Are there any Chinese playing it?" she demanded.

"No, and maybe it's why it's a good game."

She got mad. "Can't be good game," and went back to her Chinese Pai Gow tiles.

I took the walk with Mickey around the city for a couple of hours. To me it had too much history, too many Emperors, too many battles, and far too many tourists. We headed back to the hotel for dinner as the sun went behind the hump bridge at West Lake.

Mickey ordered for us and when I happened to be square in the middle of some delicious pork slices with wine this owlish looking westerner walks over to our table and hurumphs to get my attention.

"Mr. Jake Diamond, correct?"

"Am I behind in alimony?" I ask.

He smiled, a small one. Well at least he had some sense of humor. "No, Mr. Diamond, I'm disappointed you don't remember me. We met just the other week."

Where the hell is my head. That train ride did damage. "Of course, you're my Winslow Professor of Chinese Art. Wyatt? Sure. They told me you were in Hangzhou. We got things to talk about. Important things, I mean important things. You're a fraud."

Ignoring my words, he asks, "May I call you, Jake?"

I always worried about guys who buddied up too fast, especially this Berkleyite. Yeah, he appeared owlish, kind of a fat Woody Allen with extreme male pattern baldness. It appeared his waist disappeared years ago along with his humility. Kinda academic, unpressed pants and corduroy jacket with patched elbows. Still, you had the feeling a barracuda lay under all his soft pretense.

"Sure, if I can call you Wyatt." I could tell he didn't like it, but screw him, he's screwed me.

"Dr. Liu contacted me and said you might be here."

Yup, as I thought. I guess the bamboozle continues. He stands there peering at me, as though I'm supposed to say something. When he realizes it's still his dime he continues. "There is apparently some concern on your part regarding the bona fide of the *Late Autumn* scroll Mr. Liu had sold you."

He waited for some kind of recognition, but I played it straight. Let him come to me, so he continued. "You know, the certificate of authenticity I signed." I still didn't react. "I can assure you my deliberations were on the mark, and without question your painting is as described. I put it through every test, infrared analysis, X-ray, polarized light microscopy, even carbon dating, addressing every possibility." The way he's going on, its like, if you have a Ph.D. you had to talk the way he did. He ran out of breath allowing me to get on the offensive.

"Yeah, well, I think your expertise sucks." I gave the cocky expert some haughtiness of my own. "I brought some silk fibers and a fleck of the signature ink to Teddy on Hayes. You must know him."

He nodded, "Yes, a decent technician."

You condescending shit. "Well, he calculated both were about fifty years old, not the eight hundred you signed on to."

"Jake," I knew I shouldn't have given him my first name, "I don't know what you gave Teddy, and I really don't care. The brush strokes, the sense of the painting, the ink, the age of the silk, the chops, every technical aspect of the drawing tested out and made it a Zhou Mengfu. Without question my expert view is shown by the affidavit." His eyes searched around the table, maybe seeking applause.

He spoke with such confidence he almost convinced me but I knew it all to be a sham, only protecting his butt. "Look, you well scrubbed Cheshire cat, even your partner in crime, C. Liu, Ph D, curator of the Taiwan museum says I got a forgery. He tells me that the real Zhous are on the bottom of some canal and that's where we're headed. The Chinese con-man has more honesty than the fraudulent academically honored professor, you." Then it occurred to me. "How do you know what a genuine Zhou Mengfu looks like? Hell it's eight hundred years old." I start thinking about what I'm saying. "Every emperor and their eunuchs from the Sung Dynasty on had possession of *Late Autumn* at one time or another. The probability of survival of any Zhou has to be slim. How many hands have they passed through, how many emperors pawned them to fight their wars?" I watched his face as I warmed to my subject. "Damn it, the Zhou you've said it's genuine, couldn't it have been done by his students copying Zhou's style. It would give you the right silk, paint, meet all your tests."

Wyatt blanched at my attack, but recovered quickly. "Nonsense, Jake. The provenance's, research, the other paintings, all the experts, yours is the real Zhou."

Ignoring his words I started thinking out loud. "The damn thing is eight hundred years old; it's biodegradable for god's sake. Why the hell isn't it falling apart? Damn, The Last Supper is coming off the walls and it's only a few hundred years old. Even the Sistine Chapel has had its face-lift. The stuff in Christ's time can't even see the light of day without crumbling."

Now the Professor starts talking humbly. "Well what you say is true, but we do know Zhou Mengfu's work."

"Hell. There were those charlatans, Myatt and Drewe. They sold the best of the fakes of the modern masters to the experts. They made fools of the guys who said they knew. There's De Hory, right, he has more of his own homemade Matisse's and Modigliani's in museums around the world than the real guys. Compared to the Chinese those guys were still amateurs. We're dealing with Chinese, for god's sake. They can reproduce anything, even more authentic than the original. They're the master magicians. They pull goldfish bowls out of their sleeves."

Wyatt started to interrupt. No chance. I sped away, on a roll.

"How many different paintings by Zhou have survived, three, four, five? Maybe they're all fakes, copies. You know the Chinese penchant for forgery." I knew my words were falling on deaf ears figuring the only way you can get an academic to change his mind is to believe in reincarnation. First he had to die, and then come back as a new idea.

"Yes," Wyatt retorted, "The Chinese are good, excellent, technicians, but I assure you . . . ."

"You can assure me nothing. Your expertise is little more than subjective judgment, and damn it, you could be wrong." Then I stopped. Christ, what the hell am I doing? I'm building a case to destroy me. If I had given the thought to what I'm saying now back then maybe I wouldn't be in this fix.

I rose from the table unable to bear my own words, needing some air, to calm down. I walked outside. Where the hell were my cigars? You see, the trouble with experts is they can be as wrong as you but so convinced of their own self worth with all their credentials they make you doubt your own. After a while you not only accept their answers, you let them make up the questions.

I stood out there a few minutes when Mickey comes looking for me. "Jake I didn't know the trouble between you and my uncle."

"It's okay kid. I figured you didn't."

"Jake, I never meant, I mean, if I thought . . . ."

I placed my arm around his shoulder. "We'll get it straightened out kid." I threw a glance back into the hotel. "Tell mister," I searched for the right word, "high hat back in there I got a little off the handle."

"Jake," his face tells he's going to tell me something I'm not going to like, "he's coming on the boat with us. My uncle needs him in Suzhou."

"Great kid, just great." I started to walk away.

"Jake, where you going."

"No place kid, no place, but I'm going there alone, okay?"

The hotel touched West Lake and the ladies of the evening were out.

I missed Sharli. Now don't go tainted blue on me, I simply meant I needed her counsel. I've told you she's smarter than me. All of a sudden I'm getting nostalgic, reaching for simpler things, needing a little cheering up. I just about convinced myself I'm a damnable fool to buy the painting in the first place.

The shimmer of the lake soothed and I continued my walk. I sat on one of the benches. Then my personal lament began on how everything went wrong just as I thought I had it knocked? Li'l Abner's daily cartoon once had a guy who walked around with a rain cloud over his head. I understood all about him, but I knew I had to fight the feeling, yeah, you had to keep going and not give in. I learned the hardest way if you were going to win you had to keep punching to the last, but even then it wasn't a sure thing. Life's a bitch, then you die.

Yeah, I know about dying, I know all about it. Korea taught me about needless and wanton death but my father taught me about dying. You see I sat by him when the pain became so bad he needed to die. His heart, it always was his heart. Later the doctor said he didn't know how he could walk around. Manny Diamond complain about something? Not Manny, under any circumstance. His way was always to tough it out.

Sitting by his bed in a white anonymous hospital room holding his hand I thought I should have been crying, instead I stood remote, watching a process unfold. My participation lay only in rubbing his hand saying, "I love you, Dad."

I never saw my father cry, except that one time in his printing shop which was always teetering on bankruptcy. He told me the shylocks were taking everything. "They want my blood, they want my blood," and tears came, and he wiped his eyes, embarrassed before me. God, I wasn't even fourteen when he told me. I had to dry my own tears. I had some money, even then, and offered to help. His eyes misted and he slowly shook his head, no. Years later I came across a Yiddish saying, "When the father helps the son, both smile, when the son helps the father, both cry."

His white hospital room lied, it suggested calmness, hope, and life. But my dad lay there and said it hurt, it hurt so. He pulled at my arm; "Tell them to give me something, anything." His eyes focused on some spot beyond the room, as though survival required concentration at a point not of this world. "Jake, it hurts." Then his eyes shifted and found mine. He grimaced, the pain catching up to his words "This whole thing, life, it's no big deal, Jake. It's not much." His eyes cried of the hurt. "The price is too high."

The intern came in with a needle and jammed it into my father's chest. His scowl of pain relaxed and his eyes softened. His eyes closed and he whispered, "Take care of your mother." We were silent, and I rubbed his hand, his arm. I had turned away for a second when I heard the rattle. His eyes had gone to the back of his head. I stood there staring at my father, but I can't remember how I felt. I just know I didn't cry. The intern must have told my mother. She came into the room and held her husband's hand. "Manny, Manny, who's going to take care of me?"

I'll never forget it. "Who's going to take care of me?" I had watched silently as they fought over the years. I remember embarrassing scenes before relatives but at the end, husband and wife. "Manny, who's going to take care of me?"

I cried remembering, sitting there on the bench, by the lake, in Hangzhou, I cried. For myself? Nobody was going to take care of me except me, and I wouldn't let anything put me down. I had a retirement to enjoy, my golden years, they say. I couldn't let my father's last moment's serve as a lesson. No sir. My eyes went to the sky, to the moon. "Hey Liu, no matter what, I'm coming attcha.

123

In the morning I once again joined Mickey for breakfast. Blacky pulled up a chair, then Wyatt. I told them if we waited a little longer and scraped up six more we could maybe have enough for a morning prayer. Blacky had no clue, Wyatt raised one eyebrow, and the kid gave me a smile. No question, when all this is over I'm adopting him. I broke the silence following my remark. "Well, what's on the agenda for today? Anyone?"

The waitress came by and we all took a chance at ordering bacon and eggs. The gal who took our orders didn't even blink. Clearly a place used to the Westerner.

Mickey started with, "I told you last night, Jake. My uncle has tickets for us on the tourist boat going to Suzhou. We leave late afternoon."

"Oh, yeah."

"Jake," the kid said softly, "we should all be at the wharf at five."

"Oh, yeah, by boat. Kid, they sent me to Korea on a troop ship, and I threw up before we even got under the Golden Gate.

Wyatt pipes up. "I think Liu wants you to get a feeling of the canal, its importance, history, its pulsating life." He's playing with a fork, leaving the chopsticks lie lonely.

I try responding in a sardonic tone, "Pulsating life, huh," but I think I failed.

"I don't know, Jake. Uncle simply said it's where the treasures are, in the canal."

The food arrives and damned if it didn't rival what you'd get at your local Denny's.

Blacky puts in his three cents. "I caught some views of the canal last night. He's not going to get me to dive into all that filth."

I get a sharp pain in my ankle. The kid is kicking and jerks his head over his shoulder. It's the cop from the train. He's sitting there cracking Polly seeds with his teeth, smiling. There's another guy looking like his brother. They must have bought their clothes and nuts at the same state store as both are wearing steel gray Mao suits. I smiled as they kinda looked like those street art statues you see sprouting up in the squares of touristy American small towns.

"Hey kid, go over there and ask 'em what they want."

The kid starts to get up and Wyatt takes his arm. "Stay here. I'll ask. They'll be more polite to me."

I watch him walk over, hand each his card and begin talking. They bring a chair from the other table and it's like the local Rotary. The cops offer him some seeds and he cracks them professional like, between his teeth. No question, I had to reevaluate this guy.

All three bring their heads to our table and the guy from the train is pointing to me while the new guy is staring right at Blacky. What the hell did I do? I want no trouble with the local gendarme. The owl continues talking to them for another minute, then comes back to our little table filled with innocents from abroad.

The Winslow Professor speaks to me. "The good-looking one," son-of-a-gun, he has a sense of humor, "told me he had instructions to always know the whereabouts of Blacky and you." He shifted his position and gave them a half-wave and a smile. They did the same. "Wouldn't tell me why, but I suspect Blacky is considered dangerous and more important." I'm insulted. Blacky blanches. Ho boy. I have a suspicion there's trouble a brewing. As I said, with cops there's always grief.

After breakfast each of us went our own way. I just walked about West Lake with its arched bridges. Mickey had told me it has a well known for its beauty. Maybe so, but the hoards of tourists did me in again. I meandered back to the hotel for lunch ordering some Peking duck. I'm eating this stuff and the Winslow Professor of Chinese Art sits down at the table.

"I hope you don't mind."

What could I say? "Sure. But don't expect much conversation. I said about all I had last night." While surprisingly proud of what I said, I had emptied my plate.

"Despite your suspicions, Jake, I fully believe the painting you bought is a Zhou. Nevertheless, Liu now thinks maybe the one he sold you may be only a marvelous copy ordered by Chiang Kai-shek."

He could have chosen some other words. Wyatt continued. "He now believes the original is in a barge sunk some fifty years ago." His face tells me he doesn't think so.

"The one escaping from the Communists?" I ask.

I surprised him. When I get back I've got to get Teddy a little something. His little talk has come a long way.

Wyatt's eyes had more questions than facts. "Liu knew the story of the barge carrying the real Zhou sinking under lethal Communist fire between Suzhou and Wuxi. He never believed it. He once told me the canal appeared wide enough to conceal a barge, but too shallow to hide anything bigger than an old rickshaw. If it was scuttled it would have been found years ago, someone would have tripped over it."

"So why are we headed there?"

Wyatt leans over to me. "Jake," he says conspiratorially, "I've received some research money to come out here and help Liu with whatever he does. He thinks a barge containing treasures is someplace in Lake Taihu, just off the canal by Suzhou." Looking at me I give him one of those zombie stares. "You're not interested, are you?" he asks sarcastically.

Now pissed, I offered, "The little chronicle you just gave me is more academic gibberish. I don't give a damn what's under the water."

"Yes, you do, Jake, yes, you do. Liu says maybe the original of the painting he sold you is in the lake, in the barge."

"But I got your imprimaturs saying I have the real one," I said sardonically.

"It's true Jake, but my guarantee is good until someone proves me wrong. And it's what Liu wants to do."

No question, the old academic is a crowd stopper. Out of nowhere he tells me there's a chance my Zhou is safely in a lake and Liu maybe hasn't really stole my money and the prof's own word is not gospel. I'm waiting for more, his take on things, instead, he simply leans forward, picks up a pair of chopsticks and reaches to take a piece of my Peking duck.

"You don't mind do you?" He sits there chewing, hovering for his next mouthful. "Not bad," he says. "Not bad."

What he just did, reach over and take a piece of my duck, I liked it. Either it's an attempt at intimacy or sheer gluttony. The former made me smile and I become a tad warmer to this professed scholar.

So I'm sitting there watching Wyatt eat and wondering who's right, my academic here who says my painting is a legit Zhou, or my Charley Chan and his linen suits currently in Suzhou searching in the lake for the real McCoy. Life never seems to simplify.

The professor puts down the chopsticks. "Not bad. The sauce is a little stringent." Then, I swear, in an exact duplication of the white rabbit in Alice in Wonderland, he pulls out a pocket watch and exclaims, "Oh, I'm late, I'm late. Come Jake, we have a very important date with the Grand Canal." He lacked a large, floppy fedora.

CHAPTER 17

I ARRIVED AT THE ferry alone and with time to spare. Wyatt had to stop off at Zhejing University where he stayed while in town. He said he's going to run a short seminar on Chinese castings by the lost wax method. What? Anyhow, I see Blacky about a block away. He's talking to this Chinese guy with a moustache whose ends reach beneath his chin, the original Fu Manchu. You know immediately he is not of the ruling class. I also see the cop from the other day at the hotel. He's still cracking poppy seeds and keeping tabs on Blacky and his cohort. As I'm early I'm kicking stones waiting around for Mickey to show. He has the tickets. Then, sudden like, Blacky taps me on the shoulder.

"Amigo, how come you're always spying on me."

"I'm not, Blacky, just happened to see you."

His face hardened. "Fuck you. I know when someone's spying. I don't like you. Just don't fuck around with the fiddle I have going with my friend over there. You're

129

not getting hurt by it, neither is Liu, just the fucking Commies."

As he's talking I watch the cop start walking over to Fu Manchu. At the same time I see two other officers begin to close in from the other side of the quay. The Chinese guy looks this way, over to Blacky, to the cops, takes a few steps and breaks into a run that would make Jesse Owens proud. The police are after him, and the crowds on the dock part giving room to all those running, and it is a crowd.

I ask Blacky, "What's going on there?"

His face is angry, contorted. "Don't give me your fucking innocence. If you go ahead and screw things up there's more than me. Your buddy in Taiwan has just as much to lose."

If he made sense I'd know what to say. Instead, all I got is, "My buddy in Taiwan?"

He gives me a fake smile. "You wanna play it your way, it's okay with me."

"I've no reason to screw you, Blacky."

He stays with his shit-eaten grin.

"Yeah, why would you?" Then he gets this funny expression like an idea came into his head. "Tell ya what, I'll make it up to ya. If we get a chance we'll go down on a dive together. Is it good with you *compadre*?"

Like a fool I mull it over too quickly and come to the foolish conclusion, "Yeah, I'd like that." I'd been scuba diving only one time before and that was in Acapulco. Pedro sees me sitting by the pool with my second wife, and asks if I want to dive, only ten pesos. As we get over to a shack by the cove he brings out a tank, fins and mask, and gives me a quick lesson saying, "If I run out of air just pull this lever, and I'd have five more minutes." I figured, hey, I'm an ex-Coney Island lifeguard.

We're both out there in the soft, warm Acapulco bay waters and I'm enjoying it. I'm splashing around some, maybe 35 feet below the surface. I figure I can go deeper. I do. We're down about maybe fifty, fifty-five feet when I'm sucking for a little oxygen and all I get is nothing coming in. I take another hard pull, still *nada*. I think, no sweat as Pedro told me about the five-minute reserve. I pull the handle for the extra minutes. How young and foolish I was. This is Mexico. Maybe *manana* they were going to fill the tank. A little panic? Nah. A lotta terror.

I start kicking for the surface real fast, and I hear the screeching in my ear giving me a little blood on my pillow the next morning. Anyhow, I get to the beach, yell at Pedro who gentlemanly asks for his ten pesos. What am I going to do, complain to the local Chamber of Commerce? Hey, it's all an adventure.

"Go diving for treasure with you?" Hell, Mexico was a fluke and the idea of finishing something only half-done has great appeal. Yeah, a little adventure with a diving pro. "Blacky, count me in." Something stirred in the back of my mind when I said I'd go, but it wouldn't form.

Blacky gives me one of those, you know, he makes a pistol with his hand and presses down with his thumb, winks one eye and says, "Pow. Catch ya later mon ami," and walks to the boat.

I'm now shuffling my feet back and forth investigating the ferry. It's nothing but an old rusty steel flat bottomed double decked passenger scow. The old Staten Island ferry had to be an American Cup contender in comparison.

The kid comes up. "Jake, what's all the excitement? The cops were running after this guy, people were splitting in all directions. Is it something I should know about?"

"I'm not sure kid. Maybe it' all about a parking ticket."

"Very funny."

Mickey's attention first goes to the dispersing crowd then back to me. "You ready Jake? I have Blacky's diving things all stashed away. All we have to do is go aboard." He reacts to the boat's appearance. "Not much, huh. Uncle said he bought us first class tickets."

We crossed a shaky gangplank and found our outside cabin. First Class huh? I couldn't imagine Second Class. There were two steel cots fastened to the bulkhead. A bathroom more rusty than clean and an outside door missing its knob. Oh yes, it had a beat up table and a lamp without a shade. Real posh.

"We sharing this kid?"

The kid is also disappointed. "I'm sorry Jake, Uncle bought the best he could get."

I raise one eyebrow. "With my money he could have done better."

I put my bag atop the mattress and go on deck to catch the sights, particularly a famous three-arched bridge the tourist books talked about. The ferry gave a coupla short whistles, hawsers are thrown from the dock and the ship pulled softly away into the canal. Even before it floated to the center of the waterway it joined and became tied to two similar ferries. I watched the activity on the water. No boat of any size made the trip down the canal by itself.

The traffic on the waterway appeared strictly commercial. All the coal barges were loaded to the gunwales. Ancient motor launches had decks awash with rice, cords of wood piled high and bags of coal blackened the once varnished decking. Boats defying coherent description were all tied from snout to tail, like elephants in migration and clogged the waterway in all directions. I understood why the ninety miles to Suzhou would take the next fourteen hours. Everything moved a tad slower than an ambling drunk.

Wyatt had boarded earlier and had his cabin next to ours. As the sky started to darken both Wyatt and I were by the railing and caught up with the passing scene. The banks of the canal were lined with tiers of hand-laid stone now reflecting a soft purple in the retiring sun. Maybe some ten feet above the water were promenades shaded with willow and maple trees. There were benches for lovers, an occasional classic Chinese peaked pavilion with carved monkeys holding on precipitously to the roof corners, and some high-arched wooden bridges traversing the canal. And, typically, people everywhere, raucous, pulling, pushing, and holding hands. Absolutely a delightful China as drawn on a 17th Century cracked white porcelain vase.

I went to an auction in Japan about a dozen years ago, to Kamakura, a seaside town of religious significance. The society of the country had no surprises from what I had heard, orderly, polite, gentle. Standing by the city's massive Buddha statue I wondered why they brought on the devastation of World War II and the cruelty they showered on the Chinese.

To tell you the truth the Japanese never excited me. I know they're polite, their streets are safe, and sushi is good for the cholesterol, but I always see them as World War II movie pilots, buckteeth, big glasses, shooting at our guys in parachutes. It's all so nutsy with Japan so harmonious and methodical and the China I'm traveling in seemingly in a continual state of movement and anger.

Some years I got into a conversation with a customer, a Ralph something, a Sinologist, a guy who studied China, Asia. He told me if I wanted to know the difference between the natures of the Chinese and Japanese, look at their icons. The Japanese gods all have angry faces and lightening bolts. The Chinese, ha, you want to pinch their cheeks they're so cute. The guy had insight.

The professor who's standing beside me gives a little nudge. I can see he's also caught up in the shore scene. "Lovely."

I answered. "Lovely." And we both stood there watching.

After a while Professor Gourmet says, "With all the times I've been on this water it's more like a river than a canal." I stayed silent.

After about five minutes of peering at the water and smelling the air I say, "You know, it's not a canal, it's not even a river. Nope," I peered at the swirling water again, "it's really a sewer." Yup, it's what I would see coming out of the large pipes emptying into Gravesand Bay when I swam in those waters at the ass end of Coney Island. No question, pure, unadulterated garbage. I nudged the professor standing next to me. "It stinks of diesel and diapers, of chemicals and compost." I gazed at it a few more seconds, then laughed and Wyatt looked at me strangely. You see, he doesn't know Blacky offered me the opportunity to dive with him in this muck.

In the early morning hours as we approached Suzhou I came out of a restless sleep and went to the ship's rail. I again stood along side the professor wearing his green corduroy jacket with leather elbows. He shows me his education, but I don't mind.

"There," he pointed, "those falling down cottages lining the canal, they are Ming dynasty Huaihai."

I'm investigating them, and I can see they have a kind of interesting dignity as they hang over the canal with flowers dripping from their windows.

"Take a last look," he offers sadly, "they're soon to be destroyed. Monies have been allocated for modern garden apartments and," then he says something making me like him more, "with less grace, like much of this new China."

I had this friend once, Myron. A cherubic kind of guy, kind of like Wyatt. Couldn't play any kind of sports worth a damn, but excelled at schoolbooks. Anyhow, we got to talking one night. He said he knew the guys didn't like him, or the girls, but it didn't matter. We actually hit it off and stayed almost friendly, but his world's not mine. He never gets drafted, some kind of disability, and goes on to med school. Wyatt, he reminds me of Myron.

A new vibration of the ship's engines lifted my eyes showing the line of elephants had now broken the chain and our passenger scow was making its way into a narrow channel. Wyatt moved along the railing till he closed the distance between us.

"If I were you Jake, I'd be heading back to San Francisco, back to your authentic scroll. Liu is sending everyone on a wild goose chase."

"Wyatt, I'd go back in a flash if I thought I had the real Zhou. You're just protecting your ass. Besides, you never made any chemical tests on the silk and ink like the ones Teddy did."

The professor eyes me like I'm a kindly fool. "Just one more point, Jake. If I'm wrong and Liu's right, just what the hell do you think the Commies will do when Blacky comes up with the real McCoy. Under any odds you walk away with nothing, *bupkis*, as you would say."

Now he's hitting me with Yiddish, but he didn't throw anything I didn't play with earlier. Damn, I need Sharli, she'd know what to do.

Docking required the flat-bottomed ferry to do a ninety-degree pivot as it pulled to its slip. Lines were thrown out, placed around a doohickey on the pier and as faster then you could run the hundred meters the ship tied up alongside. The gangplank scraped its way down almost immediately. Definitely impressive.

Back in the cabin everything is packed and I'm ready to disembark. I carefully made my way down the shaking gangplank holding tight onto the rail and thinking I'm getting old. As soon as I hit dry land a hand came out and steadied me. It's full of blotches, the melanin kind, the hand of an old man.

"Ah, Mr. Diamond. Do be careful. I would not want your first steps into this lovely city to become an accident."

"Well, well, Mr. Liu, I sometimes think I made you up." Standing close to this old, sweet man still looking natty despite wrinkles in his linen suit, I'm thinking how I could ever consider banging him around.

"I am always at your service Mr. Diamond. My nephew should have assuaged any of your concerns."

I pause a second and come out with what's on my mind. "Liu I'll take back my six-fifty g's."

As cool as can be he says, "I'm sorry Jake, it's impossible. It is held by the museum in Taipei." He glances about, first to his nephew who had quietly ambled alongside and then back to me. "Besides Jake, there is no reason to become excited. Rest assured you will come away with more than simply our transaction."

What the hell kind of answer is that? "Liu, were you ever a three card Monte dealer?"

He gives me one confused face, shakes his head like I'm speaking in a foreign language and walks over to Blacky who's still wearing his Italian threads. They exchange a few words and Liu points to a waiting taxi. He does the same to Wyatt with some soft laughs. You could see a warmth between them bred over years of association. Great. I get an expert who's bosom buddies with the guy who's selling me the "el fako". I'm some jerk.

After walking Wyatt to the car with his arm about his shoulders, Liu comes back to me. "Jake," you could see he's kind of tasting my name, "somehow it fits you perfectly. I must commend your parents." He places his arm around my shoulders as he did to Wyatt. He walks me off to the side like we're old buddies and he's going to give me special dispensation. "I have made reservations for the first days at a delightful new hotel. I'm sure you will enjoy it. We can talk there."

We work our way through a whole bunch of streets, busy corners and high fences and come to the Bamboo Grove Hotel. It naturally gives off its aroma of newness and expense. Liu takes my arm and escorts me across the white marble floor, past the brocaded chairs and to the elevators. He hands me one of those plastic keys for my room and begins a conversation.

"Blacky will be diving for ancient works of art from the Forbidden City, five, seven, eight hundred years old, treasures like the one I sold you." Then he places his hands on mine in a special way and in a kind of conspiratorial manner says, "Maybe even another Zhou." I could have sworn he winked.

"I don't understand. Are you admitting the Zhou you sold me is a forgery? And that's why I'm here?" and I say this with my voice going up an octave.

Liu blanches, embarrassed. "Please, Jake, those are not my words." I feel he wants to say a little more but he pulls back and changes the subject. "Did you enjoy your journey on the canal? You know it's the historical avenue of Chinese commerce, a canal with an immense history."

I can't let him soft-soap me. I want to grab his lapels, to pull his sophisticated ways out of him. I try but it's just not in me. I take a step to the open elevator that's just arrived. I need to get to a bed feeling the lack of sleep from my last night's First Class stateroom. I still can't get used to these run-silent run-fast elevators preferring those open birdcage types which allowed you to see the blank walls between floors and feel the adventure. In the room I'm bushed and asleep as soon as my head hits the down. It's one thing about me, give me a quiet soft place and I'm out. Still, the Chinese have me beat. I've seen them sleep standing up, honestly.

CHAPTER 18

FIVE HOURS LATER I'm rested, downstairs, but still, what? Sullen. I needed fresh air, to see the city. I put on starched chinos and my blazer seeking to stun the females. I walk past a falling down pagoda, and then follow a moat leading me to the waterway I had left hours earlier. I find a crippled wooden bench near a high humped-back bridge and a Chinese building with maritime flags flying on a stone parapet. For more than a few minutes I'm watching Chinese life on the water flow under the tall arched bridge and my last day's tension oozes out. Last night the horns and whistles of the barges kept me awake. Now the same sounds are like a locomotive on an endless prairie, or a softly clanging bell buoy just off the Coney Island shore on a foggy night. Everything became soft and fluffy.

I thought of Harry for a while. I had always felt guilty for that night in China. Somehow it was my fault. But he always was the smart one and I've always wondered how he must of died. What I've kept from you cause he never wanted to talk about it, was his lineage—he didn't have any. His aunt took care of him without really caring. And he felt likewise, at least he said so. My parents loved me, he didn't know what happened to his. One day they were there, the next, gone. Odd for a Jewish couple. Hell, just plain strange.

When I came out of the army after those years in the cold of China I would walk the boardwalk and feel sorry for myself, Harry and my lost pinky. So far as I could tell I had no future and was too young for a past, unless you want to consider the army constituting a previous life. Somebody dealt me a hand with no hole cards worth a damn. I figured the Gods had already interpreted my character, a loser.

I worked hard to fight my pessimism and took a job as a gofer for a Chinese antique dealer on Mott Street in Manhattan's Chinatown. My Chinese boss was Robert E. Lee. While I loved his name, neither he, my job, nor the quality of the goods carried had any integrity. From my first day working I knew my knowledge exceeded his, at least for the China Trade stuff. Now and then I'd make a smart buy from Lee or any one of the other dozen down town Chinese dealers. I'd go to the Europeans on Park Avenue and flip the sale. It didn't take long for my rep to be established as a knowledgeable guy.

Uptown is where I met Abe, a slick, curly haired, fast talking, aggressive pure New York, married Jewish guy. He had some education, money and acted as a broker among the high roller art dealers. We hit it off, had some cash between us and set up a small shop on Eighty-Second and Third Avenue. You wouldn't call the place high class but it reflected our artistic moods, kind of funky mid-20th Century eclectic. We did well, at least I thought we did.

I never had the education and Abe told me to relax, said he'd take care of the books. And like a schmuck I said, "Sure." Sound familiar?

Turned out, as you've already guessed, he had this penchant for the ponies and hitting the town with sweet little things showing perky tits. Whatever we had eventually went to the bookies and Abe's wife's divorce attorney. As lawyers go he not only *shtuped* Abe but his wife as well. Hey, would you expect less?

So I took my single suitcase and all my supposed smarts and headed west. I figured I could hide in San Francisco with its fog and hills. Who knew when Liu offered the scroll like a fool I'd again say, "Sure."

A caustic horn from the river brought me out of my reverie and I figured I'd better head back to the hotel and Liu and in typical Jake fashion, I take three steps and I'm hopelessly lost.

Some guys have an unerring sense of direction. Sharli has it. But put me in the middle of San Francisco and if I can't find a bus with a number I may as well be back in Brooklyn's Prospect Park where I could never even find an exit let alone the zoo.

Just after basic training they were going to promote me to corporal. They said I had leadership potential. Well, they put me in charge of a squad and sent us on an overnight bivouac to rendezvous the next day at these certain map coordinates. Hell, I think three of my guys are still walking, lost out on those Texas plains. I taught them a thing or two about dead reckoning.

I'm wandering about in this Chinese city of canals, stunning bridges, rock gardens, falling down pagodas, and streets covered over with plane trees. I'm desperately searching for something familiar, wondering if I'd ever see Sharli or North Beach ever again. A taxi pulls up alongside.

"Jake, I've been searching all over for you." It's Mickey.

"Kid, you always got a home."

We get back to the hotel and Blacky is leaving with two of the Chinese divers. There's another cab filled with wet suits, air cylinders, a small compressor and lots of small bags.

"Blacky, where you headed?" I yell out.

I can see fire in his eyes. As he leaves he yells out the window, "Hey, Diamond, you son-of-a bitch, don't forget, I have first dibs on your ass in those lake waters."

To hell with Blacky, besides, he forgot to call me *amigo*. Then I remember I'm hungry. Seems it's all I do in China is eat. "C'mon kid, let's order." I follow the kid into the dining room where he asks for pork dumplings.

I glance up and Charley Chan is arriving along with the waiter and the victuals. "Ah, Mr. Diamond, my nephew, and dumplings. How fortunate." He sits down and is into the dumplings before I can even get my chopsticks in position. His eyes catch mine. "Blacky informed me about your impending submersion beneath the waters of China." His brow furrows. "Did you two have a row?"

"Hey, it's just his way of talking," I offered.

Liu continued, "You know he is searching for a barge in Lake Taihu, a few miles from here. I sent him and his divers to investigate two possible locations in the lake where certain information I have suggests a barge filled with scrolls was sunk just before the Communists took over."

I gave Liu a nasty smile. "I sure hope the lake is cleaner than the sewer from last night." He stares at me, what's the word, crestfallen. I could tell I disappointed him.

The kid pipes in. "Uncle, how did a barge get into the lake? Weren't they usually in the canal?"

Liu beams and you could see a kind of pride come into his face. "My sister has a suspicious and logical progeny. I must congratulate her when I see her next."

"The barge, uncle." As the kid finishes I see four cops creating a little commotion at the entrance. The headwaiter is pointing over to our table and the gendarmes are coming in a hurry, pushing aside things in their way.

Suddenly I find myself lifted out of my chair, arms yanked behind my back. I pull away, hard, and one of the cops goes flying. Then I'm shoved roughly back into the chair. I try to rise but they hold me down. Liu is yelling at the cops. The cops are yelling at him. Liu stiffens.

"Jake, they say you shot a policeman, a Colonel Qin. In Xiamen. Sunday night, early Monday morning. They say they have your gun. They checked the serial number with Interpol."

I bark out, "What are they nuts? It's my stolen gun. Tell 'em to call Sharli."

They lift me out of the chair and each cop places a hand under an armpit and with my legs trailing I'm being dragged away. I feel like a scene from one of those 1930 B type movies where the drunk is yanked out of a fancy restaurant.

I yell back over my shoulder. "Liu, for God's sake, do something."

He appears confused, helpless.

I shout over to the kid, "Mickey, get Sharli. Call Sharli."

Squirming and twisting, I break free. I should have known better. I see the cop pull out his pistol with the barrel coming to my head, the same way Qin did it with Taylor. Must be they teach such maneuvers in the local police academy. I throw my arm up, but it don't help. Everything gets black, fast.

CHAPTER 19

I'M SITTING ON cold cement hoping the world will slow down. Worse, I don't know how I got here, or even where "here" is. I do know I gotta hell of a throbbing head. Trouble is I've been here before, on the floor, with lightning leaping across my eyes. It wasn't someplace of meaning, just Weepy's poolroom in Coney Island.

"You play nine ball?" asks the guy with the, *I Love Mom* tattoo on his forearm. I don't say no. After six games I'm ahead by a buck, big deal.

He asks, "Do ya wanna go for five a game?"

"Sure, why not?"

I break, run the rack and sink the nine ball with a bank shot. He racks and again I send the balls to all corners. Like I was given the power, everything began to jell. My stroke moved like silk, the lights were bouncing off the cue ball sending me the codes. It felt fine, real fine. I ran the second rack, the third. I floated from shot to shot, stroking the stick and watching it strike true. Oh, man. Oh, man.

"You fuckin' hustler, you set me up." And I see it coming, the heavy end of his cue stick. And I wake up on my face, like I am now.

It's crazy. My eyes are open but there's nothing to see. My head is throbbing, I can feel caked blood around a bandage, and I'm lying on the cold concrete. I tell you, I could use a cigar.

Right, it's coming back, slow. The cops saying I killed Qin. Crazy bastards. I see it all over again only this time in slow motion, the uniform pulling his gun and the barrel moving inexorably toward my head. Then the blast of black.

My god. Qin is dead and they're blaming me. I don't need this. I try to rise to one knee. Can't make it. I'll wait a few minutes. I searched about on the floor's rough cement. My hands feel a metal cot, no blanket. In the corner, a ceramic bowl and the acrid urine odor filled the air. I somehow knew things would get worse. They must have heard me moving as a small window opened and a tray was pushed in containing rice, soup and some floating fat back. And then in the inimitable Chinese way, a nice cup of hot, black Oolong tea. I yelled through the opening. "Get me the American Embassy. I pay my taxes." Well, maybe I shouldn't bring that up. "Get me Liu." They shut the window in my face.

The next morning, I'm not sure, the police come in with an interpreter. I know from NYPD Blue I better not talk to Sipowicz without my lawyer. The English speaker tells me I'm charged with the murder of Colonel Qin of the Peoples Police. "You're crazy," I tell him. "For God's sake, someone stole my gun in San Francisco, from my office." They don't seem to care. "Yes," I say, "I knew Qin. Yes, I didn't care for him. But I wouldn't kill him.

Did I hate him? Not now. Sure, fifty years ago. Did I kill him? Hell, why would I kill him? My gun killed Qin?" Not all over again.

I knew it would be just a matter of time before the reported theft of my gun would free me of the murder. I mean, Sharli did report the theft, right? Sharli, where the hell are you? Don't fail me woman, don't fail me. Sam, your baby brother needs you, come and get me. I'll take the humidity, I'll buy a pair of white loafers with tassels. I'll even play pinochle with the boys and if you want I'll go out with the blue-haired women. Sam, where the hell are you?

I spent six days in solitary confinement, six days, six days. Enough to get to know your cell real good. Mine? Six by nine feet, two by three paces, ten by fourteen hand spans. Piled into a corner, dead, are twenty-three cockroaches, eleven spiders and three centipedes. The thought makes me shudder all over again. I reviewed my life. All the things I shouldn't have done are up there on the big screen of memory and try as I could the channels wouldn't change. All the things I should have done but didn't became the second feature. Every sad moment, every missed opportunity turned to life size. The images in my head had become a twenty-four hour movie with the worst one hundred features of all time.

Huddling in the corner of the dark cage all my personal horrors came together like charging Coney Island gangs. I'd run but could never escape. Turning into them I gave a few and took many, but hell, that's what life is all about. Damn, I needed to be out of my smelling clothes. I scratched my face, and little things scrunched under my fingernails. It became the cellar in the house in Manchuria with Harry and the Chinese officers. Harry, yeah. It became my worst theatre, remembering Harry in the dark. How many times have I tried to forget? Not a chance. The memory of my best friend became my *bete noir*, like the fifties movies, all shadow and fear. What did Qin say, he's alive, Harry was alive. Impossible, Harry died, out there on the tundra with me. Harry, dead? Could I be sure? What the hell. He's dead, I know. Back in the Brit's house we heard about Panmunjum and the armistice talks. The other guys were excited saying they'd let us go in a few days. Harry, he said we should run.

"Run? Where? Harry, where the hell are we? Which way Harry, where's America?"

"Jake, you know damn well they'll never send us back. There's no way for them to admit they kept American GI's in Communist China. We're at war with Korea. We've got to run before they line us up." He waited a minute. "Listen to me Jake, we head east, to the Yalu. *Carpe diem,* Jake, *carpe diem.*"

"I don't know, Harry. I think our chances are better here." Harry had a beard now, and had become thinner with a bit of a stoop and began to look well, Chinese. "We won't last long out there in the night." I had thought of saying, cold, but it wasn't anymore. I ran out of reasons not to *carpe diem*. Harry won, he always did.

We waited for a night without a moon with Harry carrying a large heavy knapsack as well as the compass. My responsibility was the food and water we were able to steal. A cinch to escape from the Brit's house, we left just after midnight. Harry told me we were walking east to North Korea but it didn't feel right.

"What's in there, Harry?" I asked pointing to his knapsack.

"Our future, Jake, our rich tomorrow." Then we heard the dogs.

"Run, Jake, run."

"No, Harry, we'll never make it," and I reached for him to pull him close, to keep my buddy with me. For a guy who feared little, "alone" terrified him. My hand went out to pull him close but he was gone. The noise of running boots, rifle shots in the dark and feeling my pinky explode. And my legs went out from under me. It was the last I saw of Harry. When they brought me back Qin never said a word. I figured Harry to be dead or lost out there, somewhere. You see, like I said, I carried the food and water. Korea and the Yalu were days away.

I waited for him when I got back to Coney Island, even kept my eye on the buses when they stopped nearby. After a while I gave up waiting, watching. Harry never showed, he never came home. And I've never forgiven myself, carrying the guilt even now. Damn Harry. Damn me.

Now why the hell did I play back this scene, couldn't I have chosen something about one of those hot nights with one of my wives? No, I knew why. Harry hated to be alone, he feared Coney Island on those dark nights when black clouds hid the moon. He told me "Jake, these black nights, they scare the hell out of me."

Qin said he was alive.

Impossible.

My cell door opened. They half dragged me out and threw me into a cold shower. It was a cool summer's squall on a hot day in Coney Island and I slowly came back to life. They give me a safety razor but watched me closely. My clean sweet smelling clothes from the hotel were on a chair, black jeans and matching jacket. Damn, the wrong stuff. The hell with it. I'm dressed and goddamn I'm starting to feel good. I look in the mirror. Hey, a few pounds less, a few wrinkles more but on the whole I'd still drive the women mad.

Okay you wise guys, yeah, you with the sneakers on, where's your boss? Hey, I'm an American citizen; I demand to see the headman. I'm Jake Diamond, dealer in Chinese antiquities. Come on, come on, talk to me, talk to me. You don't have a cigar, do you?

I see Liu in the doorway. All of a sudden he's pushed aside and Sharli bursts through. She's running, wearing a tight wove navy blue pantsuit, red blouse and yellow hanky in her breast pocket. Tears are streaming down her cheeks. With her colors and my black outfit we could belong to the Rainbow Coalition. She puts her arms around me and plants one of her very wet kisses I would have taken advantage of had we been in more private circumstance. My-oh-my. To give a kiss like that in a Chinese prison.

Then, as if she remembers why she got here, "Damn you, Jake, I had just about closed on a one-point four-million three-bedroom on Pacific." She takes my hand and places it on her cheek, and I feel the wet. I reach over to touch her fingers just to make sure she's there. Coming here when I need her, I couldn't ask for much more. It's, "I love you," for sure.

I never told you the part of Sharli that is all strength and dependability. I thought at first it might be a Chinese trait. If you want proof, stand on the corner of Stockton and Columbus in San Francisco and watch the Asian world fight for its existence. Nothing's too difficult, no burden too heavy, no insult too strong. At first I believed it character, but I learned it's all just survival. Then I met Sharli, on Market Street, by Montgomery, on the sidewalk, picking up pennies, nickels, and rags of clothing. I had watched as this cop chased two guys hell bent to get out of there. This scraggly homeless guy with a cup full of change, a sign saying, Vietnam Vet, and a dog whose coat seemed only marginally dirtier than his owner's rags, gets bowled over. Ass over teakettle as they say, and everything goes flying.

The bum has a cut chin with blood oozing out like the black stuff coming out of Starbucks espresso machines. This small lady takes out her hanky and presses it to the wound. She tells the guy to hold it tight then she's on her knees finding the coins, getting his stuff together. She embarrassed me as I watched safely from the side. I had to get down there with her even if it meant dirtying my pressed jeans. And the romance starts from there.

"What are you doing in jail?" she asks, "in San Francisco you never even go out at night." She walks over to the nearest cop, and speaks in English, "Who do I speak to here to arrange bail." Nothing like my take charge American-Chinese real estate agent.

It's funny, all my wives wanted things from me. I always felt the burden but they said they never noticed. Maybe so, but with Sharli, well, its different, she's different, it's always her doing things for me. There ain't nothing better.

Liu is watching. "Jake, you are fortunate to have a woman as this. She would not leave the police alone, pestering and badgering them everyday." He steps up close and whispers so all can hear. "Your Chai Ling, she is indeed a lovely, and charming woman." It took a second to remember he was talking about my gal.

Give Sharli a compliment and her fingers go immediately to her hair. Still, I can see she wants to come at me. "So you come to China to find the curator who sold you the painting," she nods over to Liu, "and you end up in the hoosegow."

I smile, hearing the sounds of love. "Sharli, I don't need this."

Liu takes my arm. "Come, Jake, I've spoken to the authorities. I don't think they believe you killed Qin, but they are still investigating. You cannot leave the province, at least not for the next days." As he finishes he moves away from me, almost stumbling, reaching to a desk for support. He speaks to a cop who gets him a chair and a glass of water while he pulled out those small blue pills. Everybody is quiet.

"Are you okay, Chun?" I ask. He nods yes, and motions me away. I take Sharli's hand and talk softly. "I'm sorry to drag you here. I knew I couldn't get my brother from his pinochle game. He's also the only Bar Mitzvah boy in Florida who hates Chinese food." I bring her close and speak into her hair. "You're the only other person I trust." I put my arm around her shoulders and she sees the look in my eyes.

"Jake, be careful. You know how gushy you can get when you think you owe me something."

I once suggested marriage, maybe talk to a rabbi or a Buddhist priest if she wanted. I even offered the clerk at City Hall. All I ever got for my trouble was a kick in the shins. Her golden words were, "Marry you? With your track record? You must be crazy."

I walk over to Liu and take him by the arm, lean over and whisper, "Are you alright, old man?" And I see his face tighten. "I didn't mean it like that." I straighten up.

"C'mon, let's get out of here. I could use some decent food." I run into my jailer. "No offense intended."

Returning to the Bamboo Grove Hotel is so much luxury I'm overwhelmed. I stand dazzled by the difference of one mile. We find a table in an atrium cafe. After speaking to the waiter Liu says to me, smiling broadly, "You'll be happy to know before we went for you I heard from Mickey. They have located the missing barge." Without a pause he asks, "How would you like to go to the lake?"

Emerging from days of darkness I'm not sure I'm ready for more excursions, but I suspect my original Zhou is some place under those waters. "Okay, Liu, you're on."

He's smiling at me, kinda proud like. "Jake, you have such efficiency in language. 'You're on.' How very nice."

The tea arrives and Chun takes a sip. Sharli tastes her's with a pinky extended like a question mark. Whata gal. The old man leans back into the chair as if a grandfather surrounded by his extended family. "You should really develop a taste for this, Jake. Very relaxing."

I'm not in his mood. "Will you stop it, Liu. Tell me why the barge is in the lake. Hell, why it's any place?"

He pulls himself up from the chair and places his elbows on the table. I could see the story develop in his eyes. "You know the first part I believe, about the two shipments of treasure headed for Taiwan. The third, a file of three barges sent through the Grand Canal." He takes his breath, readying himself for the story. He should have warned me.

"The rain poured continually for a week and the river reached its flood stage. The Communists spotted the barges near Wuxi, the town just north and joined in the chase." He sighs and you could tell he hadn't much strength left in either his words or body but he still had things he wanted to say.

"In the confusion of night, rain, explosion and flood, two of the barges make it downstream and finally to Shanghai." He's forcing his words, needing to finish his story. "Now the third barge tries to avoid the chasing Communists and finds sufficiently swollen streams to make it into the nearby lake. Understand, the confusion of the night, thunder, lightening, cannon shells splitting and lighting the black night. The barge captain's position was hopeless. He was somewhere in the lake but rather than give up China's legacy, the officer set off preset dynamite charges. The timbers in the hull were blown out, and the barge scuttled in the waters."

"It's the one you're searching for, the one Blacky found?" I asked.

"Jake, let me finish." He shifted his gaze to Sharli. "The crew made it back to the canal but were run down by the chasing Communist boats."

I finished it for him. "So all hands were killed and the storm and black night assured there was no one to tell where the barge lay in the lake."

"Elementary, my dear Watson." Liu smiled saying it. "But not really, Jake. There were always rumors about the sinking of the barge in the lake. Many searched, but only as adventurers, not professionally or with modern equipment. They also never had Blacky." He winked, the old rascal.

"How do you know all this big shot?" I needed the answer, but Liu's fatigue again spilled onto the conversation. Sharli is poking me softly and I get the message.

Popping up I offer, "Hey, it's been a hell of a few days for me. I'm bushed. What do you say we pick up from here tomorrow."

I could see the relief in Liu's expression. "Yes, thank you, Jake. I'm also," he finds the right word, "bushed." He reaches across and pats my hand, and a small tired smile creeps to his lips. "You would have made a good number one son."

A minute later we all follow him to the elevators.

While he's headed upstairs I have a tight grip on Sharli's arm. I give her no chance to get away. Let me tell you what I haven't told Sharli. She makes me feel like I figured William Holden did when he kissed the Eurasian beauty for the first time in "Love is a Many Splendid Thing." Finding new places in an otherwise ordinary world.

We get upstairs to our room and before I take two steps inside Sharli takes my elbow and sits me down in a brocaded armchair. "Jake, I'm missing some pieces of the story."

I know she's coming in at the tail end of a saga. So I go through the whole madness of Liu's theory of missing Forbidden City treasure, of the Zhou paintings. I tell her of Blacky diving for the barge scuttled in the lake. I also tell her of his trying to beat Liu out of some treasure and the incident of the cops at the dock. As usual she cut to the heart of the matter.

"In other words Liu won't give you your money back?"

Sometimes I wish she wasn't so bright. "You got it."

"There's a 'but', isn't there?"

"Of course, there's always a 'but'. But Wyatt, you haven't met him, the art expert, he still says I have the original." Then I feel the tired come over me. "Let's go to sleep. It'll work out."

I'm in bed and Sharli is getting undressed. I'm totally captivated. This time her routine is slightly different. She's not home and like the real estate agent she is, she's inspecting all the furniture in the room. Did you ever watch little boys in a strange place? They want to know how everything works. A lamp, they investigate the shade, a sofa, they bounce up and down. Well, that's Sharli. She's checking around as though evaluating the room's sales potential. "It's good things they have here, Jake. Expensive."

My beautiful lady sits down next to me and places her hand under the bed covers. I'm lying next to this woman who feeds my soul, who, in her tenderness allows me to look forward to the next day. No, it's a lie. She's not tender, she's a place to get lost in, to get old with. She's a country of comfort and escape. My hand is running along her back and our faces are three quarters into the pillow. We're both breathing hard, me more than her. Age has its penalty. "Sharli, did I thank you for coming here?"

She mumbles into the pillow something like, "To tell the truth, Jake, plans were made for the trip before Mickey called. I told you over the phone. My brother." There it is again, her brother. I have no idea what she's talking about and at this point I really don't care as my mind is on other things, if you get my drift.

I'm sure you've noticed lovers continually replay their first meeting, and always whisper their love for each other. Reveling in their uniqueness they will reaffirm their special place under the gaze of the gods who brought them together. Ain't so with Sharli. No, to her little of the past is relevant, to my darling lady life is always yet to be lived, and only occasionally to be remembered.

She pulls up from the goose down and kisses me. I place my hand on her waist and squeeze a little, then move it up to her arm, to the top of her head. I scrunch over and kiss her lower lip then move and give little nibbles to her neck, to her arm working my way down, taking small bites all the way. There's a little shake of her body telling me no matter what I do from here on out she's all mine.

"Jake, you are the devil," and I hear her sighs. And I get pleasure. I want to be twenty years younger, not because things were better, just so I could have this for a longer time. She gets up from the bed and walks to the closet taking things off on the journey.

Just between us, I never tire of watching a woman getting undressed, the way they reach and do those Chinese circus contortions. The straps fall away and their miraculous breasts react to the laws of gravity. Lights reflect off their special soft sides as they bulge slightly just before their cascade. It is as if polished Italian marble copied their sheen. Then the nipples harden as they meet the cool night.

"Jake, I love it when your eyes engulf me like now."

I ignored her, I was busy. My eyes followed as she placed her thumbs in the elastic of her panties. Oh, I do love those wispy things, particularly as they slide down over the rounded hips. Then she stands on one leg to remove the ruffled silk, then the other while her breasts hang suspended in pure titillation. And sometimes I wonder what happened to those nylon step-ins having the days of the week sewn onto the right side. I should have asked the girls back then whether they appropriately followed the calendar. A copy of a Picasso in Sharli's bathroom is comprised of only four lines depicting a woman's buttocks. And while the Spaniard could draw, I could only speculate how he perfectly captured Sharli's great tush.

"You're not going asleep?" she asked.

I wasn't going any place as long as she walked around naked with her pubic hair beckoning like the old Norten's Point lighthouse in Sea Gate at the tip of Coney Island. In just a matter of seconds she would put on one of my old T-shirts and the show would disappear. I slept buck-naked but she argued she'd catch cold without something on her shoulders. I'm sure she secretly believed an old T-shirt hung more appealingly than naked breasts. Women know nothing when it comes to such things.

Once in bed she snuggled close and my lips glided easily along her skin, kind of like moving along a puppy's neck. My mouth found hers and my tongue edged along her teeth finding its way to just behind her lips. I played there for a while, resting. Starting again I brought my lips to her eyes and let my tongue run along her eyebrows, then her eye lashes. I took little nips from her shoulder, and continued biting until I found the softness of her breast. I kept hearing small sighs, and I allowed my hand to lead the way between her thighs. I knew she would be wet there. I wanted her to be needing me, something of me, anything.

I lay on top, covering her completely, taking her face between my hands and letting my kisses roam as my hardness spread her. She reached out and placed me where I would be the most comfortable. I heard the first of many purrs from the cat lady below, a reassurance she thought me special, someone she would allow into places only she really knew about.

We commenced to the ballet of lovemaking. As she danced below me the crimson rose from her neck until it covered her cheeks, her forehead. I witnessed her shake as if giving herself to demons, perhaps even to rivet me to a special place. Then, at the moment, our eyes would lock in a smile and we each took a road we knew the other could never travel.

Lying on my back I'm wishing I'd never given up smoking and thinking maybe I have the strength for a little more kissing, but Sharli sees my eyes closing.

"Say good night, Jake." Seems she's always right.

CHAPTER 20

WE BOTH WOKE smiling; a kind of affirmation of our last night's joining. It's a great feeling, like maybe it's the reason life came out of the oceans and crawled upon land and into bed. After kissing her neck a few times and her pushing me away we joined the others downstairs for breakfast.

Wyatt is with Liu, and I introduce him to Sharli. Right off she looks the Prof in the eye, "You believe the painting Liu sold Jake is a genuine Zhou?"

"Absolutely."

"But Liu thinks maybe otherwise," she says.

Wyatt comes back, "Mr. Chun Liu is a very knowledgeable man, but wrong in this instance."

Liu smiles.

I'm confused.

Sharli thinks for a minute and leans close to the professor. "You'd better be right. I have a stake in this. You see, Jake is special."

I blush.

We all order. After prison food I go all out for, as the English say, an American breakfast. I'm not satisfied. Something keeps at me. I know it's yesterday's late afternoon unanswered question.

"Liu, damn it, the story last night, how did you know the barge was in the lake, and not the canal?"

Liu smiles, like he's pleased. "Jake, you listen when I speak. Like a good member of the family." He's rested, but his eyes are heavier. The trip is taking its toll on his stamina. I'm concerned about him, and surprised at my attitude. "You were wrong last night, Jake, the chasing Communists didn't kill all the crew. There was one, an officer, just as he blew up the barge he jumped into the lake grabbing onto anything that floated. As fate has these things it was a Colonel Lin, the officer who worked with Madam Chiang on the plan of sending the barges through the canal." Liu coughs. I notice he's older than when I saw him in the States.

"Lin made it to Shanghai and then to Taiwan. Mrs. Chiang had Colonel Lin write out a report of the night the barge sunk and the missing treasures were oddly forgotten. Madam Chiang kept the report of only some three pages but apparently lost interest in the scuttled barge.

Liu cleared his throat and said the strangest thing. "Jake, I was born in Chengdu, in China's West. When I die I would like to be cremated and my ashes placed near my parents, my family. Mickey knows this, he also knows my brother's remains should be brought to China from Taiwan. I am telling you this as my nephew may need help."

I don't care for compliments. No, those are the wrong words. What I don't know is how to handle them, they embarrass me. I needed to change the subject. "Chun, the barge, the barge." His eyes stayed on me a second longer and a small smile edged to the corners of his mouth. He went back to the Colonel Lin story.

"For some unknown reason, whenever the Madame shuttled her residence between Taiwan and the United States she took Lin's report. When she permanently left America she auctioned off her New York furniture. An unattractive, out-dated bedroom set came up for sale and our museum bought it for no particular reason except as an interesting addition for some possible future exhibits. I went through it just after I returned selling you the Zhou, Jake." He paused and looked earnestly at each one of us in turn. "In the second drawer of the night table lay the sealed report filed by the now long dead Colonel." He mopped his brow and again took some water. "I called the Generalissimo's wife, related the report's contents and expected anything but what I got. She said she felt too old to search for treasure, that I should do as I felt best." The old man now turned his head to meet my astonished stare. "Jake it's how I know the barge is in the lake."

Wyatt now asks the real question. "What's in the barge, Chun? You think it's a stack of the original Zhou's, don't you?"

Liu turned his eyes first to the professor, then me, Sharli, and finally back to Wyatt. "Professor, it's a little more complicated. I have seen letters by Zhou praising the work of his young student Yuan Chi. He had written how his skills were exceptional to the point of having difficulty defining his own *Late Autumn* from that of his student's.

I'm staring at Liu. "What the hell does that mean?" I glance over to Sharli. She's not disturbed. Am I the only fool?

Wyatt pulls out a pipe. Oh hell. There's nothing more pretentious than a pipe-smoking academic. Between puffs he says, "So you think one of the barges contained the original Zhou's while another held the students works."

Liu's eyes lit. "Exactly."

I think I'm beginning to understand so I throw in two cents. "The barge in the lake has the real Zhou's. The student's works made it to Taipei and easily passed for the originals. The museum people accepted the copies shipment as the originals and that's where the one you sold me came from."

Liu pats my hand. Maybe he should scratch me behind my ear. I'm just a dumb little cocker spaniel. Wow. Talk about morning pick-me-ups. This breakfast makes, "Wheaties, Breakfast of Champions," pale in comparison.

Sharli whispered we should leave and all agreed to again meet for dinner. Now she's up and running. "C'mon, Jake, lets go see this town. I hear it's one of the better ones." We take in a couple of the famous rock gardens and walk for a while on Ganjlang Road when Sharli suggests some noodles. Hey, why not.

Entering the crowded place there's a guy in a stained white gown by the front window taking dough and twisting it all kinds of ways. He reminded me of those salt-water taffy machines on the Coney Island boardwalk where the metal arms keep turning and more strands of the stuff kept appearing.

The guy with the big white Cat-In-The-Hat cook's hat spreads his arms and like a magician makes strings of dough appear. He does it again and again, and in the hand-is-faster-than-the-eye business his fingers were quickly filled with long, strung out noodles. A Chinese waitress comes by and barely swipes off our not so clean table. Sharli takes out a tissue and wipes the top clear. The noodles come in a clear broth. We join in the slurping we hear around us. We're sitting on these high stools sucking up the magician's handiwork when a cop walks in. He's with yesterday's interpreter at the jail. Now I get nervous. There ain't no place for me to run and I don't want to go back into the clink. The cop comes over and begins to talk in Chinese. The interpreter chirps in with his parakeet's voice, "Mr. Diamond, I believe we have found the man who killed Qin." Relief is an understatement. My life, once again my own. But curiosity grabs me, naturally.

"Terrific. Anyone I know?" I ask cutely.

"As a matter of fact, yes." He checks a piece of paper he's holding. "It's a Mr. Davis," his eyes go back to the paper. "Yes, Taylor Davis."

It takes me a moment. "Taylor Davis? My Taylor Davis," and heads about the room snap to my direction. Maybe I shouldn't have shouted.

Both Sharli and I look at each other. The interpreter chirped on. "You were there when Qin struck Davis, correct? Apparently your Mr. Davis took his revenge. That same night he entered Qin's home and shot him four times, with your gun, I may add. We have a witness." I stared at the cop, waiting for more. He had finished. Now I shifted to Sharli. "Could it have been Taylor who broke into my office?"

"It could have been anybody, Jake. But why did he break in?" She shook her head. "Not simply to get your gun?"

The Chinese is twittering once more. "We advise you stay in China until all matters are concluded." For some reason he turned to Sharli, as if she's my keeper. "It should not be long."

Sharli and I are about to leave our wonderful noodles and proceed out the door when the cop waves a blue booklet above his head. His mouthpiece tells me, "We have your passport," and both disappear out the door before I could react.

Oh my, I have no passport and Taylor killed Qin? What the hell? I no longer have a buyer of my Zhou Mengfu, even if it is a forgery and I can't go home without a passport. I tell you, this Taylor business definitely complicates things.

Both my sweet lady and I exit the noodle shop passing Shuangta Gardens braced by twin falling down pagodas which are damn impressive. I guide Sharli to a bench, look back toward the pagodas and wonder if I could get inside one of those multi-storied, many-sided relics. I then tell Sharli about Allie and Taylor, and she's concerned only in the religious part of the relationship. She asked about the talking in tongues and Allie's efforts to convert the Chinese to Christianity. I offer, "The police didn't look kindly at Allie and the other teachers. They said they were breaking Chinese laws. Allie said she followed God's law. I could tell it wasn't a winning argument."

Sharli is giving thought to my words and I can see she's bothered. "Jake, you can see Chinese life is difficult. Confucius offered no hereafter, and neither does Communism. It's not right for Christianity to promise them eternal salvation." Her intensity toward the Christian pledge of deliverance surprised me, but she's always a package of the unexpected. Then she eases the air with,

"Jake, this whole China thing is getting complicated isn't it?"

My head is shaking up and down. "Yeah, It's like a movie I love, Chinatown, with Jack Nickelson. It seems anything can happen." I'm sitting back into the bench just staring, but events just won't stay still. Here comes Mickey.

I'm insulted, instead of coming to me he first talks to Sharli and in an excited tone. "Am I glad to see you. When did you get here?" Finally he comes to me "My uncle told me to find you. We're all back." He ends up with a big smile. "We found the barge." I guess he expected us to be as gripped as he. We weren't. He shrugs and goes on giving me one of those one raised eyebrow kind of things. "Jake, did you and Blacky have an argument?"

Now what? "Blacky and I? Naw. We're good buddies."

He says, "I don't think so."

Now it's my turn to try to raise that single eyebrow. I fail, but it doesn't stop the kid.

"He called you a son-of-a-bitch. He wasn't smiling."

I hoped it's the kid's protected up bringing not picking up on Blacky's sarcasm. I knew he would do most anything if he thought you wronged him. You get on his bad side and he'll come down on you with blood in his eyes.

"Kid, you must have heard it all wrong," I say hopefully.

"Jake, he is blaming you for the cops who are following him. He said you squealed, something about, a . . . ." He thought for a second, "Blacky said a 'fiddle'."

"He said a what? Kid, don't worry, he's spent too much time in London." But I knew I had to talk to him. He could blow at any time.

"What's this fiddle, Jake?"

Sharli asked the same question. I told her what I believed Blacky was up to, stealing whatever he could. I also figured I better face Blacky right up front. I don't want anything smoldering.

We all walked back to the hotel. In the lobby are Liu, Blacky and Wyatt. The professor's greeting to Sharli borders on the unctuous, learned, I'm sure, from faculty teas and museum openings. Sharli flutters to the sweet words, but I know what she'll say about the flattery.

Blacky, on the other hand, does his best to show what an ass he is. He kisses the back of her hand. Someone must have told him it showed culture and charm. In the meantime his eyes are devouring each part of her body. He's such a slob.

Liu gave one of his big smiles, almost gushing. "Jake, good news. Blacky has found the barge. He says it's where we estimated, a depression in the middle of the lake's channel." He has to contain his effusiveness. "Jake, Jake, it's there. And if I believe rightly you will end up with another Zhou replacing the one I sold you." The old man is almost jumping as he pirouettes back to Blacky. "You say it's in the channel?"

Blacky then gives me a gaze with tight lips. "Yeah, *bubeleh*, sweetheart, in the middle of the channel." *Bubeleh*, huh. Blacky went on. "Just where we figured. It's in about fifty, sixty, feet. It's going to be an easy dive. Water is murky as hell but seeable. There's a further depression next to it. Goes down about another hundred. It gets black quick. And, yeah, there's some nasty ledges." He's the man of the moment and we listen.

Liu is still beaming "Jake you'll come with us to the treasures." He reaches over and takes my gal's hand in a proper fatherly fashion. "And of course, you too, Sharli."

While Liu's gesture binds us together, I still needed information. "Where's it at?"

Liu pulls out a small map. "It's between this island here, Xidongingshan, and the end of a peninsula jutting into the lake. This town," and he points to a small dot in the middle of no place, "Dongshan. It's our base. Blacky has all his equipment there. The other divers are waiting."

I get up close to the map and turn it every possible way. "You know Liu, I'm not too big on camping out."

Chun first gave me a puzzled expression but he's learning Coney Island short hand. "No, you're right, Jake. Hardly anything you'd call a hotel." He tries to get Sharli on his side. "It won't be comfortable, but we'll only be there for two, possibly three days." He brings his words back to me. "But think of it, Jake, a modern treasure trove. A piece of the Forbidden City." Liu was getting impatient with his own words and wanted to get things moving. "Jake, why don't you and Sharli go upstairs and pack, I've already checked you out."

I noticed Liu had bought a more stout cane. "You okay?"

Blacky came close, actually crowding me. "You're diving with me, at the barge, right?".

"Okay Blacky, I think it'll be interesting."

Then I ask a wrong question. "Did the cops catch the guy by the ferry?"

Blacky's face blanches and just as quickly it became red, and not a blushing red. I could see him holding his hands rigidly at his side. "Those fuckin' cops. They caught him. My good buddy." He edged close to me. "Someone snitched on him. Some no good son-of-a-bitch told the cops he filched things, national treasures. Whoever he is, dead meat. I'm telling ya, the guy is going to live with the fishes."

CHAPTER 21

TWO CARS PULL up. Liu, Sharli, Blacky, and I go in one. The kid, the professor and all the luggage in the other. I'd like to tell you about dazzling Chinese countryside of the ancient city of Suzhou but the best I can do is say the pollution from the new industrializing China wasn't too overpowering. Not until we reached the mountains west of the city did things improve.

The car is quiet as everyone is lost in thought and we all had to be thinking about tomorrow. Blacky's next remarks told us his thoughts. "There's a cabin section looking pretty intact. We should be hitting it tomorrow. I don't think there are more than one, two, days diving left."

Liu glanced over to Sharli and me and says in a matter of fact tone, "There are some masterpieces down there, Jake."

Blacky picked up on the last words. "Hey, Liu, for your sake I hope so. You're paying the bill."

The tender subject of money also bothered me. I asked, "Yeah, Liu, who's financing this whole caper. It's gotta cost a pretty penny."

"Just between us, Jake, it's jointly financed, half–Taiwan, half–Beijing. Keep it quiet, the parties prefer the illusion of incipient war." His last words trailed off. I could see the long day had done him in. We all kinda settled back and watch the hour grow later.

When we arrived to the dot on the map no surprise greeted us; a dusty street, a few shops with fluttering banners announcing their wares. The local, hell, the only hotel reeked of disinfectant and long unattended care. Liu spoke to a Chinese guy in a frayed jacket and the rest of us ambled over to a side room with tables and chairs. This little guy comes out in dirty apron and a three days growth, with a half-smoked butt dangling from his lower lip. I could have sworn he owned a *kosher* delicatessen on Manhattan's East Side. Liu strides over to him and they exchange a few words. Next thing he comes back out with one of those simple but miraculous meals a Chinese country chef can whip together.

On the table sits a whole lake fish. I could tell it was a Chinese Perch by its flattened high backed body. Sharli leaned into it and smacked her lips. "Jake it's a Mandarin fish." Hell, a perch is a perch. Along lay a side dish of shredded pork with mushrooms and a must for any Chinese table, an abundant plate of bok choy cooked in peanut oil and laced with garlic. There's some tofu with broccoli and a super bowl of steaming rice set in the middle of the table. The perch, my taste buds tell me, was cooked in slivers of ginger, onion and a delicate soy sauce. About as good as anything on Grant Avenue. The masterpiece doesn't last long as we all had an appetite. And as in a typical Chinese dinner no one lingered for conversation.

Sharli and I head for the sack. It's been a long day and neither of us had any strength for more then a goodnight kiss. Well, not quite. I snuck in a squeeze where I always love to squeeze. I had plans to sleep late and go out to the dive site mid-morning.

CHAPTER 22

I'M WAY ASLEEP, deep, not even dreaming. In a long way off I'm hearing, "Jake, Jake." Right. Then this soft knock and the kid's voice. "Jake, Jake."

I look at my watch. What the hell, it's not even five. I get up and notch open the door getting a smiling young, slightly flattened Chinese face framed by the intrusive light of his lantern. I remembered, we're out in the, well, boondocks, away from that lovely town of Suzhou. Should have stayed and not been so heroic coming out here, if heroic is the word.

"For crying out loud kid, the stars are out."

"Jake, Blacky said that we should be there by first light. Less interference with the fishing guys. Besides, he said it's best when you're fresh," he paused, smiling "he thinks you're too old."

"Oh yeah. I told him I'd be there, didn't I?" I ended with, "Give me a minute, kid." I mean there are certain necessary things to do with an aging prostate.

I'm looking down over this toilet, this hole in the floor and wondering what the hell I'm doing in the middle of China heading for a dive in a lake for a sunken barge supposedly full of 13th Century Chinese scrolls with an almost pirate crew I read about someplace in 8th grade.

I look over my shoulder and shout to the kid, "What's your opinion? We smart doing this? Your uncle, Liu, that sweet old man, you think he's right? There's a boatload of antique Chinese scrolls down below?" I knew it was an unfair question. I'm here 'cause I'm believing that beautiful 19th Century gentleman sold me a forged Chinese painting. Now he thinks maybe he did but he's sure the real one's at the bottom of this damned lake. Who's more crazy, him, Blacky or me? Yeah, Blacky, the only albino diver gangster I know. He's a piece of work, as close to the killers of the 20's Chicago as you can get.

I close the door and start getting dressed. Sharli is up on one elbow and I can make out her most charming, well-formed, well, architecture. She asks if she should go with me.

"Stay in bed. Everything'll be under water. It's just Blacky me and the kid."

I follow down the narrow wooden steps to the kitchen. There's some hard rice and last night's masterful fish cooked in ginger and fried in oil, now congealed. Last night it was a feast, this morning, well . . . .

"Kid, understand, getting this stuff down, it's no way to start a day."

The kid looks at me funny as he's into the rice and stuff, "You sure you want to go?" he asks. "Blacky seemed awfully pissed at you. His friend, the one the police picked up. He believes you're responsible, says he'd get even."

"Kid, that's just Blacky."

He comes back with, "He said you busted his fiddle."

"His fiddle?" I ask, giving the kid my best smile telling him I knew his meaning.

Blacky's outside waiting. There's a slight break of light off to the east and some cool sweet smelling air hits me. I think how I should get out more often in these early hours. We take a short walk to a small boat alongside a longer dock. I can tell you it wasn't much, like the old fishing boats I would see in Sheepshead Bay in Brooklyn back then. Seems most of these small Chinese towns without new factories look like a kind of Brooklyn of 50 years ago. The boat sits there bobbing up against the sea weedy pier. Nothing to look at, about thirty feet long a small cabin, peeling paint, stinking of fish and rust where rust just ain't supposed to be

"Blacky, where did you get this scow?" He ignores me.

The deck is filled with diving things, fins, masks, lead weights, depth gauges, yellow flashlights, all kinds of stuff. There's an air compressor right in the middle of the mess. The kid is about to follow me on board when Blacky cuts him off.

"Not today. It's just Jake and me."

"Jake?" the kid says, with a touch of concern in his eyes. I just shrug. Something to worry about? Naw, it's just Blacky. Maybe a little bananas but not like that nasty jailer in that odd place on the other side of the Korean border from so many years ago. Now he was a real son-of-a-gun, a vicious piece of work.

The Chinese divers are already into their wet suits, reaching behind for the tie that pulls up the zipper. I look at them getting into their air cylinders, masks, fins. Hell, why not? Should be fun.

"Jake," Blacky commands, "put this wet suit on. It's one of my older ones," then he does something unusual, he smiles, "when I was thinner."

I've never worn one before and all I could think of are those sleek young blond surfers I'd seen at Oceanside, north of San Diego, and me a chunky *alta cocker*. Handing it back I say, "Blacky, I can't get into that. You have a bigger size? Maybe a double breasted forty-two regular."

"Put it on Jake, put it on." His coal eyes narrowed making his albino skin and face shine all the brighter.

It's like a rubberized jump suit but with some squiggling and twisting I got it around me. It's a good thing it bent where I bend and gave at places where there was more of me than it. When I'm all done I couldn't breath then wish my sweet lady was there cause I sure must have looked good.

Blacky pushed the starter of the boat and we chugged slowly out about half mile to some floating buoys. He cut the engine and we tied up. "Here, put these on." Blacky hands me a mask, fins, a floating dive light, weight belt, and a pressure and depth gauge. I'm ready for a walk on the moon.

I'm amazed how all this diving machinery makes me think I can do things I know I can't. I reach for this shoulder harness next to the compressor. It's already rigged up with a bright red aluminum tank that I know from the damned first dive with Pedro in Mexico. I almost have it on when Blacky rushes over, almost in a panic.

"Dammit, Jake, not that one," yanking at the tank. His other hand is holding a harness with the same kind of cylinder, only that one is green, a dark unpleasant green. "Take this one," he orders.

I say, "Blacky, red is my good luck color."

"Stop bullshitting me." He pulls the cylinder off and I'm losing my balance. "This one is better for you Jake, and don't hand me no crap." He gains some composure. "Its a little lighter."

Now what the hell was that all about? I pick the tank up. Seems just as heavy to me. I get the cylinder on, stand up and it takes me backwards. Blacky is laughing.

"What are ya, a wuss? Put some strength into those shoulders." He gives me the air regulator and shows me how to breathe. I tell him I know how. He points to a round doohickey and says, "Jake when the pressure gets even close to 500 PSI you'd better be on the surface or you're in trouble. Ya got enough air for maybe forty-five minutes"

I look at the gauge. "Okay. Gotcha."

He puts my flippers on. I tell him I know how. Last, he demonstrates the mask. I tell him I know how.

"Look Jake, I'll go down first. We'll follow this line," and he points to a bobbing buoy, "its tied to an anchor down where the barge is sitting. We're going down slow. Get used to the depth. Each time I raise my hand you pick up the bottom of the mask and blow through your nose. That'll adjust the pressure." He gives me a demonstration. "See that kid," I say silently to no one, "he's on my side." Blacky finishes with, "We gotta go down sixty-sixty five feet. Keep your light on me."

I'm curious. "Blacky, how come after all these years the local fishing guys never found the barge?"

"Dunno. Maybe cause it's a shallow lake, no more than 15-20 feet except here where there's a big depression. The perch in the lake don't like that depth so not much fish here so not many fisherman."

Sounded okay. Looking over I see the albino got the same diving stuff I have except for a knife 'bout 9 inches. It's not at all nice looking having that serrated edge of Sharli's good kitchen knives. Blacky gets into the water first and I follow holding my mask tight to my face and go over backward, off the gunwales, like Blacky.

The water is warmer than I thought and not at all clear, besides there's things suspended, just hanging there. Not dirt exactly, like what I'd seen in my aquarium I once kept loaded with guppies and mollies. At the lake floor all kinds of sea plants are twisting up and touching me, ugly like. I'd scamper up in a second if my curiosity about the supposed treasure hadn't been stronger. There's no barge like Blacky said would be here. All I see are some metal ribs laying flat in a pattern looking like the bones of an animal carcass that had been stripped clean by some scavengers.

This business of being underwater, the whole sensation is weird. My hands, face and feet feel pressure but not the water; it's this wet suit. And oddly I'm beginning to feel, what? Detached? I don't know how to explain it, like I'm getting a little high, kind of drunk. I'm really sucking in the air but it feels not enough.

Pointing my light off to the right I see a hulking shape, the last whole section of the sunken barge. I'm a little disappointed. I thought it would be like the Titanic, you know, swimming into an open hatch way, fish coming in and out of port holes, a giant squid with tentacles swishing, dead bodies floating about. That sort of good stuff.

I let go of the guideline and start kicking to get some motion. Gangbusters feeling. While dark around me, the portable light creates a real ambiance. Hell, it creates shadow and mystery. I start to kick to the hulk where

I'm told the art scrolls of the Chinese masters survived the barge's scuttling. All this supposedly some 60 years ago when Chiang fled to Taiwan taking as many Imperial Palace treasures as he could. I'm looking around for Blacky so I know what to do but can't find him. I'm a little light headed, and I figure that's okay. I look at my depth gauge, 60 feet. No problem.

The Chinese divers who got here before us are using a kind of vacuum cleaner to pull up the loose debris to get at the lake floor and I'm having a good old time watching. Then, strangely, I giggle. Must be the beer from last night. I just kind of lean back and watch my bubbles rise. I'm happy, and when I exhale the bubbles really get agitated.

Blacky is back, grabs my air tank and takes me to the right about 50 feet and points down to a black hole. Sure Blacky, let's go. I take in a deep breath, and then another. I can't seem to get enough. We keep heading down and I look at my gauge. I see a one and a bunch of zeros. I have no idea what it means. I look for Blacky, but he's gone. Goodbye Blacky, have a nice trip. Blacky don't leave me alone. Blacky. Oh, that's okay. Bye, Blacky.

Whee, I'm doing cartwheels. I'm watching the light go round and round. Then I giggle again. I imagine Sharli's with me and we're dancing. A little two-step. I'm drunk. That's what I am, drunk. Damn, where the hell did Sharli go? Did she go up? Up? Where the hell is up?

I hit a rock outcropping and feel a sharp pain, take in a deep breath and hardly get any oxygen. I try again with little success figuring the thing in my mouth is blocking the air so I take it out to get a good gulp. My mouth fills with water. I don't understand but put the contraption back. Where the hell am I? I'm fighting for control. I yell out, "Blacky, where the hell are you?" All I get for my trouble is another mouth full of water.

"Jake," I say to myself, "get out of here. You're in trouble. Go up, Jake, up." I shake the light loose and watch it float. I know it has to go up, or I think I know it has to go up. I'm reaching for it like I'm a student in a wall climbing class. I take off the weights around my waist, accelerating.

Blacky comes swimming by and gives a swipe with his knife and suddenly there's no air at all only a dangling hose and shit tasting lake water in my mouth. I throw the harness off as the cylinder falls away. I start to kick, to follow the light above. I need to breath. I have no air. I hear a screeching in my ears. Oh, not again. I open my mouth to get air. I'm going to die. No, please, not this way, I have to retire, collect Social Security. Bush promised. And then, as they say in the picture business, everything fades to black.

CHAPTER 23

I NEVER TOLD YOU I had a deviated septum, did I? It's no big deal. Almost all kids get them breaking their noses and don't even know it. Me? Touch football, an elbow in the face. Lots of blood, but I wouldn't cry until I got home. Anyhow, about the same time I started taking vitamin E my nose started to make breathing difficult particularly if I lay on the wrong side when I went to sleep. Sometimes I'd get the same dream, and all because of the deviated septum.

It's pitch black. I know I'm in a coffin. I can hardly move and my nose scraps against the wood. I'm yelling but I'm not hearing any sound. I bang on the pine boards. "Down here! Help me! I'm alive! Don't bury me," I sob, and all the time I hear the shovels full of dirt thudding above me. "I can't breathe. I can't breathe. Help. Help me, please."

"Jake, open your eyes. Jake, for crying out loud. Open your eyes." Then it's an exasperated, "Jake," and I'm shaken from side to side.

"Who you pushing?" I yell in anger. My eyes open. It's Sharli's face.

She leans over and kisses me, strokes my face and I don't want the feeling to go away. I'm beginning to believe I've been cheated. Maybe I'm not dead.

"How do you feel, Jake?"

I smile, not sure why. "I'm fine, Sharli." All of a sudden I realize I am fine. "What happened."? I remembered. I drowned. Yup, no question about it. I drowned. The crazy feeling, no air, the screech in my ears.

"Sharli, is there blood on the pillow?"

She looks at me like I became clairvoyant. "How did you know?"

Damn. I take in my surroundings. It's all white but replete with water stains about the ceiling and walls and some chipping of the bed's enamel. Must be a Chinese hospital. I smell the disinfectant. How do they expect you to get better with that stink all around?

"How long have I been here?"

"Since yesterday."

Not so bad. I feel some bandages, and see a whole slew of black and blue spots on my arms, legs. I wonder how the other guy came out. I see the kid, Liu, and even the professor, who I ask, "Got a cigar?"

Mickey smiles at my words. It's a good feeling. I turned back to my gal. "Sharli, tell somebody I'm hungry."

I see her leave, and feel my eyes closing. Then, like a second later, they're open again. Past the windows it's nighttime and the kid's in the corner, dozing. There's a tray of cold, unappetizing food next to me. Caked rice, dried dumplings, and wilted greens.

"Hey, Mickey," I call softly remembering I'm in a hospital, "where is everybody?" He comes out of his doze, gives me one of his unpatented smiles and walks over to the end of the bed.

"They're out to dinner. I go next."

"What happened to me, kid?"

"We're not sure, Jake. We think nitrogen narcosis. The divers said they watched you trying to swim underwater, the Australian crawl." He liked his own joke. "They pulled you out, gave you oxygen and at first you came around but then went unconscious after a few minutes."

Where the hell had I been when all those exciting things happened? "Where's Blacky?" I asked with good reason. If he wasn't caught or dead I know he'd still be after me. He'd never been the kind to give up after just one try.

"Gone, Jake. He's gone."

Then I'm back sleeping. I wake up again and Sharli and Liu are there. He appears just as white as the hospital walls. I'm worrying about him, but he still gives me good words.

"My good friend Jake. You had us worried. First Blacky says he lost you in the water, that you foolishly swam into the big hole. Then you're underwater for almost an hour."

"An hour?"

"The next thing the other divers are bringing you to the boat. The way you looked, I thought I had lost a dear friend."

"Liu, where's my good friend Blacky? I'd like to belt him out if he doesn't kill me first."

"I believe the expression is, you will have to stand in line. The police are searching for him. They suspect he is headed to Hong Kong."

"Why they chasing him? Don't tell me he gave them diving lessons?"

"Jake, are you ever serious? No. They know he stole some of the antiques he uncovered. He committed crimes against the Peoples Republic."

I place my feet on the floor and try to stand holding onto the bed. I wondered who put my bikini shorts on. I'm a sexy guy, if you didn't know by now.

"Where's the professor?"

Sharli answers. "He's out by the dive site examining what they brought up from the barge. They had to cut the salvage operation short. You've became somewhat of a celebrity."

So this became my allotted fifteen minutes of fame. I should have taken a rain check.

There's a knock on the door, and as the old expression goes, you could of knocked me over with an AK-47. "Allison?" Ms. Banana Cream Pie. My born again Christian, Taylor's main squeeze. "What in the world are you doing here?" I ask crudely, unthinking. Actually, I don't think I want to know. It could only mean trouble. Well, not really trouble cause nothing happened between us, thankfully. Allison ignored my question. She had her own agenda.

"Jake, the police in Xiamen told me I could find you here." She looks blankly at Sharli, at Liu, and finally back to me. Oh yeah, my manners. I introduce Allie and everyone says hello with some understandable caution on my girl's part.

Allie's attention is back to her message and me. "Taylor says it's important he speak to you." She seems tentative, unsure of her place, of her words. I tell her everyone knows the story of Taylor. I could see she gave battle to her forming tears. "They sent him to the police headquarters in Shanghai. He told me to say he needs to see you, to apologize."

Sharli speaks for me, "Of course he'll go." Then, in a stage whisper to me, "There are relatives to visit. I promised my mother."

I'm not convinced. I have bigger fish to fry, namely to see what the Chinese divers are bringing up. Liu steps right in and eases my problem. What an old man. He's smart and comforting.

"Don't worry Jake. I'll be here when you return. My Chinese divers have a barge to plumb."

Damn. I didn't have a single excuse. Shanghai's not even an hour and a half away. I'm evaluating my Banana Cream Pie and she's still tearfully delicious. There's no way out.

CHAPTER 24

Taylor, what the hell are you making me do? Now I'm on another train at eight in the morning and I'm getting mad. What are you going to tell me, you're sorry you killed Qin? Fine, but Taylor you're the one who put me in solitary.

You know, I'm not the kinda guy to stay angry, usually it blows over fast but first it's a cold, bug filled jail then Blacky tries to kill me. I'm entitled to be pissed. And now Taylor's bringing me to police headquarters? It's not a place I cotton to under the circumstance.

Sharli is sitting opposite me, by the window. She's staring out but I can tell she's not seeing anything. She has her mother's Chinese skin and her father's blue eyes. Did I tell you she had an American father, thrown off the roof of the Chinese Overseas Hospital in Shanghai by her cousins? Sounds nuts doesn't it? Yeah, she tells me all kinds of stories, but this one I pieced together on my own. Once in a while a sadness comes across her face and it seems she wants to tell me something important, like maybe a confession. But she never really gets there. I get a little crushed as a bit of trust is still missing. I figure the suspicious Chinese part of her keeps me from getting inside to those private places. Time, I figured, would eventually let me in. My second wife and I had this kind of game we'd play just after some great sex. I'd ask her to tell me a secret, something she kept from the others. I'd usually hear something surprising, new, even extraordinary. I'd give you an example but I'd be breaking confidences. Then I'd tell her something from the same hidden vein. The exchange of secrets brought us closer, created a bond, trust, but as you can see, not enough to keep us together. Anyhow, it generated a kind of freeing of the soul, if you know what I mean. Maybe some day Sharli and I will find a similar kind of faith.

Allie is across from me. She asks, "Jake, how do you feel about Taylor?"

Going by my best instincts I answer as though she asked the question a month ago. "I envy Taylor. I don't think he's like the other successful Anglo-Saxons I know who have too much money, confidence, and arrogance." I thought about the tennis pro, our conversations. He once admitted he had luck on his side, God smiled on him. "I like him for his humility."

"Jake," Sharli said, "sometimes you say good things."

She got me thinking. What do I really know about those who believe like Taylor? Hell, the first time I came across a guy who believed in Christ was back in Mark Twain Junior High School when Italians and Jewish kids first crossed swords. This dark skinny guy with the shiny hair and big pompadour walks over to me.

"Fuck you, Christ killer."

Christ killer? Who? Me? I'd always lived a life outside of religion. Even the guys with the *yamulkas* were from a distant planet. The life I understood had no room for liturgy and powers beyond myself. Sure, on the occasion I prayed for divine intervention but only to get into the pants of some lovely or hit a tricky combination to sink the nine ball for ten bucks.

Back when I first arrived at San Francisco I met this lovely Presbyterian, Sandy. She often talked against the church, about Calvinism and how it demanded too much with an unknown payoff. I figured she had my kind of enlightened view to all those things. Anyway, in late December, Christmas time, we walked along Polk Street. A couple of the stores had done up real good for the holidays. This one liquor store had an elaborate and colorful window display of the Nativity scene, palm trees, camels, a manger, three wise men, Mary, the Christ child and whatever else you could fit in behind six feet of glass. You could see they put some bucks into it, none of those cheap plastic things fruit stores put on the sidewalk.

I'm gazing at the three wise men, the donkeys, and all the rest and she's by my side. I say, "You know, I still can't figure how this gets to people the way it does." I look at her innocently, confident in my irreligiousness.

"Damn you, Jake. You don't know anything. You don't say that to me." She peered at me as though I'm some kind of heretic. She never said a word to me after, ever.

We pulled into Shanghai station where the crowds were like nothing I'd seen before. What hit me again were the clumps of peasants sitting on concrete, waiting. They appeared like those turn-of-the-century grainy brown and white photographs of immigrants on Ellis Island, wide-eyed and uncomprehending.

The three of us are standing around, not quite sure how to proceed. It's cloudy out and faces are unsmiling. Shanghai reminds me of New York. The hustle, the noise, the controlled chaos. Sharli pokes me.

"Jake, you and Allie go see Taylor. I'm going to see my aunts."

"Your relatives? Now? What about your father? Didn't you tell me they killed him?"

"Jake I never told you such things. You made the whole thing up, him being pushed off the roof. It seemed to please you to tell the story and it harmed no one. But I'm in Shanghai and I haven't seen my family for more than thirty years. Much too long for Chinese to be apart."

Now she tells me I made up the story about her dad. Imagine, I concocted a whole fable about her father and she never said a word. Still, I had to admit it was pretty inventive. Then I felt dumb, considering the number of people I've misled. I moved away from my foolishness by asking Allie, "Where's a good place for Sharli to meet me later?"

Her eyes searched the street, thinking. "Oh. The Peace Hotel, by the Bund, the river. It's a lovely old building, and everybody knows where it is."

Sharli shook her head, okay. Well at least she agreed to meet for the trip back. I could imagine myself alone in this town. I gave her a sweet kiss and watched her walk off. So did about four thousand other Chinese. I guessed kissing in public wasn't a Chinese thing.

Allie and I caught a cab to the Public Security Bureau where the local constabulary was holding Taylor. Half way

into the cab I caught sight of the cop who had dogged
my trail since Xiamen. I turned away from him to get to
the business at hand. The police building mirrored the
way I felt, gray and depressing. The Chinese had allowed
this large stately brick structure to deteriorate. Seems
maintenance is not a word in their vocabulary or they
haven't had the wherewithal to keep the structures up to
their original stateliness. Pity. Its three huge Doric pillars
dated its construction back to the 20's when western
money and architecture dominated. I figured a defunct
English bank.

There were two guards with side arms, shoulder to
shoulder by the huge metal embossed front doors. Allie
gave them her well-intoned Chinese along with an official
looking document. They spread apart like paramecium
in binary mitosis. I got that from my biology class.
Weird stuff. Inside, a domed sky light brought some of
the outside in and the marble floor echoed the squeal of
Chinese military sneakers. In the center light sat a metal
desk where another uniform demanded our papers.

We were led up a circular staircase to a windowless
room divided in two by heavy chicken wire. There were
two empty chairs and two guards, one on each side of the
mesh barrier. One puffed away at a Chinese cigarette. My
cop Friday walks in and sits against the wall behind me.
The overhead fluorescent bleached any life from faces.
Man, this place intimidated. I reached into my pocket
for a cigar and put it between my teeth. I let it sit there,
unlit.

Taylor comes in with operating room green prison
clothes, thinning blond hair and his inherited Connecticut
manners. His shoulders slump, and his eyes are hooded.
His face paid the price of Qin's pistol. His left cheek

was bandaged, nose splintered and both eyes blackened. Allie let out a small wounded animal sound. I've got contradictory emotions, sorrow for the hell he's been given and hatred for what he put me through. I want to tear through the screen and shake the patrician head to somehow even the score. I also want to lean over and touch him softly and say everything will be okay. But my darker side won out.

"Damn you Taylor, you kill Qin and I'm in solitary for six days."

Softly, calmly but in a labored voice Taylor answered, "Jake, you shouldn't blaspheme." How's that for making me feel like a fool? He sat down and gripped his fingers through the wire mesh, and spoke in tired, measured tones. I didn't want to but I felt sorry for him.

"I'm not sorry for killing Qin, Jake. I regret you became involved." He placed his hands in his lap and stared at them. "I broke into your San Francisco place searching for the money I gave you for the Red Official. I watched you place it in your safe. I needed it."

"You're the one who broke in? You needed the money? But I thought . . . ."

He raised his hand, "Your safe almost begged to be opened. But the cash wasn't there. I thought maybe you put it in your desk so I started rummaging. I found the gun." He reached out to take my hand but hit the screen. "Jake, I don't know why, I just took it. I had no use for it."

The .45 wasn't my concern for the moment. "You needed the money? You broke in to steal the cash you gave me?" I almost couldn't believe him. "What about your trust fund?"

191

"I had borrowed to buy your Red Official. The shylocks gave me two days to get the cash." Then he tried to raise his eyes to meet mine. He gives me an expression puppies have just after they tinkle on the kitchen floor. "When I couldn't find the money, the cloisonné, I had to sell it." Davis turns his head to the cop who's puffing away creating a cloud of blue-gray smoke and Taylor says to him in what I figured to be exquisite, but demanding Chinese, "Would you please stop smoking." The cop hardly pays any attention, checks out the other cop, ponders unperturbed but nevertheless grinds out the cigarette on the floor.

I stare back to Taylor incredulously. "You sold what I sold you?" Then my dealer curiosity got the better of me. "Who did you sell it to?"

"To the curator of the museum in Taiwan. I knew he'd be interested."

It took a second. "You sold it to Chung Liu?" I asked incredulously.

In a monotone, "Do you know him, Jake?"

Do I know Liu? I can't believe this. "Yeah, Taylor, I know Liu. We've had some business dealings." I'm riveted to this guy, this tennis pro who at one time ranked twenty-sixth internationally, "Why the hell did you sell it, I thought you were loaded. You said you'd buy the Zhou Mengfu."

"My World Christian University, Jake. Allison told you. The costs of finding the right Christians to teach at Chinese universities, Jake, the costs." He paused, leaned into the screen, "The Chinese Generals, all those petty officials, they had their palms out. Jake they were bleeding me."

"But your trust fund? You're flush."

His eyes were now wide, inflamed, tortured. "My teachers, Jake, they are good Christians. All they want is to show the Chinese the loving heart of Christ."

This is a show, something I had never seen before and I'm caught up in all its drama.

"Jake, the constant expense of bringing new teachers to China to replace the ones Qin chased away. My trust fund, almost gone." He gaped at me with a pained expression. "He was evil," and he put his head in his hands.

I'm sitting there staring at this poster child for good bloodlines and I realize I'm outraged. I'm up on my feet grabbing and rattling the mesh wire separating us. Allie told me later she thought I'd gone mad. I could see the guards rushing. Dammit, I was going to have my piece. "He destroyed your good works? Great, Taylor, just great. The hell with you, Taylor. You killed Qin because of money, because he broke your bank and you couldn't handle it."

There were hands on my shoulders pulling me away and pushing me back down into my chair. Either my tirade or his guilt had him react and his hands went to his face. As they came away his eyes were lit in both confusion and denial.

"No, no, Jake. I could never kill him for that, Jesus would never allow me."

"Then why the hell did you kill him?" I screamed softly.

And now, even more softly he says, "For you, Jake. For you." He waits a split second. "For Harry."

What the hell?

"Jake, don't you know, Qin killed Harry."

Do you know how it is to be punched in the chest, for the air to get knocked out of you? Your mouth is open and all you can think about is a next breath.

"What the hell you talking about, Taylor. Harry died in Manchuria, just as the war ended, with me, in the night, out on the tundra." And I can't hold it back, "Just how the hell do you know about Harry."

"No, Jake. Harry didn't die then. He told me he used the escape as an excuse. He wasn't aiming for the Yalu but to walk to Mukden. He needed you for a diversion, knowing you'd be safe."

Now I'm sitting down in a kind of stupor, listening, fascinated.

"When Harry reached Mukden he convinced the Chinese he had deserted from the Russian army. His almost perfect Chinese enabled him to make it to Japan, and from there to Taiwan."

"Taiwan?'

"He told me returning to Brooklyn would be too boring. He decided to take as many of those priceless Chinese antiquities in the Brits house he could carry in his knapsack to set up an antiquities business in Taipei. As he said, that's where the market would be." I was looking at innocent eyes with nothing made up. "He became a wealthy man, Jake, and we became," and his eyes found mine, "very good friends."

"His knapsack? The knapsack he carried? Those marvelous Chinese works of art in the closed room were in his knapsack?" My god, Harry you old thief, you carried your inventory on your back while I carried water. Harry a dealer in stolen Chinese stuff? I always knew he'd make good.

"Taylor where is he?"

"He's dead Jake, I told you, Qin killed him. Harry came back, Jake, to China. An ex-Nationalist general sold him a bill of goods of a barge scuttled in a lake. He felt sure the Chinese had forgotten all about him, and besides, they wouldn't recognize him as he had aged so. But for the first time he proved wrong, Jake. Qin was waiting."

Could any body believe this? It had become the Gong Show, all craziness. I sat transfixed watching Taylor's lips forming syllables, words. While I heard his voice it came across as though he spoke to me underwater, garbled, inaudible. Incredibly I could understand every word.

"Qin put Harry in solitary for stealing treasures from some Englishman's house. He could have had him shot, but he didn't." A moment passed, a silence took over the room. Taylor continued, "Qin kept tormenting him, saying the rest of his life he'd be in solitary, sitting in blackness with food passed through a hole in his cell door. Jake, you know Harry to be a clever man but certainly never a brave one." His eyes almost teared. His next sounds were wrenching words. "Harry hung himself."

What was the movie? The Third Man? Where Harry is supposed dead and the cat walks over his shoes? Is this what it is, a series of old scenes in old movies? Was I Joseph Cotton, disappointed in the shenanigans of my old friend? "Taylor, you killed Qin for Harry? Revenge? Is this what it is, revenge?" I asked, incredulously.

"Jake, Harry told me Qin helped arrange both your escapes. The arrangement had Harry sharing the proceeds with Qin after the war. And Harry, being Harry, reneged. He kept it all."

"Son-of-a-bitch," I said softly, almost to my self, "that Harry, a tried and true thief."

"You don't understand, Jake. Qin was evil. He killed all things good."

I'm disoriented. Words are piling up too fast. Rising, I make a circle about my chair and sit down. I think I see things clearly. I want to grab his green jacket and scream, "Don't kid yourself Taylor, you killed Qin for the money he cost you, for money, for nothing. You robbed my store so don't use Harry as an excuse. You're nothing but a cheap thief."

But I can't do it. Here's a guy who's future is a Chinese prison. I can't let him go without some absolution. Besides, what would it cost me? Hey, life is difficult for us all, any help should always be offered. I've tried to live by that.

"Taylor, you did right. That son of a bitch Qin needed killing. It was long overdue. Harry would have appreciated the revenge." His face brightened as somehow I spoke the right words. I got up not wanting to hear any more of my make-believe, pushed the chair under the ledge by the screen, turned and without even a glance back walked out of the room and down the steps.

Do you think me harsh, uncaring, for not staying longer, giving more warmth to my words? You have the wrong guy. It's Taylor you want about uncaring. But I'll tell you, what stays with me, sympathy, and maybe some admiration. To believe as strongly as Taylor, to dedicate your life for a belief, Christianity. Yeah. Maybe it's all envy. Who knows?

I say to the marble hallway as I'm rushing out, "Harry, you bastard, a letter to your old buddy would have been nice. Not even a Hanukkah card?"

CHAPTER 25

I WAITED FOR ALLIE in the lobby, standing quietly on the hard floor. Sunlight now came in from the glass dome above. My thoughts were like the steps I just walked, cold, impersonal. Taylor kills Qin because of Harry? Harry, my boyhood buddy, the friend I deserted there in the black night. What were Izzy Klien's words about Harry? "Your friend Harry, Jakeala, he's, he's, maybe not so good." I should have listened to the old man who let me take over his 25-cent, "Guess Your Weight" gig by the Cyclone, the last wooden roller coaster in Coney Island.

"Jake," he said, "you're a good boy. I'm getting tired and you have the experience, you know the spiel. Take over the concession for the summer. I'll be in Miami where a man can relax and enjoy the women.

"Yeah, sure Izzy, it sounds great. I'll even get Harry to do a day or two a week." He gave me a face telling me he didn't like my words.

"Jake, maybe for those days you should close down. Your friend Harry is not a good boy like you. You, you're

BERNARD KATZ

a mensch, your friend, I'll be kind and only call him an opportunist." I told Izzy he didn't know Harry like I did. "Yes, I do, Jakeala, better."

Screw it all. I wasn't going to feel sorry for Taylor in killing Qin or for trying to save his World Christian University. Hell, he even tried to rob me to send his Pentecostals to China. I now had myself to cry over, my Zhou no longer had a buyer. You know what this taught me? I'll tell you. There's nothing in all the sideshows of Coney Island could ever compare with complexities of us humans.

I go outside and suddenly I'm feeling better. Harry's death is no longer on my hands, he didn't die because of me deserting him. All these years of seeing him fade away into the Manchuria dark like Sherlock Holmes's Hound of the Baskervilles engulfed by the fog on the moors. That son-of-a-gun Harry took off on his own dime. Imagine, he hung himself. I think about it for a minute and you know what, I don't buy it. No sir, not Harry. He may have feared the dark but death terrified him even more. I run it through my head once more. Not a chance of killing himself. The hell with it.

I study the bustle of the avenue. I'm beginning to like the entertainment value of the Shanghai street scene. Even in San Francisco walking in Chinese neighborhoods had an uninhibited feel. Maybe that's it. The streets present honest activity, the way the Chinese lived, hard and to the core of things.

Allie comes out of the Doric column building. She peers with a softness in her eyes. "Jake, that was good of you to say those last words to Taylor. He appreciated them."

I couldn't tell they were just words, no feelings but there's no sense in making Allison's life any more difficult. Yeah, maybe so, maybe so." When you see him next tell him I'm sorry about his trouble, okay?"

I felt the sun fully on my face and realized the true impact of his confessions. Taylor had returned my freedom, my guilt about Harry. It was a relief sixty years coming. "No, wait. Tell Taylor he changed my life, and I'll be ever grateful." Allie smiled, and I walked away freed from my memories of my boyhood friend.

Allie and I found a little tea shop on a main shopping street. I asked Allison about Taylor's trial, his defense. She said he hired a Chinese lawyer but there's little hope. A neighbor had watched Taylor enter Qin's apartment. There was a loud argument then two pistol shots. The apartment building residents emptied to their doors and all the tenants watched Taylor running away.

"He hasn't confessed, has he?" I didn't think China ever heard of the Miranda rule. I hoped Taylor hadn't followed confession–is–good–for–the–soul business. And if by chance it is, it's certainly not good for the neck, at least not in China.

We walked to the Peace Hotel down by the river where the boats docked. Standing before the entrance I kissed Allie's cheek and a slowly falling tear. Her eyes looked needing. "Jake, say goodbye to Sharli for me." She shook my hand. "God bless you, Jake," and she walked away.

The lobby of the Peace Hotel became a trip back to an earlier era. The wood paneling, marble floors, overstuffed chairs, and chic art–deco arcade shops suggested the beginning of the flapper period. A modern video game parlor worked hard at destroying the overall effect.

Sitting down opposite a polished mahogany reception counter I waited for Sharli. Two minutes later I'm up and searching for a phone. With only a little help from the concierge I connected to the Bamboo Grove in Suzhou but neither the kid nor Liu answered. Leaving a message and the phone number of my booth I went back to my chair, picked up a day old South China Morning Post and believed myself an old Tai Pan. No question, I entered my senile period.

Reading wasn't my best suit as Liu kept popping up in my head. If I hadn't gone chasing after him I wouldn't have sold the Red Official and Taylor wouldn't have had to borrow money. If he didn't borrow he wouldn't have had to steal it back and there would be no theft of the gun, no killing of Qin. Damn you old man, look at the sequence of events you've caused. And me? Liu's saying there's a good chance the original Zhou is on the bottom of the lake, in a recoverable position. If so, then I did buy a forgery making the professor wrong and Teddy right. We'll see. But even if I do end up with the real Zhou I no longer have a buyer, and to a make matters worse, my first payment to both banks I borrowed from is coming up real soon.

The phone rings in the booth and I'm up in a second but fearful it might be in Chinese.

"Jake?" The kid's voice is dull, sad.

"What's up, Mickey? Did they find the paintings?"

"Jake." It's in his voice.

"What's wrong?"

"Jake, Uncle Liu died. Just after breakfast, by the dive site, in the boat. They said a stroke."

I hear the tears in his voice. Damn, damn, damn. Which do I ask about first? The important one. "Kid, are you okay? I mean, I mean . . . . Stay there, I'll come right back."

"Jake, he wanted you to take him home to Chengdu, remember?"

"What? Sure, kid. Stay there. We'll take him together."

"Jake, he wanted you here. I need you here."

As I'm hanging up I say, "I'm coming kid, I'm coming."

What the hell did I say? I can't even get to the railroad station by myself. I gotta wait for Sharli to point me in the right direction. Then there she is, coming through the door. Oh, God, yes. When things happen they come fast.

I rushed over to her. "Sharli, We're heading back to Suzhou. The sweet old man Liu, he died, a heart attack." I started walking out, then back, not sure where to go. Liu is dead. It can't be. He owes me a picture, he owes me six hundred and fifty big ones. Oh, God, not the nice old man. What am I saying, he's the son-of-a-bitch who may well put me in jail, again. What the hell do I do now?

Sharli studies me as I'm spinning around the lobby imitating a Whirling Dervish. "Jake, what's wrong?" she asks. I tell her about Liu and she comes back, "Jake, you know I'm sorry about Liu, but I'm staying here with my cousins. They're my family. I haven't seen them since my childhood. We have a bit of talking to do. It's my Chinese family." She hesitates. "I'm going to see my brother."

Now I looked at her, unbelieving. "Your brother?"

"Don't yell, Jake. I'm sorry I never told you but you understand, a family secret," she then added a word, "an embarrassment."

"Embarrassment? Sharli, what are you talking about? No, not now, tell me about it on the train." She stared at me the way you would with a little boy who didn't understand when told he's not going to the movies. "Jake, back during the Cultural Revolution, when our family returned to Shanghai from the country side, my parents had another child. A boy. He was a, a," and it came out with difficulty, "a Mongoloid." She began crying, softly. "The authorities took him away and placed him in an institution. They said defective children were not allowed to live with their parents. Jake, they called him defective." She breaks down into a terrible weep. "It's the truth, Jake. Its true." She wipes the tears away. "My father, he couldn't handle it all. First my leg forever distorted then his new son, a Mongoloid. He couldn't handle it. He wasn't pushed off the hospital roof, Jake, he jumped." She tugged me to a corner of the lobby. "I could never tell you the story, I couldn't face the sadness."

The world spins too fast and my heart goes out to this woman I love.

"Your brother is alive?" I ask foolishly.

"Yes, but he's ill. Mongoloid children don't live out normal lives." She stopped crying and regained control. She leaned against the dark wood paneling of the hotel's lobby.

"It's all so long ago," she sighed. "The family called my mother last week telling her he wouldn't live much longer. Then Mickey called about you being in jail, in Suzhou." Her tears were starting again. "Mother told me to go, to say goodbye to my brother."

"Sharli, Mickey wants me to go with him to Chengdu and bury Liu. I need you, Sharli to go to Chengdu with me."

"Chengdu? Oh Jake, not Chengdu. You know I can't go there"

The way she said it I knew it had to be important, and then I remembered. Chengdu, Oh damn, yes.

I told you Sharli limped. It's her left knee. During those crazy Red Guard days they sent her family out west to the no-place town of Luding, near Chengdu, to learn humility among the peasants. Small, tiny, delicate Sharli picked up the streptococcus bacteria in December of the first year. Without antibiotics it grew in intensity like a Caribbean storm in September. Her father appealed to the Luding Farmer Cooperative hospital.

"Please, my daughter, she needs an antibiotic. Penicillin."

They ignored the capitalist running dog. He went to the nearest big city, Chengdu. "You can't say no," he said, "I need the penicillin now, the infection will spread." They stood there, implacable to the Boston doctor. He ran to Shanghai, to his old colleagues.

"For god's sake man, my daughter, she could, she could . . . ." They gave him drugs the Catholic Church had already sent in his name. Returning to Luding he saved Sharli's life but not her leg. He diagnosed it as septic arthritis, the streptococcus infection has worked its way to her left knee joint. Speaking to Sharli softly, he prepared her for a limp she would carry for the rest of life. To the little girl it became just another part of growing up. To the doctor, the father, it was a calamity.

I knew Sharli had to stay here in Shanghai. I had no argument, Liu dead, Sharli alive and worried. I only asked her to take me to the train station and buy my ticket. We waited silently as the train pulled in.

A child, that's what I am, a child. Back in the states I'm a functioning adult, here I'm a prepubescent, needing to be led about by an adult's hand. I took Sharli's fingers in mine. "You'll call Mickey as soon as you can, right? To tell him to meet me?"

"Yes, Jake, as soon as you leave."

"You promise. Cross your heart? You won't leave me out there alone?"

She brought her pinky up to her lips, kissed it and drew it away quickly up and to the right. The child's sign it's a promise. I told her I felt better. She smiled. We kissed goodbye.

To hell with the gaping crowds.

CHAPTER 26

I'M SITTING IN soft seat and going back to Suzhou, alone. Me, Jake Diamond, alone in China, a very scary event. Sharli told the conductor to let me off in Suzhou. He'd better, otherwise I'm liable to end up in Paris, Texas.

Liu is dead. Taylor is almost as good as dead. Blacky wanted me dead and is gone somewhere, hiding from the Chinese who probably want him dead. And Harry, I'm told he's also dead. There's just the kid and me. Oh yeah, the professor. I know I wanted him dead, but only for a crazy moment. A couple of hours go by and the guy who collected my train ticket opens the door and gestures I should be getting off. I follow the crowds toward the exit. I'm a piece of flotsam on the roiling waters of exiting Chinese. There's Mickey waiting for me at the end of the platform. The kid grabs my arm and escorts me out to where we catch a taxi.

"Jake, gee, thanks for coming." He glances about. "Where's Sharli?"

I ignore his question. "You should never say 'gee' kid. It makes you sound as old as you look." Mickey ignores me. "When did he die?" I ask.

"About noon, Jake. In the morning the divers were bringing up the scrolls wrapped in tin foil and thick wax when my uncle just collapsed. We brought him here."

"Where is he?"

"I have him in a Chinese cloisonné in turquoise and green on a dark blue background with a matching cover."

"What're you talking about kid?"

"Just after the stroke he managed to say he wanted to be cremated. It's where I was when you first called, the crematorium. His ashes are in the cloisonné." The kid's face is streaming tears as he's telling me this.

You know tears are like yawns. Somebody does it and you do it right back. I let go and all of a sudden I'm a tiny Niagara.

We pull up to the hotel and go to my room. I want to ask about the stuff they're bringing up from the lake bottom, but not sure if it's appropriate. The hell with it. "Kid, the things they're getting from the lake, the paintings, I mean did the water hurt them."

The kid peeks at me with those red eyes. "I'm not sure. They haven't been opened, but Dr. Wyatt said they knew what they were doing when they packed them."

If they find the Zhou and it's authentic I may come out of this in reasonable shape. But if the real Zhou is recovered how could I claim it? I mean the old man is dead. Who would accept an exchange of a forgery for the real one?

"Dr. Wyatt said they would bring everything up and truck the batch to Hangzhou. The university has a laboratory for just this sort of thing. Skilled people with the right instruments."

"All right kid, let's start talking about your uncle. First, why do you think he wanted me to tag along to Chengdu?" No doubt the old man and I liked each other but we didn't have any kind of history. Hell, he wasn't born anyplace near Brooklyn.

"I'm not sure Jake. He said something about giving you back something for what you gave the family."

"Did he say what he had in mind?"

"Nothing beyond what I told you."

"When we leaving?"

"Is tonight okay? I bought plane tickets. It's pretty far. We come back in two days."

I figured it to be perfect. By then Wyatt would have separated the wheat from the chaff and I'd be ready to blow this burg. I had enough of this Middle Kingdom, the Grand Canal and Chinese masters. I needed the soft fog of San Francisco and the dark roast coffee in North Beach. I also needed Sharli for myself.

We arrived at the airport, to the Air China desk. The guy is checking his computer, asking about our luggage, stapling tickets, and then he requests our passports. The kid gives the attendant his then the guy glances to me.

"I don't have it," I say, "the police do."

The clerk with the blue shirt and blue epaulets stares at me and in reasonable English says, "You must have passport. You cannot go on plane, you cannot go any place without it."

I'm standing there explaining everything to the kid when my shadow, the cop who's been following me pops up. He hands my passport to the airline guy who doesn't even blink but makes some notations on a page.

He's handing me back my passport when the cop plucks it from my fingers. He smiles and walks away. I can see I'm not leaving this country without my man Friday.

I have nothing to say about the flight except their menu. It consisted of jellied chicken, claws and all. Just after we landed we headed to a local restaurant in the home of Szechwan cooking. "Mickey," I said, "Would you tell the cook to go easy on the fire they put into those dishes with the pork. And maybe they could cut down on some of the red stuff, and those green things."

"Jake, I can't do it. The cook would be insulted."

Prima donnas for cooks, just great. I mean you gotta remember there's nothing blander than a Jewish mother's cooking or her son's palate. Besides, my stomach ain't what it used to be. Come to think of it neither was my uncle's, you know, the vaudeville guy, the one who left his money to buy trees in Israel. No question a generous gesture, but he could have left a little over for my brother and me. Well, not to my brother, he has plenty. Anyhow, when I was a kid all the aunts and uncles would come over to our house. I remember my aunt Suri saying to my mother, "Lana, please no more invitations. It's such a trip from Manhattan. The trains, the buses."

Jewish delicatessen dominated the Sunday brunch. Hot pastrami, corned beef, stuffing, things you see in old time windows in Katz's delicatessen, near Houston Street. Now for the point of all of this. This one time they're passing around the pastrami. It comes around to my uncle, Mr. Vaudeville.

"Not for me. I'll pass" he says. I can tell you heads turned. He knows his shock value and confesses, "It's my stomach. I'd be up all night."

I figured my uncle's words had to be a code for something else. I mean here's a guy who would devour anything free, and hot pastrami, a gift of the Gods. And now fifty years later I understand. It must be in the genes 'cause kosher hot pastrami, like Szechwan peppers, would just about kill me now. Yeah, as I've said all along life's a bitch, then you die.

We stayed in Chengdu for just over two days. I met the kid's relatives. Nice people, but no English at all. We simply smiled at each other. I'll tell you, they were not easy days. The family would gape at me like I represented some kind of, well, American. You gotta remember these were old line Communists. When Mao took over from Chiang Kai-shek Liu and his sister ran with the Generalissimo to Taiwan. All the others, the parents and aunts and uncles stayed in the old country, here in Chengdu. And this wasn't Beijing, American tourists were still rare as Edsels.

When we handed over the urn containing Chun's ashes they placed it in front of a small but very complicated red family shrine. There were lots of crying, clapping of the hands to summon the gods, and incense burning. Not too big on any of that stuff, I'm tapping my feet waiting for the whole thing to be over.

"Mickey, I hope there's not much more of this. I'm getting tired of asking you 'whatta he say, whatta he say'?"

The kid laughed. "I don't mind Jake. I know it's a little tough, but they all like you, my aunts and uncles. I never met them before. I like them. Just one more day, Jake. We'll leave tomorrow."

The next morning we went back to the family house a few miles out of downtown where we had stayed.

The place they lived in had this mausoleum quality. A three-room concrete cell in a four-story cement building, an early reproduction of the Russian apartment house. With linoleum on the floor, a pull chain squat toilet, a small kitchen added two water spigots. Everything looked similar to Ms. Banana Crème Pie's place. One of the water spigots had this contraption which turned on gas jets heating an above the sink holding tank. When you wanted hot water the gas ignited with a whoosh. Kind of exciting. I expected the whole building to go up in a blaze. A small refrigerator sat in the living room covered by a large silk wrap with a fading picture of Mao. You really couldn't escape the guy. The road out to their place went past a tall, massive Mao Zedong statue sitting in the middle of town. I loved it. It had just the right touch of theater; a benevolent face, a soft arm gesture, but I thought his middle finger was raised a tad too high. Anyway, Mickey said the family would read Liu's will.

The aunts and uncles are still staring. Make no mistake; polite, sweet, charming, they couldn't do enough. At the same time no amount of watching would satisfy them. It started to get annoying. But what the hell, now I'm a movie matinee idol. We all gathered in the largest room of the house and the guy with the longest whiskers began reading from a small scroll. There were all kinds of quiet noises, ooh's and aah's. Heads turned to a particular person and smiles would follow. Pieces of paper would be exchanged, jade, in all forms and fashion would change hands. I could see it became the distribution of Chun Liu's fortune. At least the part held by the mainland family. Then, unexpectedly, all heads came around to me, and the room hushed. I ran my eyes about the room, not sure what happened. They began to clap, softly, demurely. My eyes pleaded to Mickey, he smiled. What's this I asked myself, my Bar Mitzvah?

"Jake, they're clapping because you are mentioned in Uncle Liu's will. They all like what he left you."

"I'm in his will? He left me something?" I'm touched, I really am.

From another room Chun Liu's cousin, Sheng, appeared carrying Liu's stout walking stick and a big armful covered by a gold silk cloth.

I'm handed the armful, carefully. Oh, damn you, Liu. The minute I got my mitts on it I knew it would never leave my possession again. The old reprobate, that sweet old man, the aces kind a guy. Old Liu left me his, no, he willed back to me my Red Official.

Can't you just picture it, a jowly Jewish guy in the middle of China surrounded by sympathetic Chinese, awash in his own tears. I needed to get at my handkerchief but didn't want to let go of the Red Official. After everything kinda quieted down I read the little note attached from Liu:

> Jake, I like calling you my friend. I have
> caused you much trouble. Please accept this,
> as you would say, to even the score. I know
> you are its true owner. While I believe we
> both appreciate the Red Scholar as wonderful
> craftsmanship, the gentleman was always yours.
> I just borrowed him for a short while.

Well I'll be a son-of-a-gun. I wiped away the tear that had gathered in the corner of my eye before some wise guy could see it. I think Mickey did the same. I figured whatever happens next has to be anticlimactic. As usual, I miscalculated.

CHAPTER 27

T HE DAY AFTER the dispersal of Liu's worldly goods the kid and I are headed to the airport. I'm trying to juggle both my inheritances, Liu's walking stick and the Red Official. At the ticket counter it's business as usual. Not too many Chinese ever heard of 'queuing up'. It looked to me if you had half a mind you simply stepped to the front and shoved your ticket into the face of the attendant. The kid gives me an explanation. "Jake, no one's objecting because they figure it's an emergency and at some time they may be forced to do the same." I don't buy it. There are always gatecrashers. Now I'm waiting for the cop to show with my passport so I can get on the plane. He does. He looks different. I realize he's shaved and I'm impressed. Tall for a Chinese, also heavy in the chest. He had a small scar along his chin. His eyebrows allowed me to pick him out of a crowd as they appeared as two fighting black caterpillars. I'm impressed and can honestly say he's a handsome Chinese man, except of course for the garlic.

It's a long flight ahead and I'm trying to get comfortable. Mickey sat gazing at the Official. He finally asked, "Jake, why would Liu leave you the statue?" I had asked myself the same question.

"I don't know kid. But I'll say this, he seemed to know quite a bit about me."

We landed on time, caught a cab from the airport straight to the ferry ticket office for an overnight trip back down the canal to Hangzhou. Luck was on our side as we picked up the last of the first-class cabins. On the way to buy some food for the boat we passed my cop standing in line.

"You going first class?" I asked him, always enjoying his confused face when I give it to him in English.

"Of course, and it shall be paid from your purse," he says in American, straight faced, without a trace of smile and only a touch of an accent.

I'm stunned, the gumshoe could do the English right along. I had to laugh. "You son of a gun. You fraud. Here I thought you some ordinary cop, and instead I get a Harvard Ph.D. You sound better than the kid or me."

He gives me an ear-to-ear grin. "You? Certainly, or should I say "soitenly". But for the young Mr. Mickey? I think not. He has the advantage of the native born. It wasn't necessary for him to live in Singapore to learn proper pronunciation."

The ferry appeared to be the same beaten up scow we had in getting here only with a different name. We put our things away and I again stood on the deck. I had my inheritance, the Red Official in the stateroom behind and I wasn't about to wander far. The Chinese cop walks up and stands next to me by the rail like Wyatt did coming here. Now he's talkative.

"Do you like China?"

What kinda question is that? "Yeah, it's okay." I won't tell him it's an experience I'll treasure, particularly yesterday.

He stands there staring absently into the opposite shore. "We came this way from Hangzhou," he says looking out along the opposite shore, at the houses dipping their eaves into the canal.

"Uh huh," I offer. Now what. We're by the railing watching the passing scene, the smokestacks, the scows, barges, tugs, and bridges. The cop nudges me.

"You would think everything would be a duplicate of what we had seen coming up here, but it's not the way it is, is it?"

I inspect him. What the hell is this all about?

"Did you ever notice when you go back from the place you came from in the opposite direction it's as though everything is new." He gives me a glance, smiles, and walks away.

He's right. I had seen nothing of this before. My cop, a Chinese philosopher.

It's all Sharli's fault I'm traveling alone subject to the observations of the Chinese police. But she wouldn't care about what he just said. No, she's not as romantic as me. Now you may not believe this, especially as I've had two wives, but I'm more loyal and romantic than most of the women I've known. And I'm including all my wives, and certainly Sharli. Women confuse romance with romantic. I suspect it needs some explanation. For example, the movies always gave us romantic characters.

Take Errol Flynn, in any of his flicks, he always risked his life no matter the circumstance for the maiden who captured his heart. He's the pure romantic. Women, on the other hand sought Errol for dancing in the moonlight and for a squeeze of her thigh. Perhaps even a little gift on her birthday. You see, they don't understand. What they see as romantic is unimportant romance. Now, I'm a romantic. Give me a moment.

I'm in Texas waiting to be shipped overseas and to kill time I go to the service club to shoot pool. This young hostess, a Texas gal with corn fed boobs and hips made for, well never you mind, comes over. She liked the way I moved around the table, my stroke, my position. Now all them's clean words. She asks me to teach her the game. We became friendly, quickly.

My young lady embodied all the attributes of a great chocolate fudge sundae, sweet, succulent, tasty and over the days I devoured her. When I received word my unit would be shipping out I didn't even have a last night. I ran to her place with enough time only to kiss and pledge my undying devotion.

"Mitzi, meet me in New York."

"Oh yes, Jake. When?"

How the hell would I know? "Christmas Eve, eight o'clock, by the Astor Hotel in New York," then I did some quick figuring, "1954."

"Oh, Jake. You'll be there, honestly?"

Well, 1954 comes around and I'm back in Brooklyn dressing to meet my little Texas gal. I had to pick a damned freezing December night. Taking the subway and waiting by the Astor Hotel I figured Mal was right when he said I must be nuts. He guaranteed I'd be wasting my time.

What the hell did he know, she'd show up, besides, I promised to be there.

I arrived early, naturally. I'm waiting under the hotel marquee and eight o'clock had come and gone, and I still waited. What an ass, but I had faith, well, more like an outside hope. Cabs would pull up with a single woman getting out. I would stare real hard but some older guy would walk up and take her arm. After another half-hour I admitted defeat and took the subway back to Brooklyn, freezing feet and all. All of this is to tell you something of my romanticism, either that or I'm a total schnook when it comes to women. I once told Sharli the story.

"Jake," she said, "you are a schnook. You're silly, and foolish." She glowered at me in a sideways fashion with her eyes narrowed. "You were probably just horny."

You see, it's the Chinese part of Sharli, the pragmatic, the realistic. Then again, maybe if I wasn't in China I'd say she showed wisdom, common sense. I don't know. I've always said she had more smarts than me.

The ferry pulled into Hangzhou right on time and I stood on the the dock holding my inheritances with the kid alongside. We're figuring what to do when the Winslow Professor pulls up in a small van with a Zhejing University written its side. He comes bounding out of the van.

"Welcome to Hangzhou, ancient capital of the ancient Chinese. Good to see both of you."

He glances at what I'm holding then places his hand on the kid's shoulder. "I'm sorry about your uncle. He and I went back a few years. A man of principle, not too many left."

The kid's face screwed up as though a tear would pop through. "Thank you. He would appreciate your words."

I asked the kid quietly how Wyatt knew we'd be here. He said he wired him from Suzhou. Smart kid.

Wyatt's enthusiasm couldn't be contained. "Your timing couldn't have been better. The divers brought up the last of the trove from the barge day before yesterday. We've placed everything in the Ancient Art Department of the University."

"Is my *Late Autumn* there?" I ask.

"Patience, Jake." He peruses my armful, "If you don't have any more luggage we can get in the van." Wyatt opens the door to the small bus. We're about to get in when the garlic chewing, peasant faced, omnipresent, English speaking, passport-holding cop walks up. He pulls out his identification cards and badge and bows.

"I do hope you gentleman don't mind but I shall be traveling with you to the University." He then steps on my toe, the brute. "And for you. Mr. Diamond, I shall be by your side for the balance of time you are in China."

"To hell you are," I said. "I'm not about to share anything with you, not with your garlic breath." He didn't like that. I'm still staring at the cop and not liking it. "It wasn't so bad when you were just sniffing about at my heels, but I don't want to live with you."

"My name is Yang. You may call me Yang," and he gives me a half smile. "While I do enjoy your quiet hysterics, Mr. Diamond, we are, regrettably, stuck with each other. You have a national treasure illegally taken out of our country and we wish to retrieve our Zhou Mengfu."

The jerk, didn't even know I had a forgery.

Wyatt simply accepted this kind of personal infringement. He had spent more time in China. "Come alongYang, you can be there when we open our treasures from the lake."

I can't believe what I hear. Doesn't Mr. Owl know cops just bring trouble. "Wyatt, are you nuts? You want a cop there?"

"Jake, it makes little difference. The arrangement between Liu and the Chinese government held great simplicity. Everything found belonged to China. Liu's museum would get reimbursed for his time and expenses. Liu thought the adventure would be a fit closing chapter to his life. I don't think there's any question it has."

Which explains Blacky's disappearance. The government came in on the entire enterprise from the start. They knew about every piece coming up from the briny as well of its disposition. They probably cataloged the antiquities, knew their ancestry and if any appeared to be missing they knew where to go. The bureaucrats also screwed me, big time. What happens if the Zhou they brought up from the lake is the original? I'm filleted nicely, I'd never get possession of it. And I didn't think they would trade my forgery for the real one.

Yang explores what I'm carrying. "I do hope it's not a national treasure."

"Don't even let your mitts get close to this." Some nerve.

Turning to see if the cop is joining us in the van there's an old kinda shriveled Chinese guy leaning against a plane tree; watching. He's wearing a faded cheongsam with a brocade collar like it comes from a different age. Dammit if he ain't smiling at me. And I gotta look again. Something familiar.

Wyatt calls out, "Jake, you coming?"

"Sure, sure. Give me a second." I look back to the tree and the old guy is gone.

I'm in the van and feel a kind of tension. All of us know we're headed toward an artistic Armageddon, the fiction or fact of my Chinese masterpiece. But I'm looking out the window thinking about that long ago cold Brit's house.

CHAPTER 28

"WYATT, WHERE ARE you taking us?"

"To the paintings, Jake, to Zhejiang University, to the scrolls. It's what you want isn't it?"

We pass through a wrought iron gate appearing like an entrance to a large estate. Easy like he pulls into a space in front of a series of old buildings, not at all Chinese, more like an American university out of the Northeast. The one we entered even had ivy clinging to its old stone. I glance around.

"Hey, Wyatt, is this the low tuition section?" The plaster walls are chipped, and in some places the wood lathe is exposed. The oak floor had patches of differing boards, pine mainly. At the wall the planks had bulged away.

"Jake, maintenance has not been a major priority, particularly for the arts. The budgets go to Engineering."

I've heard that before.

We come to a room where the ribbed glass in the door had the painted words, "Classical Art." Wyatt walks in, I follow. A pungent odor hits me.

"Smells like Coney Island at low tide," I offer with a wry smirk.

Wyatt tries to imitate my smirkyness. "Well, you're half-right, Jake, it's the algae from the lake. The artifacts were submerged for fifty years. They carried the odor with them." He sniffs the air. "Yes, quite pungent. You have a good nose."

Good? It's more than good. I've always been able to smell cheap perfume a good six bar stools down. Damn, what a scene. In conjunction with the smell were the tatters of the tin foil preserving the scrolls. Slime, mud and wax were piled in the corners, deposits from the bottom of the lake. Wyatt strode to a stubby, gray haired middle-aged Chinese woman and conferred in hushed Chinese. He kept shifting his view to me and then back to her. The kid walked over to me.

"She's Fan Jin, the Chinese art historian."

He stared at her with his eyes wide in complete admiration. She had to have a reputation. The way she spoke to Wyatt and his deference to her said she clearly had authority here. For the first time I noticed there were no windows, no natural light in the room. Floodlights placed in corners and in the middle of the floor dominated. They bounced their intense white off the ceiling onto the walls and floor.

Mickey suddenly pointed to the rear corner of the room. I had to take a deep breath. There they were, eleven scroll hangings all bunched together. We quickly walked over. As we came close I heard Mickey give a short exclamation. They were simply marvelous, breathtaking.

Wyatt walked up to us and repeated the obvious. "Classics. All signed by a master."

My breath caught in the back of my throat. There it was, shining, hanging apart from the others. Undoubtedly done by Zhou, my *Late Autumn*. It's what I should have gotten for my 650 G's, the reason I came to China. Now how the hell would I be able to leave with it? Wyatt came to me as I strode up close to the scroll.

"You know, Jake the man had his place in China. Zhou played a unique role in Hangzhou's history." I turned from the scroll to Wyatt, the man who knew everything.

"Tell me." My hunger had to be insatiable.

"You're viewing the works of a Renaissance man. He became artist, scholar, warrior, poet. For years he headed a literary group of the great writers of the time, all living in and around East Lake, in Hangzhou. For ten years he directed the local province schools of Confucius. For a short period he even shaped the Yuan Dynasty as part of the War Ministry. Jake, his resume is impressive."

I stepped over to another scroll hanging along side the *Late Autumn*. Significantly larger, a full quarter of this scroll consisted of blocks of signatures and Chinese characters laid out as poems or short essays. I asked Wyatt its name. I disturbed him.

"You see how different this one is from yours, Jake? The artificial distance and scale shift. There is an uncertain quality to the painting. Very disquieting." I'm following his fingers as he makes each of his points. Mickey is beside me. Wyatt steps back from the painting. "It's Zhou's, 'Autumn Colors'". Then he said the strangest thing. "Not my cup of tea." He turned his back and walked to a different part of the wall. "Come here, Jake. Here, this one is also a Zhou, he named it, '*Layered Rivers and Tiered Peaks*'."

Wyatt came around and fixed his gaze at me and I see his eyes, different than before. His iris's are as round camera lenses, registering the entire room. He headed back to the scroll. "Jake, this scroll, it's the minimalist's art. Everything is stripped to its basic skeletal nature. There is no atmosphere, no source of light, no shadow, no mass. It is all brushstroke, Jake, all line on silk." He finishes, pleased with himself. He stays and stares as if he should be anointed.

Off to the side I see the policeman Yang using his finger to trace the Chinese characters of the *Late Autumn*, trying to copy the words.

You know life always kids you. Take now for instance. Is it really my decision all of this is great stuff? Is it possible after having been told so often they are masterpieces I see them as impressive without even looking? Are we now all prisoners of the expert? I take a deep breath and I'm back to Wyatt. He's peering at me, walks over and places his arm about my shoulders. Now what? "You know Jake, it's too bad. Ordinarily these scrolls would be overwhelming."

I must have forgotten my vitamins as his words took a second to register. "Ordinarily? What do mean, ordinarily?"

"Jake can't you tell? They are all forgeries. Copies. Good ones mind you, excellent ones actually, but still only copies"

Did this arbiter of Chinese classic beauty say everything in this room is a counterfeit, a reproduction, a phony? The only sound in the large windowless room became the flood lights vibrating filaments. First a buzz, and then a crackling of falling trees in the forest, finally a cacophony of ear splitting static.

"Copies? Frauds? Fakes? You're sure? All of them? The Zhou's?"

The small owl appearing man stood alone in the middle of the room. His head shook up and down like one of those little fake Chihuahua dogs in the back windows of a Chicano's low rider. Wyatt says casually, "Yes, Jake, without question. They are inspiring, wonderful, brilliant, but just copies."

I'm frozen in place. I need time to thaw. Mickey had walked up to the scroll, ran his finger along its surface, inspected it from different angles. He spoke to Wyatt. "How do you know?"

The professor stayed cool, scholarly. "You see it's all wrong. Here," he took a step back to the *Autumn Colors*, "the ends of the strokes turn down. It's not Zhou's style. His always swung to the top of the scroll. In all of his paintings we know the sweep of his brush always ended with a clean, upward flip. It became his signature." Over his shoulder he says, "In your Zhou, Jake, the one in your office, didn't you notice the ending of the stroke? How surgical they were, like a cut with a surgeon's scalpel. Here, look at this," and I follow him to the wall scrolls, "the fuzziness of the serif," he's searching for the word, the best description, "like a torn piece of thread." He peered at me. "The forger's brush must have been very worn."

His words were beginning to sink in. I wanted him to repeat each syllable at least twice. Don't you see? I needed those scrolls to be the fakes. It meant I had the real goods. Under the floorboards at Gold Street the real Zhou wore its regal robes, I had the authentic *Late Autumn*. If given a chance I'd embrace Wyatt, the kid, Yang and even the old professor lady who stood off to the side watching these funny Americans.

For crying out loud, I'm rich! I'm back on the beaches of Cancun. From now on its fillet mignon and lobster. Wait a minute. Better let my euphoria take a breather. I'd been taken in before, a history of premature celebration.

I asked, "I suppose all the others, the scrolls, they're also fakes, copies, all of them?"

"That they are, Jake, yes, indeed." I could see Wyatt being cute, playful, content with himself.

I ask, "And they all had the wrong brushstrokes?"

"Not at all, Jake. There are a number of reasons why they're fakes. Come here, I need to show you something." He pulled at one of the landscape paintings and spread the silk fibers of the scroll. "Here the forger took an old scroll painting, washed it clean and painted over it to appear as a Li Sung. This one," we moved to the next in line, "is a copy of a Ma Lin."

"Painted on somebody else's scroll?" I asked.

Wyatt smiled and told Mickey, "Tell him."

The kid walked over. Stood for a few seconds in puzzlement, then his face lit. "The perspective, it's too deep. Ma Lin always sought a single dimensional space in his paintings."

"Excellent, Mickey. Very good." Wyatt stood still taking in the scrolls. Then with a puzzled expression walked back to the Li Sung. He pulled at the silk, ran his fingers along the vermilion signatures. "Very amateurish. In this one the signature ink hasn't totally dried." He walked over to the Ma Lin. "Mickey, come here. Does it appear some recent silk became woven in with the older threads?"

Yikes!

The kid walked over and examined it closely. "I can't tell." He gave it a hmmm there and a hummm here and then concludes, "but I would need a microscope and some alcohol."

I didn't say a word as I'm still confused. Now I speak up. "Wait a second, Wyatt, Liu was sure the barge contained the originals. And what ever happened to Zhou's student and his copy of the *Late Autumn*?"

The professor gazes at me almost sadly. "Jake, Liu grasped at straws. A romantic at heart he wanted the lake to contain the originals. It would have satisfied his idealism of the original Nationalist cause and given Mrs. Chiang even greater stature. This, in turn, would have given him pleasure, and, if I may, bring Liu considerable fame." He paused for a moment and as an afterthought tells me, "The supposed student, Yuan Chi, I believe he's just Chinese slight of hand, a kind of myth made up by scholars to increase their own stature."

I don't follow his words exactly and let it go, hell, I've got an original. "Wyatt. I take back every nasty thing I ever said or thought about you. Actually. I'm in love with you. I have back my two million-dollar painting. I'm going to buy you a dinner, in San Francisco and I know just the place."

"Wu Chow's? Chinatown?" Mickey asked.

"Naw, Six Prophets out on Taraval. A lot cheaper."

The cop walked over to us from where he had been studying the Zhou. "Good copy of Mengfu, but the calligraphy is wrong." Wyatt raised one eyebrow. Yang continued. "Not as elegant as I have seen in studies of comparative drawings among the masters."

Just terrific. Now my once dumb cop is an expert in calligraphy. Everybody knows the real Zhou except me and the strange thing is, I got one. I'm back in business.

All of us are walking down a tree-lined lane on the school's campus. It's a good feeling. A touch of cool in the air, a few trees with some color, students all around. We have to move as the bicycle bells tell us they're coming. The professor smiles at me.

"Jake, I said you had an authentic Zhou back in San Francisco."

I'm thinking about Teddy, back in Hayes Valley. The guy I gave the samples of the ink and silk. He had the microscope, the tools. Well, damned if he didn't prove right with the few slivers I had supplied. My mistake was not giving him the entire scroll. If I hadn't been such a jerk thinking myself an expert and figuring somebody was out to screw me I could have saved myself this headache.

Then I'm thinking it's been kind of fun, a fitting way to discover China. An adventure with tour leaders the average tourist seldom comes across. But I'm not through, there are still some questions, like how Wyatt knew the real scrolls weren't in the lake and why Liu thought they were. The dinner with the little owl should turn out to be interesting. I'm missing Sharli. It would have been better if she were here.

CHAPTER 29

Wᴴɪʟᴇ I'ᴍ ᴀɢᴀɪɴ a millionaire I still don't have the bucks in my pocket, meaning I still had to pay attention to my expenses. As Wyatt drove us back into town I told him to stop at the downtown East Lake Hotel. I knew it to be reasonably priced from the last time we were here. I figured we'd be there for one night, catch the train, pick up Sharli in Shanghai and we'd be off to San Francisco.

"Jake," Wyatt said, "for a farewell let's eat at the Song Dynasty Restaurant. They have excellent roast duck and it's near your place."

We agreed to meet at seven. That gave the kid and me some time to put our things away. I only had the Red Official, my small bag and Liu's walking staff. I took Liu's bequest and checked it at the desk, making sure I had a receipt and assurances.

I'm downstairs, outside, waiting for the kid to show. Across the street I see this guy squatting in front of a blanket he's laid out on the sidewalk. You could tell he was a mountain of a man. I think I'm seeing bloody animal heads, and entrails. Inspecting the guy more carefully I take a step back, he's more frightening than what he's got before him. Remember those old pirate flags, the skull and crossbones. Well somebody removed the crossbones and left the rest with hair as wild as his eyes. The animal skins he wore didn't help any. Then he fixes on me. Oh man, it stopped me cold. I inched back to a bench by the hotel.

A voice behind me says, "He's a bit scary, isn't he Jake."

"Harry," I scream to myself. While the timbre of a voice deepens, the trace of all accents rarely disappears. You can't get the Brooklyn out no matter how long you stay away.

This little old man then steps in front wearing a faded blue Mao jacket and a stained green cap that came down to his ears. The lines of his face were etched mahogany but the shape of his eyes told you he wasn't Chinese.

"I heard you were dead, Harry."

"We both know about Mark Twain and the report of his death, don't we, Jake."

"Yeah, I guess, but the word of your demise came from a good source."

He laughed softly. "Despite rumors to the contrary, Jake, Qin, the cop and I were on good terms. Who the hell do you think bought him his rank and how the hell do you think he lived so well?"

"Yeah, I shoulda had more faith that you'd only double cross me."

He sat down next to me.

"Let it lie, Jake. It's been what? Some 45 years. Besides, I knew you'd be okay out there in the dark. Qin and I worked it out."

"Qin, huh? He cost me my pinky, Harry."

Maybe Harry was right, it's the past, but he didn't know and probably couldn't care for all my nights awake wondering whether the son-of-a-bitch lived or died.

"I've been following you, Jake since you came to China." There was a second. "You do get around."

"Following me, how come?" I asked

"You have a Zhou and I'd like to buy it."

I shoulda been surprised but wasn't. "Still dealing in stolen merchandise, Harry?"

"Stop it, Jake. You can't break our friendship."

I thought about what he said. "Maybe so, Harry, but I don't have to like you." It took me a second for his offer to register. "How do you know it's not a forgery?"

"Jake, Liu took it from his museum and wanted to give you a present, to make your life easier, to make you rich."

"How do you know this."

"C'mon, Jake, I'm a Taiwanese dealer in legit and stolen high priced artifacts. Sometimes the National Museum uses my services for authentication. They suspected something when they heard an expert in the States was looking at a Zhou. All rumor, mind you, but I knew Liu stole it and gave it to you for a pittance. You saved his brother's life. In his Chinese way he needed to clear up obligations."

"You always were the clever one, Harry, but you're wrong you know."

"About what, Jake?"

"Us, still being friends. You turned out to be an opportunist and a thieving bastard. I want no part of you."

"Jake, you always played to the dramatic. It's what makes you so lovable."

"No chance, Harry, you're not laying your hands on the painting. if only for principle." I had a thought running around. "You were sure what I had was legit?"

He gave me a smile that broke a whole bunch of ridges about his mouth. "I heard about the barge from Blacky and figured I'd better come up. Who knows, there could have been a harvest."

This time I smiled. "Your boy, Blacky, seems he ran out on us."

"Never, 'my boy,' Jake. T'was always strictly money. Even I have scruples." He waited a moment. "It's worth about 3 million to me, Jake."

It didn't take a second. "Not a chance, Harry. Not to you."

Mickey waved to me as he came out of the hotel. Harry caught it. He rose, walked behind me, softly squeezed my shoulder as a last goodbye. "Carpe diem, Harry, carpe diem."

When I turned to face him he had already folded in among all the other very old men in Mao jackets and green caps. I didn't care. He made his choice long ago.

Mickey asked, "What did the old Chinese guy want?"

I stood up. "Just wanted to give me some Latin lessons."

The kid looked at me strangely.

I needed to rid myself of my attitude toward Harry. I know I wasn't nice, but it was honest. So was turning my eyes back to the guy with the bones and voodoo across the way. Mickey's followed.

"Jake, he's a kind of medicine man, selling witchcraft, magic stuff, you know, snake oil. There's a long history there. The Chinese believe in spooks and gods. Ask Sharli."

Yeah, just where the hell is my darlin?

We started walking to the lake looking for a bench away from the traffic, near the restaurant. Something bothered me I needed to ask the kid.

"Mickey, how come your uncle willed me the Red Official."

The kid gives me a warm smile. "Jake, my uncle liked you. He told me you outbid him for the porcelain figure in some Amsterdam auction years ago. You impressed him as you inspected the piece, the way you held it, touched it. He knew you were captivated and showed your passions. But its more than that Jake, Liu always spoke kindly about you. It almost seemed he owed you something." A quizzical expression appeared, "Do you know?"

I think about his question and have no real answer, just a suspicion and there was that remark by Harry, about saving his brother's life. I let my eyes fall to my watch. "Hey, Kid, it's Chinese restaurant time. C'mon, we gotta meet Wyatt."

The Song Dynasty restaurant Wyatt chose was but a step above a cheap-eat place. Dingy indeed and the table cloth at our bench was stained with yesterday's food. Wyatt arrived the same time we did. I guessed it to be a local's place, not clean but good chow. We let the Prof do the ordering as it appeared he knew the waiter. The kid told me he ordered the duck, lake fish, green pea pods laced with garlic and some egg plant in black bean sauce.

While I'm screwing around trying to manipulate the chopsticks all the pros are way ahead of me into the choice pieces. I'd ask for a fork only I don't know how. I needed a way to slow down my ravenous companions.

"Hey, Wyatt, how come Liu was sure the *Late Autumn* lay at the bottom of the lake, and you knew I had the original."

He put the chopsticks down, sucked in a little of the tea, and wiped his mouth. "Mickey, no offense, your uncle was a bureaucrat, not an expert. He joined Chiang Kai-shek's as a loyal follower and made curator of the museum in Taiwan as payment. A fine gentleman, and a good guardian of Chinese art history, but no expert." His chopsticks start to the duck, but he thinks better of it and he comes back to the conversation.

"There are a couple of things you don't know, Jake. With the confusion of the new Chiang government and the new museum sorting the authentic from forgeries depended somewhat upon inventory lists. A shipment of the Sung Dynasty scrolls arrived in Taiwan in 1951 without an inventory. The missing invoice always made that particular shipment suspect for Liu." Mickey and I are eating while Wyatt is talking. Wyatt is not to be out maneuvered. "I'll take the rest of the fish if nobody wants it."

"It's all yours." I would be happy to see the fish's open mouth and pearly eyes disappear. Wyatt does a quick job on it. The only thing left is the head and spine. The Winslow Professor wipes his mouth and picks up his part of the conversation.

"Liu gave too much credit to the Colonel's report to Madame Chiang. The generals in Nanjing knew they sent the masterpieces directly to Taipei and the forgeries down the canal. They just never bothered to tell anyone which shipment contained the forgeries. After all, they were generals." Wyatt beamed at me, "I'm pretty sure it's the way it happened, Jake." The Winslow Professor then picked up the last of the eggplant. Just perfect.

We all looked at each other, went to the remaining food and didn't look up again until all plates were wiped clean. As we rose from the table the waiter with the bill walked over to Wyatt. The owl confers with the Chinese guy who then takes a step away and gives the tab to Mickey. The kid looks up to me, I shake my head yes and Micky pays the bill. He leaves a little extra on the table. Wyatt comes by and picks up the change. "There's no tipping in China, it's insulting to the Communist spirit," and walks away as calm and slick as can be. You had to love the guy.

We're outside but it's still too early for bed, even for me. As we were near our hotel I asked the professor if I could buy him a beer. We took a table in the hotel lounge. Now I had a question, and it's been bugging me all night, all last week.

"How come my Zhou, the original, had both silk and ink only fifty years old?"

"I'll take a guess, Jake. Everything happened fast that night, confusion was Chiang's ally. The men who did the copies also put some fake details into the originals in case they fell into Communist hands. A quick, unstudied investigation would find the ink and silk telling the searchers they had forgeries. The Commies would leave those and continue hunting for the originals." He keeps his eyes on me. "Like I said, Jake, it's a guess but it's consistent with other inconsistencies among the museum's holdings. We have faked signatures on genuine first cast bronzes and added chops to original paintings. Someone worked hard to create uncertainty." He paused as though going over what he had said. His gaze moved from me to the kid. "Maybe the uncle had the story right. Maybe it was all Madame Chiang."

Me, I didn't care. Let them all play around seeking logic and cause. I had the scroll and even Harry offered 3 million. Now it's going to be just a matter of finding another buyer. Tomorrow I'd get Sharli in Shanghai, and then back to Fog City and retirement in luxury. It's about time. It's been a helluva of a few days. But it's over. Over? I had forgotten I currently resided in the original Chinatown.

CHAPTER 30

MICKEY AND I take the elevator to our floor. There's a little desk for a young Chinese woman who oversees the goings on. I go to my bare room, bed, table, chair and lamp. Mickey is next door. I take off my jacket and I'm sitting on the bed kicking off my shoes. There's a knock. "In a second kid." Before I can put on my shoe the door explodes. Damn.

"Blacky. You son of bitch. Where the hell did you come from?" I'm still trying to get the shoe on. I'm up, half-walking, half-dragging my shoe to get to him. "Damn you, you tried to kill me." I forget his size, his strength. I foolishly grab the lamp by the bed. He's standing there with his impressive ten-inch serrated diving knife. A mean looking thing. The threatening lamp seemed of no concern to Blacky. He had his purpose.

"You mother" he said, "I couldn't kill ya then but I can now. If they catch my friend it's going to be a bullet to the back of his head. Did you know that? Did you know that?"

I'll tell you I was scared. No, terrified. I'm hardly a match for Blacky even at my best day but I would have given it a shot without the knife in his hand.

"Hold up a second, Blacky. Hold on. You can't pin your friend's troubles on me. I would never go near the police. Never my style."

"Shut your fucking lying mouth."

So much for truthful explanations. Now I had my immediate problem, Blacky and his knife. With no place to hide, I edged around to Liu's walking staff, the only weapon of meaning.

"Get away from there." He came at me with the knife.

I threw the lamp and grabbed Liu's cane. It was a worthy weapon, about an inch in diameter—it would have made a hell of a good stickball bat, but I'm not back in Coney Island. I move quickly and get the staff up, pushing the tip at Blacky who now backs off. I know it's just a matter of seconds before he'll be all over me. There's only one thing I can do and I do it. "Fire! Fire!" Seems my yelling got somebody to move, yeah, Blacky. He's coming in a crouch and the knife is in his right hand in the classic knife fighter's stance. I know I have one swing, maybe two, no more. I choke up on the stick as I don't have the room to fully come around and swing from my toes. While I'm aiming for his head he jumps to the side and I miss my target but get a shot to his ribs. I put power behind what I gave him and he's backing away, holding his side. I'm left holding a cracked piece of wood.

Now I'm moving away from him, trying to keep the bed between us, swinging what's left of my stickball bat. He lunges, I grab at his knife hand and swing the walking stick like Babe Ruth, one for the bleachers. Feeling his fist crash onto my cheek, I get my foot between us and push him away. I'm puffing and know one more charge by Blacky and this little boy would seriously need his mama. Where the hell is there a cop when you need one?

I hear another crash and the splintering of whatever was left of the door. Both Blacky's and my attention is shifted to the newcomer. Yang burst into the room. Most impressive, aside from his new black shiny Italian silk suit like the one Blacky wore, is a small .38 pistol in his right hand. He yells to Blacky in perfect copdom English.

"Drop it!"

Blacky's quick and without any hesitation goes for the cop, gun and all. Zhou points his weapon upward. There's a hell of an explosion in the small space and quite a bit of falling plaster. Blacky stopped in mid-step. I think the fight is over, but it seems I'm never right. The gorilla again lurches for the cop's gun. Yang, in classic Shaolin form, spins and his right foot shoots out and catches Blacky in his Adams apple. It's the end of the battle. Blacky is now upright with his hands around his neck, trying to breathe.

I'm going to remind myself to write and commend Beijing on their cop training. I'm out of breath and sit down. Yang walks over.

"Do you need help Mr. Diamond?"

I reach up and grab him by his upper arm. I feel the long, sinewy muscles beneath his shirt. I see his body taut, intense. Even in my best days I wouldn't have measured up. It's obvious *tai chi* must sure beat Mr. Atlas in the body building department.

"No, Yang, I'm fine."

In minutes there's a whole slew of police in my room forcing me into the hall where I'm talking to the kid telling him everything that happened. I'm laughing but only to cover my shaking hands.

I know I'm not going to sleep so the kid and I go back downstairs and sit at the bar. I buy him a beer. A couple of police guys follow us down. I figured we're important witnesses. There are a few women hanging around, they must have known Blacky was back to town. I don't know who's going to break the news to them.

I say to no one. "That Blacky, he's a mean son-of-a-gun." I'm still shook up. I replay the last five minutes. Could there be anything I should have done? Then I get a little reflective. "It's been a hellava trip hasn't it kid? But what the hell, you know the cliché: all's well that ends well."

"I guess so, Jake." His face brightens, like the start of a new day. "I've seen China, my relatives, and you have the real Zhou." And the sun in his face darkened as fast as it rose. "I lost an uncle."

"Yeah, I'm sorry, but c'mon kid, he had a full life."

I'm thinking over things the old man did. "Mickey, you know the furniture maker we met in Xiamen, Si Huang? Do you know why your uncle give him the photographs of the scroll paintings to be copied by every artist within a thirty minute pedi cab trip?"

"I asked him about that, Jake. He said it was for the folks of China. My uncle wanted copies of great paintings to be spread among the people. He said it would give them a sense of China's magnificent past."

Yeah, given Liu's sense of China I could accept it.

"Kid, about Huang. Do you trust him? Is he a good guy?"

"Oh yes, Jake. The guy's aces."

I laughed.

"Why do you ask?" the kid continued.

"I don't know. Maybe you could hitch up with him. Seems a good business."

I'm sitting there and I'm cold. I know it's not the temperature, I'm just not accustomed to this kind of drama. Yang comes out of the elevator with a bunch of cops and Blacky in tow. The garlic eater peers at me, says some words to the others and walks over.

"Good evening, Mr. Diamond. You do lead an exciting life."

This guy kills me. He saves me from Blacky's knife and he maintains a straight face and flat, gentle, manly language.

"How did you get there so fast?" I ask.

"No mystery, Mr. Diamond. I waited downstairs for you to be tucked away for the night. Then I see this Mr. Blacky go in the elevator. I took the stairs."

I'm impressed by the guy's efficiency. "Can I buy you a beer? You saved my life."

"By all means."

He calls the bartender, "Tsingtao." He takes a long pull. "As for Mr. Blacky and saving your life, I think you would have thought of something, Mr. Diamond. You have always appeared to be a resourceful man."

Yeah, it's not what I thought. Yang isn't finished.

"You know Mr. Diamond, the men you associate with have not been the best influence." He waits to see my reaction. I don't give him any but it doesn't stop him. "Your Mr. Blacky, you interrupted his embezzling scheme and spoiled it for him or at least he thought so."

"For an inscrutable Oriental you're always right out front. Rare and commendable."

"Mr. Jake, you are, like your Zhou painting, very much hot stuff," and he gives me a wink.

I said, in the right tone, "You are a cheeky bastard."

While it got a smile from him he still wasn't finished with me. "By the way, Mr. Diamond, you will be coming to Shanghai with me in the morning."

"Sure." I figure it had to be about Blacky.

"I'll get the tickets," he said, "and I'll charge your account."

Now he's telling jokes.

"Soft seat," he continued.

I properly smiled. "Of course," I offered, "and don't forget to get the kid one. And, oh yeah, while you're at it, can you get me any discounts for my flight back to San Francisco." I take a good look at my savior. "By the way, nice suit."

"When are you flying home,?" he asks.

"Oh, hell, no later than the day after tomorrow."

He looked to me with a grimace. "I wouldn't count on it, Mr. Diamond, I wouldn't count on it."

Oy vey.

CHAPTER 31

A FTER A GOOD night's sleep I'm walking across the hotel lobby with my Red Official in hand when I see Mickey at the front desk. "Hey, kid, you're checking us out right?"

"Yes, Jake, go on ahead. I'll meet you in the breakfast room."

I felt pretty good despite Yang's late night remarks. Blacky's in the slammer, my Zhou is legit, I had the Red Official back in my hands and pretty soon I'd be leaving for the States with Sharli The kid said he missed good Chinese restaurants and the Forty-Niners. His priorities were right on.

Yang, just finishing his breakfast asked Mickey and I to join him. "I see you have the porcelain there, Mr. Diamond. May I see it?"

"Oh, this." I handed him the Red Official. "Yeah, Mr. Liu, Mickey's uncle gave it to me."

"Yes. I know." I could see he had experience in handling fine art. He went on, "It is a good thing it is not an historic piece."

I thought it kind of an insult. "And if considered historic?" I asked.

He comes back in an almost righteous tone. "Why then it couldn't leave the country without proper permission. You see, we protect our Chinese heritage. We do not like unscrupulous people stealing them, like Generalissimo Chiang," and he peers at me straight on, "or your friend, Harry." He handed me back my Official.

"No, not you too. Everybody knew Harry as a dealer but me"

"You were too harsh with Mr. Taylor Davis. He and Harry were good friends, very close. They both loved China's past. I believe Mr. Davis killed Colonel Qin in revenge for Harry."

It was reassuring he didn't know everything. Then he said some scary words. "There will be a car waiting for us in Shanghai."

I didn't care for the tone of his words, although the kid didn't seem concerned. When cops are good to you, worrying is the thing to do.

We all boarded the late morning train for Shanghai, went to our soft seat cabin and hardly said a word to each other during the entire journey. True to Zhou's word, a car waited taking us to the police station with the three Doric columns.

"Mr. Diamond would you please tell your friend Mickey to wait in the lobby. We shouldn't be too long."

I gave the kid the Red Official to hold and Yang and I went up the circular staircase, my steps making the

243

same sounds as before. The room I entered had good size windows and a large mahogany desk as dark as the Chinese cop sitting behind it. He had enough gold leaf on his shoulders to replace all my silver fillings. There were also three straight back chairs over by the wall. I began to wonder where they kept the rubber hose.

"Good morning, Mr. Diamond." Certainly an American voice and it came from behind me. I swiveled around and sure enough, a Yank. He walked up to me. "I am Reginald Dawes, American Consulate." He stuck out his hand.

I knew it, trouble. There's always something about State Department people. Their pursed mouths said they were there not to serve, but to be admired. I sure hoped he didn't want me to call him Reggie.

Isn't it the truth when you start a day in a good mood with little trouble it never ends that way. I thought I'd get things moving. "What's up, Mr. Dawes?" If he says London Bridge I'm out of there, passport or no.

"Call me Reggie." Great, another prissy guy with soft features and dainty moves, watery eyes, rounded chin and a zit a little to the left of his nose. Where the hell do they find 'em. At least he didn't give me any chit-chat. "I'll get right to the point. The Chinese Government has told us you illegally purchased a Chinese national treasure and holding it in San Francisco. They wish it to be returned."

Oh, screw you. All of a sudden the stars and stripes has the same construct as a black and white striped prison uniform. This guy comes out of the blue and wants to bankrupt me or put me in jail, certainly to ruin the rest of my life.

I just spent a couple of weeks of hell but I gotta admit, interesting, to find out I had the real goods. And now this schnook wants me to give it up. Friggen guy is crazy. To make matters worse, he's my government, he's supposed to help me, not screw me. I gave him my answer. "I have no idea what you're talking about."

Ole Reggie over there gave me a blank face. He thinks maybe he has the wrong information and peeks at Yang and the Chinese guy behind the big desk. The two cops walk over to him, like coaches walking out of the dugout to talk to a tiring pitcher. After giving him the old pep talk they walk back to the dugout.

Ole Reggie goes on. "Come now, Mr. Diamond. They know you have the painting. Zhou's *Late Autumn* was taken illegally from the National Palace in Beijing and sent to Taiwan. It's known the late Mr. Liu of the National Museum sold you the painting. Rather place you in jail and start an incident they would prefer you simply give back the scroll in question."

The late Mr. Liu. It had a sad sound. This little stinker wasn't simply going to tell me to do something and expect me to do it and certainly not by referring to the, "Late Dr. Liu. "Look, you *putz*. I paid for it, legal tender, an honest transaction from the owner to me. I'll be damned if I'll just hand it over." I wondered about the savvy of this State Department guy. "I'll tell you what I'm going to do," I went on, "I'm going to walk out of here to the French Embassy and ask for political asylum from both China and my turncoat country." Screw him.

Yang comes over with two chairs. "Jake, sit down, relax." Now its Jake, is it. "We know you have the Zhou. We even know Mr. Taylor Davis had plans to buy it from you. He told us," he hesitated, questioning his next words, "for almost 3 million dollars."

"Okay, you wanna buy it? I give a five percent discount to friends." He didn't move a facial muscle. "Okay, for you, make it ten percent."

Yang's face stayed cop placid. "Jake, you will never have a chance to sell it. We will place word in the art market the Chinese government has declared it illegal to purchase any work removed from the National Museum in Taiwan. We will say possession carries a jail sentence. And Jake, we will keep a special eye on you."

This guy saves my life from Blacky's knife then turns and puts one into my financial heart. "To hell with you and your government, Yang." I took one step to good ole Reggie boy. "And you, you can crawl back into your gilded embassy." And with a flourish I walked out, stomping harder on those slate steps. I'll show them. Mickey watched as I bounded down the staircase and he caught up to me outside.

"I guess things didn't go too well upstairs, did they, Jake?"

"Let's get out of here kid." I knew what I had to do. "I'm going to get Sharli, then go to our Consulate and tell them I lost my passport." I'm thinking, the damned Chinese can't arrest me and they can't keep me here. The American bureaucrats may want me to hand over the Zhou to keep the peace, but I'm outta here.

"Where we going Jake?"

"The only place I know. the Peace Hotel. C'mon." I'm wondering whether the hotel will live up to its name. Now where the hell did I put Sharli's number?

CHAPTER 32

I FIGURED THE PEACE Hotel would become my base of operations. But I had trepidation, I'm on my own bank account and I knew this place cost bucks. The young woman with the good English and stylish bow tie said, "A single sir, is one hundred and twenty, the double is one hundred and sixty."

She's a pleasant looking Chinese young woman in a blue uniform, white blouse and red tie. Alongside is a handsome young man similarly dressed. And his English? How come they all sounded better than I?

"Is that dollars? American?" I ask.

"Yes, sir."

I glanced over at Mickey, then I thought of Sharli, and the possibility of her staying over.

"I'll take a double and a single."

In my room I find the number of Sharli's relatives. I bring Mickey from next door to make the call, telling him to ask for Chai Ling. I figured Sharli's too foreign for China. The kid gets the number, works through a couple of family members and finally reaches my gal. He hands me the phone and smiles. "Chai Ling, huh?"

I never did tell you why I prefer Sharli, well, it's just a matter of tongue placement. When a kid, fourth grade exactly, they sent me to the school nurse because I couldn't pronounce my l's, they came out w's. The sweet woman with her white uniform and wood depressor gave me tongue exercises. She would have me repeat what she said, only with me it came out, "Wittle Wouie woves wovly Waura."

After one term little Louie finally loved lovely Laura. Anyhow, from then on I preferred to stay away from the letter, l. No big deal.

"Sharli, where are you, I need you."

"Jake, you could have said you missed me or, 'How are you Sharli,' or, "Is it good to be with your family. Oh, no. It's, 'Sharli I need you.' Well Jake, it just so happened I missed you."

"Sharli, they won't let me out of the country. They want my Zhou."

"Where are you?" she asked. I told her. "I'm going to take the subway and I'll be there in about forty-five minutes."

"The subway? I'm not worth a taxi?" I ask.

I could hear exasperation. "In Shanghai, Jake the new subway is faster than even a newer cab. I'll be there as soon as I can."

In about an hour Sharli calls from the lobby. "Jake, come on down. Let's take a walk."

I didn't like the tone of things. There were no sweet words suggesting a little cheer or even a timid, "Darling." When we meet she gives me a polite kiss on the cheek, but the whisper in my ear becomes the necessary tonic. "I missed you, Jake."

Now you may think I became disappointed by not getting one of those big wet ones full on the face. Not really. There's something gross about two adults our age kissing that way in public. I'm talking about full, you know, on the lips kind, where the lady is bent back and the guy looks as though he hadn't had any in weeks. It's okay when you're twenty-five but when you're in the sixties, hell, it can be gross, despite the onlookers who would say how cute a couple they were.

"Sharli, there are too many things happening around here. It all swamps me."

"We'll get it straightened out, Jake. Everything will end up fine, just fine."

She understood all our worlds and nothing could throw her off balance. She had those genetic characteristics crossing two continents. Some passing biologist once told me about hybrid vigor, telling me when you cross two species the offspring is greater than the sum of the parent parts. To me America is only a couple of generations away from becoming the cross of a dozen genetic pools. I knew it to be a dazzling future.

When I first started my China trade business this woman comes into my place, a black woman, no, a Chinese woman. You could tell she turned guys heads in her time. "Mr. Diamond, I have a house full of furniture in Georgetown, Guyana." She gave my place a once over. "The kind you have here." Well, if she wanted my attention, she got it. Taking out a sheath of papers, an inventory list with matching pictures, she asked if I had any interest.

We flew right on down and after three days of negotiation agreed on a price. As Izzy Klein said to do, we both walked away smiling. But Guyana had to be the ultimate dazzler, the mixes of the races, the ex-black slaves with Chinese merchants, with East Indians, with the Arab Muslim, British sea captains, first mates and common seamen of the world, all a dazzling array of color, a world's fair of human construction. Yeah, it's what I figured America to be. It's all just a matter of time.

Sharli and I left the hotel and took a short stroll to the Bund, the riverfront. We found a bench along the Huangyu River, and watched the ships, barges, tugs, and whatever else floated. I looked to Sharli. "I got the Official back, the one I sold Davis." I told her how, and it sat comfortably upstairs in my room.

She said, "Good," unenthusiastically. I felt let down.

The river wasn't a pretty place. All kinds of flotsam, oil slicks, ugly sea gulls and noisy buoys. In front of us were the stately buildings of China's old Wall Street, the financial center of the European powers of the twenties and thirties.

I said, "That cop, the one whose been following me. Turned out he's a pretty smart guy. Saved my life." Then I told her about Blacky, and the melee we had in my room.

Sharli asked, with out any real concern. "Any bruises, cuts?"

"No. The cop came in just as Blacky readied to cut me up for fish bait." From where we sat I could see the old Teng Fong Hotel that housed the pre-war Shanghai Club with its longest bar in the world. It appeared to be run down like so many of the other once stately buildings.

"The best thing," I said, "is the *Late Autumn*, the one I have, well, it's the real McCoy."

"So you're a rich man?"

Without any intensity I said, "I guess so."

She could see I wasn't as keen as I would normally be finding I had become a millionaire.

"What's wrong Jake? Does China say it's theirs?"

Absolutely bewildering. "How did you know?"

"My relatives suggested it. They said it's a Chinese treasure and the government will claim it, like they did Tibet."

I peered over to a park on my left where animated conversations were taking place between Chinese and Westerners. Sharli followed my gaze. She spoke softly. "That's Huangpu Park. The Chinese go there to practice English. Back then they called it the British Public Gardens. It had a nasty sign about Chinese and canines not allowed." Her eyes looked to me and she asked softly. "What are you going to do, Jake?"

I responded, sullenly, "I don't know."

A couple of minutes went by. She speaks excitedly. "Jake, you're a businessman. Why don't you make them an offer?"

What a gal. I leaned over and kissed the top of her head. "Yeah, make them an offer, why don't I?" I thought about it. I wished my name Corleone. "How much should I ask for?"

"Don't play around, Jake. Davis probably told them what he agreed to pay." She thought a second longer. "They may have more cards than you." She thought for another second. "But you're the art dealer, you figure what they'll pay."

I thought of what she said. This wasn't a free market, and it wasn't going to be what the traffic would bear. I stood up.

"C'mon, Sharli, I gotta make a phone call."

We went back to the hotel and I searched for the card Yang had given me. I dialed the number and expected to fight secretaries and petty bureaucrats till I could get someone who spoke English. Instead, I went right through like he had alerted every telephone operator in the building to expect my call. Sure, I'd surprise him. Fat chance.

"Yes, Mr. Diamond, this is policeman Yang."

"Look, Yang, maybe there is a solution to our problem."

"My superior anticipated you would find one."

"Could we meet to discuss it?"

"Absolutely, Mr. Diamond. We could do it right away and without your American State Department. We did not think him too, what shall I say, diplomatic."

"That's fine with me." Sharli's nudging me. I get her message. "In the hotel dining room, the Peace Hotel, in an hour."

There's a moment's hesitation. "No, Mr. Diamond. If it's jake with you," and he laughed at his own joke, "I wouldn't mind some Tex-Mex food tonight. I know a rip-roaring good place, the Rio Grande, in the old French Concession. Your lady friend Sharli can find it. In an hour-and-a-half. Good bye."

I hang up feeling abused. They follow me, keep tabs of Sharli and now control my eating habits. Tex-Mex huh, shades of hot pastrami. How the hell do I lay in a good supply of Tums around here?

CHAPTER 33

I'M FEELING A little frisky lying down on the double bed with Sharli next to me. We're meeting the cop for dinner in about an hour. I figured what I had to say and what he'd say and how the negotiation would go. I'm prepared. I reach over for Sharli. She's there and then again she's not.

"Jake." I didn't like the sound of her voice. It has to be trouble "We must talk." It sure sounded like trouble.

"Can't we save it for after?"

"I'm not going back with you."

It's not only my chin that drops. I've just about got my life back in the groove when she hits me with this. This is the love of my life, a woman I should have met at the start and she comes at me with the worst.

"C'mon, Sharli, you can't be serious. You know how I feel about you. I'll even learn how to use chopsticks properly. We're good for each other."

"I know we are, Jake. It's something else. It's the family, my Chinese family. We made up, and, well, my mother's coming over to Shanghai. She wants to see her son one more time. We're going to spend some time here, maybe even travel around."

"Don't tell me, Chengdu."

"Well, maybe."

I know this lady of mine. When she talks like that it's going to happen. Now I'm worrying. I'm not sure what all of this means, I mean to me.

Actually, I'm kinda jealous. Me, I don't have any family in the old country, hell, I don't think I have an old country. My mother came here as a child born in Russia. Her brother said Poland and not any of the seven kids knew the name of the *shtetel,* the small town they left from someplace. I guess you had to be a three thousand-year-old civilization to know such things. Being God's chosen don't rate.

I'm looking at the lady of my life and everything is not hunky dory. "What's the matter?"

A three-second pause. "Nothing."

"Who you kidding."

"It's just, it's just. I'm not so sure my mother could take living in China. It's not San Francisco conveniences."

I remembered squat toilets. "Wasn't your mother born here? She should know."

"Well, maybe I can't deal with it".

Ah, the truth. "Sharli, it's your game, you call it."

There's only silence. I knew I couldn't push any further. We'll just wait and see how things play out between Sharli, China, and me. We're each an important part of the other's life. I'd better not go on, I'd only get maudlin.

Now we had to meet Yang to discuss how I can get out of China and keep the Zhou intact. I know I didn't want to play Solomon and split the scroll in half. Sharli gets a taxi and we're off to the Rio Grande Restaurant. Hi Yo, Silver, away!

To tell you the truth, Mex food, I'm just not too big on it. The way they make in the States, where all the stuff on your plate seems to ooze together. I can never tell where the refried beans end and the guacamole begins.

Yang waited inside. I had planned to introduce Sharli when they began chatting like old friends. I gave the restaurant a once over. All ersatz Mexico with a few flags strung across the walls, some old San Miguel De Allende and Acapulco posters, and a number of those wide brimmed sombrero hats. Not at all convincing.

My cop walked over to a guy who's dressed like a Disney character portraying a Mexican gunfighter. I'm figuring he owns the place. A big walrus moustache, wide hat, cowboy pants, two pistols slung across his hips, and a bandolier of shot gun shells crisscrossed his shoulders. Zapata he wasn't, still it could have been carried off if the props didn't appear like they came from the local Five and Dime.

Sharli is reading the Chinese menu when the waiter comes over and our cop gives him an extensive order. Sharli kicks my legs and grimaces in dissatisfaction. I can only imagine what's coming.

"Ah, good," Yang says, "you should enjoy the meal. I know it to be quite authentic." He smiles. "A Mexican told me," he winks. How can you dislike cops when they're like that?

"I can't wait," I murmured.

"And now, Mr. Diamond, you have something to tell me. About the Zhou scroll."

"There's no sweet talking you, is there? Ok, let's get this over with so I can get back to San Francisco." And before I can say anything he's at me, smiling.

"We are not prepared to pay anything for something stolen from us."

Now I knew it's not a good beginning to a negotiation. "I had a different figure in mind, something greater than zero."

"Hear me out, Jake. We are also mindful it is in your possession, and we believe the situation could become unpleasant if we pressed our point." Zhou took a swig of the *Dos Equis* beer that just arrived. He smacked his lips. I would have liked to do the same but I luckily remembered those muscles of his. "We are prepared to give you the six hundred and fifty thousand American, the amount you paid to Liu plus accumulated interest owed." He sees my face drop. "And not a Yankee dollar more."

My six-fifty back? That's it? We both knew what the Zhou would fetch on the open market but I'm not sure I can ever get close. No, I'm certain of it.

"Now, Yang, let's be reasonable. The market . . . ."

He cuts in. "We believe we can keep you here in China despite any of your California Congress people. In all probability we can provide your retirement and even your burial plot."

I'm thinking you never pick a fight with a cop in his territory. I wanted to say, "You bastard, with those kinds of terms you don't give me much of a choice." Instead, I blurt out, "Your offer. I'll take it."

Sharli chirps in. "Now that's what I call hard bargaining, Jake. You must teach me your technique."

"Stop it, Sharli. I don't need your cutesy observations, I already have Yang." I had little alternative as he could get away with a lot less. I figured China didn't want any more bad publicly over private property rights. So I guess it's finished. I'm back where I started. All I get to show for all of this China business is a bunch of railroad and plane stubs.

Yeah, life's a bitch, but you know, things are not so bad. I took one hell-of-a-trip I wouldn't have missed for the world. Qin got what he deserved and Liu proved to be a hellava guy. Me, everything I did came out okay, no major mistakes. I feel good about it.

Then Yang says, "Six hundred and fifty thousand, less expenses."

I do one of those comedy double takes Lou Costello had mastered. My head flips from Yang to Sharli back to Yang. My snappy come back is, "What? What expenses?"

The waiter comes with the food and stops the conversation. He puts down another three bottles of *Dos Equis*, a table full of nachos, chicken fajitas, beef tacos, refried beans, guacamole and saffron rice. The smells are good, the colors on the plate appetizing, we dig in. Good stuff and even Sharli who's a real *dim sum* fan and never even expressed a liking for Taco Bell is feeding her face and nodding her head, yes. I finally come up for air and pick up without losing a beat. "Expenses? What expenses?"

"Why, Jake, the cost of my government to keep you under surveillance during the time you were in our country." He gives me a big grin, "My salary, Jake, marvelous Szechwan and Shanghai restaurants," he grins a little wider, "Tex-Mex."

He begins again. "Boat trips, soft seat train and air fares, and, of course, there are hotels." This guy's raking me over the coals. "And oh, yes, the cost of an Italian silk jacket to replace the one your friend Blacky ripped." He pulls out a list and his eyes check off entries. "Also, the cost of your solitary confinement in Suzhou." He smiled over to Sharli. "Not at all expensive," and he laughs. There's always something nasty about cops, isn't there.

"What is this, a Chinese laundry? I'm getting charged for missing buttons?" I could tell he didn't like my last words.

"The total, Mr. Diamond is eleven thousand three hundred and fifty two dollars," a pause, "American." I asked to see the accounting. He gave me an indignant scowl. "Don't be so bourgeois."

I had to laugh. What the hell, in for a penny, in for a pound. "Done," I said. "Sharli let's get out of here. Yang, you can finish the tacos, and I'll expect a check in the morning." Mao's protégé gives me a deep once over. I could see I'm up for an evaluation, and I don't think I'm looking forward to it.

"Mr. Diamond, what you have been through, the way you handled it, all class, Jake, real class."

Stunned, yeah, a bang-up compliment, or else he's is a real pro at flattery and will go far in the cop world.

"Thanks. And you too, style, pure style."

He actually blushed. "I am a policeman, Jake. We do not have style, just discipline."

Then he does the strangest thing, he puts his muscled arm about my shoulders and pulls me close. "Mr. Diamond, there is something you should know about Mr. Liu." He waited a moment as if to convince himself he should continue. He did.

"I believe you know Liu's brother left China to die in Taipei, to be near Chun. You should also know before he left China he had risen in the ranks of the army, a very respected officer. He also never forgot what you did for him."

Now that took me aback. I'd never help a Communist. "Yang, I'm surprised, you should know I've never spoken to Generals and their ilk."

"No, Jake, it is you who should know better. Liu's brother was the Chinese lieutenant in the North of China, the officer Qin would have killed, the life you saved."

I needed a moment to take in what Yang just told me. Yeah, I remember zonking Qin with the dead Englishman's delightful Canton blue tureen. Then it all cleared up for me, Of course, Liu and his brother, the Lieutenant. Damn, damn, no wonder the old man's face was so familiar when he first came into my place in San Francisco. They were spitting images. Why the hell didn't it come to me earlier? Why didn't the old man say something? Liu and I, we could have swapped family secrets.

"You see, Mr. Diamond, when you were sold the Zhou scroll it became Liu's way of saying, "Thank you. All the Liu's are grateful."

I'm still trying to come to grips with the revelation. Son-of-a-bitch, life has a way of leading you by the nose into the strangest of corners. "Thanks for the information Yang. It helps in so many ways." He wasn't used to compliments and blushed slightly, again, but only for a moment. He had more to tell me.

"Jake, I will meet you at the plane tomorrow with your passport and three tickets." He turned to Sharli. "I believe you will be staying on in China?"

Sharli, never perturbed, says, "Yes," but I think she even wondered how he knew.

I looked to the cop. "Meaning you'll be going to the States with Mickey and me?"

"Of course. I will bring back the Zhou to its rightful place within the Forbidden City collection."

"Not to Taiwan?"

"Makes no difference, Jake," then he gives me an exaggerated wink, "one China, two systems."

I love it. He gets up and is heading for the door. As he leaves he's laughing. Two-Gun Jose is running over waving the bill and Yang is pointing to me.

I yell out, "Yang, it's been a kick."

My last night in China, in Shanghai, so I take a short walk from the Peace Hotel to the Bund, to the park that once proclaimed, "No Chinese allowed". I sit with my back to the city and watch the freighters and ferries pass on the river. There's not much to see in the rapidly fading day, just a bunch of confusing lights here and those on the opposite shore.

"Jake, don't turn around."

Not again, for Christ sake. Harry, get outta my life. I started to turn but felt his hand restrain my movement.

"Don't Jake" A moment passed. "I know I used you."

"You also screwed me up for all these years."

With a puzzlement, "How so?"

"You're a bastard, Harry. I worried about you."

"I've paid you back. You know all those good deals you made in Taiwan?"

"I would have traded them in a second to know you were alive, Harry" Then I come to the thought, "You've been following me, haven't you?"

. "I'm glad I got to talk to you, Jake. I've missed you. Those early days, the Englishmen's house." He paused. "There was never anything to go home to. Coney Island seemed so, so, tame. Certainly not for me." There was a pause. Then his voice. "Take care of yourself, Jake. It was great seeing you again. And, oh yeah, she's a lovely woman." Another pause and I felt all those years rushing back. The hand restraining me was now gone.

"Harry? Harry?' I turned to see his face, to touch his hands and all I got were a bunch of Chinese faces staring at me. "Harry. You bastard, where the hell did you go. Stay dammit, there's too much to talk about." I said it softly, with no malice, to no one. How can you stay mad with a boyhood friend? But I knew he was gone, forever.

EPILOGUE

I NEVER DID TELL you much about my mortgaged condo in the city, did I? Just a one bedroom along the Powell Street cable car line at the edge of Chinatown and Nob Hill. And as it's San Francisco it has a required view, well, from one window. My red flambé Official is sitting on a *tansu* in my living room. He's staring out to Alcatraz, and if he peeks across the room he can almost catch the Golden Gate.

The weather forecast is for sun but right now there's a chill and it's drizzly. I'm sitting on the living room's brown leather couch that has deep creases like the old World War II Flying Tiger jackets. And the last weeks are on my mind. Actually, I feel good about them, oddly enough, damn good. I mean, I survived China, Blacky, the Peoples Republic police and even got a moment with a boyhood pal. More important, the guilt I carried for Harry is gone and, thankfully, I wasn't the bad guy. The lieutenant's life I saved from Qin's wrath paid off in Liu's strong friendship, and also a close tie to Mickey.

And Sharli, what we survived, well, we couldn't get more, what, intimate. Sure, things happened I couldn't plan for but I stayed on top of them. And my decisions, look at it this way, if you're correct six out of ten guesses you win the game. As long as I've been more right than wrong, I mean, what more can you ask? Excuse me, the telephone.

"Yeah, Mickey, it's okay, I'm not busy." The kid's my partner now, and we're pretty chummy, he's even gone to wearing pressed chinos or Levi's with blue blazers. He looks good. We have a small shop in Hayes Valley, near Teddy's. I can tell you it's not much. While I shipped my inventory over from Gold Street half of what I got is crammed on the floor and the rest is in the back. Once I'm sold out I figure that's it. So it won't be Cancun, big deal. But the kid, well, he has an eye for quality. He'll do gangbusters. I should tell you while the rent is a lot less I kinda miss Gold Street, it had class.

"No kid, I still don't have my computer working." You see Mickey is into all this online stuff. He even set up a web site for The China Trade. He tells me we get a respectable number of hits. "Give me a break kid, I just learned how to turn the damn thing on."

We have good business on the internet, in fact, we have a hell of a line of merchandise for China Trade furniture lovers. You see, we're the world rep for Huang of Xiamen. Yeah, the kid went back before we left and negotiated a sole distributorship agreement. I told you right along he's smart. Maybe I'll sell my stuff to the kid. We'll see.

Mickey tells me his mother likes the two of us together, thinks his future is okay now that he's set up in business with Mr. Diamond. I should tell her the kid'll do better than I ever did.

"What's that, kid? C'mon, you know I won't sell your uncle's legacy, the Red Official. He's like family." Then he says something weird, but I'm not surprised. "What? You wanna buy it?" I'm laughing. "Hey kid, don't worry, I just made out my will. Find a place on your mantel, it's yours when I kick off." I could hear him get mad. "What? Okay kid, I'll stop talking."

Yeah, the kid knows I'm still planning to retire. But actually, between you and me, I'm in no hurry. You see while I offered Sharli my hand in marriage she's still not sure. In fact, I'm going to meet her for lunch in about an hour.

Sharli's mother landed in Shanghai some months ago and is planning to come back to San Francisco pretty soon. Sharli said she only planned to stay a few days but I knew she'd stay on longer despite the rough living of the old taipan town. Hell, what could overcome the Chinese attraction of family and history. Sharli first thought her mother might, well, stay on and die in Shanghai as she first wrote she liked it so much. Her more recent letters changed and Sharli laughed when she told me her mother's new words. "Chai Ling, I love my family but those Chinese women, I forgot how they gossip." It's tough to be an American.

When Sharli came back from China I asked her why she didn't stay on with her mother? She said she's lived too long in San Francisco; she loved me, and would never give up either. I think about what she said and figure all the punches I took in China were nothing and the God's have been on my side all along. My father was wrong, you know, when he said it wasn't worth it. This life stuff is just one hell of a fine party.

I'm about to say goodbye to the kid when he says something that nails the phone tight to my ear. "What? You got an email from Yang, from Yang? You sure it came from Yang?" I'll tell you, there's nothing stranger than people. "He wants to what? He's offering to sell us a line of Chinese classic art reproductions of the old masters? C'mon kid, he's pulling your leg." I gotta laugh or I'd be in the asylum. Yang comes to the States with me, picks up my Zhou Mengfu, and gives me a check for six hundred and fifty thousand plus interest, less expenses. He takes in the city, eats in Chinatown and then, straight faced, tells me he's going to divorce his wife and quit the police. He says he's in his mid-life crisis. Hell, I didn't think Chinese were allowed to have such things.

So anyway, after I pay off the banks I'm back where I started before Liu paid me his first visit. Well, almost to the same place. From a cash position I'm actually a few bucks ahead. The costs Yang hit me with and my expenses in China were a couple of dollars less than what Davis paid me for the Red Official. Actually, I'm going to take what I have left over and donate it to the World Christian University. I figure it's the least I can do, besides, I hear Allison is running it now.

Oh yeah, there's a big brouhaha over Davis. The church and Taylor's family are going to the Chinese Communist Party asking for clemency. They're arguing extenuating circumstances and are trying to get our State Department involved. Me, I think the tennis pro will escape the bullet in the back of the head but no more. As I read it, China's pretty tough when it comes to things like murdering a cop, just like the States.

"What's that kid? You say Yang's serious? Yeah, sure. Tell 'em to send over a few of those scrolls. If he has good stuff I guess there's got to be a market for 'em." Hell, I'm living proof.

I thought of telling the kid to first send them over to Wyatt for authentication, but I wasn't sure Mickey or the Winslow Professor would get the irony. Sharli would. I haven't seen the professor since we've all come back. In all honesty I'm kinda hesitant, I mean, wouldn't you? I made one big ass of myself with the Zhou painting. I don't need to keep reminding myself by socializing with the expert.

"No kid, I'm not coming in today. I have a date, I'm meeting Sharli at Ghirardelli Square, by the sweet little baroque fountain in the middle of the upper plaza, the one with the mermaid and small turtles." The Japanese lady who designed it died a couple of years ago. She has attractive little water shows all over the city. I figure from there we'll decide where to go for lunch. For me a little fish wouldn't be bad. They tell me it's good for my cholesterol.

By the time I get to the fountain the sun is out and making little silver bursts out of the spritzing water. I watch the kids dipping their fingers into the pool, playing with the cast iron turtles, splashing each other. Their mothers step in, pull them away, fingers waving, scolding. You know, its pictures like that keep you joyful inside.

Sharli comes up the steps onto the plaza and she's smiling so I'm also smiling. Did I tell you we're now into telling each other little secrets, things we've never told anyone else? Still a few feet away I see her hand go to the gold chain around her neck. She brings her jade amulet out, fingers smoothing its shimmering green surface. She walks over and kisses my cheek. I know she's got her mojo working. I'd like to give her a big one on those lovely lips, but she wouldn't like it with all the people around. Did I ever tell you she hardly ever wears lipstick? I like that.

"Jake, lets go to Torelli's, I'd like some of the mustard dressing they serve with the broiled salmon."

She always brings the best part of the day.